"No list of thrillers is complete without Robyn Harding."
—*Real Simple*

"A master of domestic suspense."
—Kathleen Barber, author of *Are You Sleeping*

PRAISE FOR THE WORKS OF ROBYN HARDING

The Party

"Tense and riveting . . . I was hooked from the opening scene and could not look away until I reached the very last page."
—Megan Miranda, *New York Times* bestselling author of *All the Missing Girls*

"Cleverly constructed and brilliantly paced, *The Party* is a raw telling of a family coming apart at the seams. . . . Impossible to put down."
—Bill Clegg, *New York Times* bestselling author of *Did You Ever Have a Family*

"Everyone is flawed in this contemporary tale of mothers and daughters. Everyone behaves badly. And the story is a pure delight."
—Lucy Ferriss, author of *A Sister to Honor*

"Fast-paced and tension-filled, *The Party* explodes the myth of the perfect family and is one invitation you can't turn down."
—Rebecca Drake, author of *Only Ever You*

"An innocent sweet-sixteen sleepover goes terribly awry when a wealthy San Francisco couple awakes to find their daughter crying and covered in blood. . . . Shades of *The Dinner* and *Big Little Lies*."
—*New York Post*

"With teenagers worthy of *Mean Girls*, and a healthy dose of suspense, *The Party* reads like a cross between Megan Abbott and Jodi Picoult by way of James Patterson."
—*Booklist*

Her Pretty Face

"A fast-paced, thrilling, gut-wrenching novel."
—Taylor Jenkins Reid, *New York Times* bestselling author of *Daisy Jones & The Six*

"A haunting tale of friendship and loyalty, secrets and betrayal—a book that will grab your insides and give them a twist."
—Janelle Brown, *New York Times* bestselling author of *Watch Me Disappear*

"Harding expertly builds subtle menace. . . . Creepy and compelling."
—*Kirkus Reviews*

"A fierce and blazing one-sitting read that will make you question even your closest friendships . . . Will undoubtedly spike paranoia levels in school car lines everywhere."
—Carter Wilson, *USA Today* bestselling author of *Mister Tender's Girl*

"A powerhouse of twists and turns."
—Roz Nay, internationally bestselling author of *Hurry Home* and *Our Little Secret*

"A smart, darkly witty, and perfectly constructed thriller."
—David Bell, *USA Today* bestselling author of *Since She Went Away*

"This one might be the thriller of the summer."
—*Toronto Star*

"The tony setting and the slowly revealed secrets make this a good read-alike for Liane Moriarty's *Big Little Lies*."
—*Booklist*

"Robyn Harding knows exactly what she's doing, and she did *not* come to play."
—*Hello Giggles*

The Arrangement

"An insider's look into the world of sugar daddies . . . full of shocking revelations, volatile characters, and vice. Look out: *The Arrangement* will blow your mind."

—Mary Kubica, *New York Times* bestselling author of *The Good Girl*

"A nightmarish deep dive into the underbelly of a secret world. Rivetingly dark, *The Arrangement* delivers on every level—a shocking premise, a forbidden obsession, and a plot that builds slowly and masterfully escalates to a chilling end. Prepare to be blindsided."

—Heather Gudenkauf, *New York Times* bestselling author of *The Weight of Silence*

"The most compelling, gripping, and entertaining book I've read in a long time. Nobody writes about young people and their obsessions as authentically as Robyn."

—Liz Nugent, bestselling author of *Unraveling Oliver*

"*Pretty Woman* meets *Fatal Attraction*, with a twist . . . or three. . . . Deliciously seductive from start to finish. Hang on for the ride, because this tantalizing thriller will knock you sideways."

—Jennifer Hillier, author of *Jar of Hearts*

"Welcome to the sugar bowl. . . . The world of sugar babies and their daddies is fascinating."

—*Kirkus Reviews*

"*Pretty Woman*'s creepy counterpart . . . Throw a little murder in there, and you have yourself a page-turner."

—*29Secrets*

"A must-read novel."

—*Real Simple*

the swap

~~~~~~

ROBYN HARDING

SCOUT PRESS

New York   London   Toronto   Sydney   New Delhi

Scout Press
An Imprint of Simon & Schuster, Inc.
1230 Avenue of the Americas
New York, NY 10020

First Scout Press trade paperback edition June 2020

For information about special discounts for bulk purchases, please contact Simon & Schuster Special Sales at 1-866-506-1949 or business@simonandschuster.com.

The Simon & Schuster Speakers Bureau can bring authors to your live event. For more information or to book an event, contact the Simon & Schuster Speakers Bureau at 1-866-248-3049 or visit our website at www.simonspeakers.com.

Interior design by Jaime Putorti

Manufactured in the United States of America

10 9 8 7 6 5 4 3 2 1

Library of Congress Cataloging-in-Publication Data has been applied for.

ISBN 978-1-9821-4176-9
ISBN 978-1-9821-4178-3 (ebook)

To my writing companion, Ozzie.
I miss you.

Men, some to business, some to pleasure take;
But every woman is at heart a rake:
Men, some to quiet, some to public strife;
But every lady would be queen for life.

—Alexander Pope

Epistle II: To a Lady, of the Characters of Women

1743

spring 2019

1

low morrison

I first saw Freya at my high school. I hated school, found the classes as dull and simple as my fellow students. This attitude did not endear me to my teachers nor my classmates, so I was alone, as usual, when she walked through the double front doors. No one noticed her, which seemed to be her intent. She wore a ball cap and aviator sunglasses that she did not remove under the fluorescent lights. Her shoulder-length blond hair was pulled back into a low ponytail, her heart-shaped face free of makeup. She was petite but curvaceous in her faded jeans and plain white T, with the kind of figure rarely seen outside of comic books. I had a comic-book figure, too . . . Popeye's girlfriend Olive Oyl.

Even through the crowd in the hallway, I could tell she was *somebody*. There was no way I could have known then that she would come into my life and change it, change *me*, but I felt a magnetic pull toward her, like I had to meet her. It was destiny. The other kids were immune to her presence. It was lunch break, so they were all wrapped up in their pathetic social jockeying— gossiping, flirting, or roughhousing. We would graduate in less than three months, and everyone was already obsessing about prom, pre-parties, after-parties, and college. Everyone but me, that is.

I watched the woman head to the office as Morrissey warbled through my earbuds (unlike my pop- and rap-loving peers, I preferred to listen to angsty classics: the Smiths, Nirvana, R.E.M.). She was too old to be a student, too young to be a parent, too cool to be a teacher. As she disappeared into the principal's domain, I wondered: Who was this woman? What was she doing at Bayview High? And why was she dressed like an incognito celebrity?

A few minutes later, she emerged from the office with Principal Graph beside her. He was enamored with her; it was obvious in his attentive posture, his fawning mannerisms, the color in his meaty cheeks. The portly administrator led Freya (who had removed her shades but not her hat) to the bulletin board in the main hall. As always, it was covered in ignored bills: school-play announcements, lost-phone notices, guest-speaker posters . . . Mr. Graph cleared a space for her, handed her a pushpin, and she posted a piece of paper on the board. They chatted for a few seconds, the principal clearly trying to bask in her aura for as long as possible, before she donned her sunglasses and left.

I hurried to the vacated bulletin board, eyes trained on the standard white sheet she had put up. It was a typewritten advertisement in Times New Roman font.

Pottery Classes

Learn to throw, glaze, and fire in a cozy home studio.

Make beautiful mugs, bowls, and vases.

Ten classes for $100.

Contact Freya Light.

Casually, I snapped a photo of her contact details just as the bell rang to signal the end of lunch.

I waited two days to text her. I didn't want her to know that I'd watched her pin the notice on the board, that I'd recorded the information directly, that I had been thinking about her ever since. It's not as creepy as it sounds. My life was exceptionally boring. I had no friends, no hobbies, no extracurricular activities. I did, however, have a lot of chores. My family had a small hobby farm with chickens, a couple of goats, and a pig. There were always animals to feed, eggs to collect, kindling to be chopped for the woodstove. Whenever I escaped to my room to watch Netflix, my mom would insist she needed help with something. She worked from home as a bookkeeper, but she was obsessed with canning: peaches, green beans, dill pickles, kimchi, applesauce . . . As if we had to prepare for a nuclear war.

Sometimes, I'd escape to the beach or into the forest to take photographs of seals, driftwood, birds, and trees. My photography teacher, Mr. Pelman, said I had a good eye. He even let me sign out the school cameras, a privilege usually reserved for yearbook club members. Other times, I used my phone. I liked viewing the world through a smaller, more intimate lens. I liked the solitude. And my singular hobby gave me time to think. For the past two days, about little other than Freya.

She fascinated me, this woman who looked like she'd walked off the set of some Beverly Hills reality show. The town of Hawking, where my high school was located, had some wealthy residents. There were the bankers, the real-estate moguls, the captains of industry who summered in the waterfront mansions set along the island's rugged coastline. Year-round, the town housed a handful of professionals—doctors and lawyers and accountants. But mostly, our island was populated with organic farmers, beekeepers, or artisan candle/soap/pickle makers and those who ran the shops and restaurants servicing the seasonal tourist trade. We had the occasional celebrity pass through town, usually some washed-up old actor en route to the fishing lodge on the island's northern tip. But Freya was different. She exuded glamour, significance, and a palpable sense of cool.

After deliberating over my words for several hours, I texted:

I'd like to sign up for pottery classes

With a trembling finger, I sent the message.

When she didn't respond, I fretted. Were my carefully chosen words somehow off-putting? Or had she seen me in the school hallway watching her with barely concealed wonder? Could she read my thoughts—which, while harmless, were perhaps a little . . . *much*? It was possible that she had reconsidered offering classes to teens. Why had she wanted to in the first place? Kids my age were assholes. They wouldn't take learning pottery seriously. They'd joke around, make a mess, show up stoned. Except me. I would treat it like surgery.

Finally, a week later, she texted back.

Hi. Classes start next Monday at 4. Bring a friend!

Ha.

I had one more problem. Or should I say, I had sixty-two more problems.

I decided to steal the shortfall from my younger brothers. I didn't feel guilty as I rifled under their twin beds for their piggy banks. They were nine and eleven; they had significant birthday money and no expenses. When I got a summer job, I would pay them back . . . if the little brats even noticed the money was missing. And I would have held up a bank to get the cash I needed. I would have rolled an old lady. These pottery classes, my meeting with Freya, had to happen. It was fated.

That Monday, I drove my battered 1997 Ford F-150 SuperCab pickup truck from school to the address Freya had texted me. I hadn't fussed with my appearance; there wasn't much point. But my hair was washed, my lips were coated in enough cherry ChapStick to give them some sheen, and I'd doubled up on deodorant . . . which was a good thing. My anticipation had me sweating like a hog.

Freya's isolated home was stunning—a cedar-and-glass structure perched on a rocky cliff above the ocean. It was surrounded by arbutus trees, their naked limbs straining toward the water, and seaside juniper perfuming the air with the tangy scent of gin. The building wasn't large, but it was sleek, modern, and expensive. The opulence of Freya's home did not surprise me. She was clearly a somebody, her effortless glamour indicative of wealth. This house, with its ocean view and modern architectural design, would be worth millions. My curiosity about her was further piqued.

I parked in the drive and headed toward the pottery studio. It was a small cottage nestled in the trees about fifty yards to the right of the main house. With its clapboard siding, multipaned windows, and wood-shingled roof, it must have been a remnant of the home's previous iteration. A chalkboard sign mounted next to the door read: *Welcome to the Studio*, in a swirly script.

My height allowed me to view her through the window at the top of the door. Freya wore black tights and a loose denim shirt—her pottery smock—her blond hair pulled back in a stylishly messy bun. I watched her plunk a heavy bag of gray clay onto a slab table, arrange her various tools into plastic containers.

She was preparing for my arrival, and I found it oddly touching. Before I became mesmerized by my observations, I knocked briefly and entered.

"Hi." Her smile was broad and white and sincere. "I'm Freya."

She held out her hand, and I took it. It was smooth and warm, her grip strong from the clay work.

"I'm Low."

"I'm so happy you came." Her eyes flitted behind me. "Just you?"

"Yep."

But she wasn't disappointed. "One-on-one always works best. Let's get started."

Freya handed me a man's plaid shirt that was too big even for me. As I rolled the sleeves, Freya sliced several one-inch pieces from a block of clay using a wire with two wooden handles—a garrote. We began by "wedging," pressing the clay into itself, making it malleable and releasing any air bubbles. I watched Freya intently, copying the movement of her small but powerful hands. Afterward, we filled two metal containers with warm water from the back sink and moved to the wheels. Here, we encountered our first hurdle.

"Are you right-handed?" she asked me.

"No, I'm left-handed."

"Oh." Her brow furrowed. "You'll turn your wheel clockwise then. I'll try to do a left-handed demonstration, but I'm not very ambidextrous."

"It's okay," I assured her. "I'm used to learning everything opposite."

And so we began. Freya chatted as I got used to the feel of wet clay spinning beneath my hands, of the force of my touch to morph it into a vessel. She had moved to the island just four months ago, she told me. It was her husband's idea. She had a husband. Of course she did. A beautiful woman her age would not be single.

"He wanted a fresh start," she elaborated, eyes on the perfect clay cone taking shape upon her wheel.

"And you?" I asked.

She didn't answer right away. Her hand slipped over the top of the mini mountain, palm compressing it into a small, round hill. "I don't want to be here. But I have no choice."

"That makes two of us," I muttered.

She looked up at me, a slow smile spreading across her face. She saw me. She really saw me. I was not simply a misfit teenager, tall and awkward and outcast.

I was a kindred spirit.

2

Mondays quickly became my favorite day. After school, I drove toward Freya's waterfront property, pulling over at the secluded boat launch to eat a snack in my truck. Thankfully, my job as egg collector provided a share of the profits, which I promptly spent on meat. My mom was a vegetarian, and since she did most of the cooking, so were the rest of us. This diet was not the most satiating for someone with my height and metabolism, so I would often buy burgers or subs loaded with ham, turkey, and salami—no onions. I was conscious of my breath in the small studio environment. After checking my teeth in the rearview mirror, I drove to Freya's home, arriving each day at precisely four o'clock.

She was always there, always prepping, as if she were as eager for our sessions as I was. Her smile, when I entered, was bright and welcoming even if her blue eyes were sometimes sad, sometimes red and puffy (From allergies? From crying? From a hangover?). Each time, I tried to hand her a ten-dollar bill, and each time, she waved it away. "We can deal with that later." Eventually,

I stopped offering and slipped most of the money back into my brothers' stashes.

On my second lesson, I arrived to find that the side-by-side pottery wheels had been moved to face each other. "This way, you can mirror what I do," Freya said. It was the most considerate thing anyone had ever done for left-handed me. As I took my seat across from her, a lump of gratitude formed in my throat.

I was not particularly good with my hands, but Freya was a patient and encouraging teacher. Within a few lessons, I was creating slightly lopsided bowls, mugs that were a tad off-center, and vases that wobbled on flat surfaces. Pottery is quite a forgiving craft. Freya would help me trim and patch my creations, would suggest a heavier glaze that would better hide the flaws in my work. In time, I created giftable, even salable crockery. But the product of my lessons was not the point.

Freya was the point.

As we worked, I learned more about her. She had grown up in Pacific Palisades, a coastal neighborhood west of Los Angeles. Freya's mother was Icelandic, had gifted her only child her Nordic good looks and artistic talent.

"She taught me to work with clay when I was five years old," Freya said. "By the time I was eight, my pieces were good enough to sell. We spent hours together in her backyard studio. I didn't realize she was batshit crazy until I was thirteen."

"She was *crazy*?"

"Bipolar. But she never got diagnosed, so she never took medication," Freya stated. "She'd stay up all night making pottery, then she'd sleep all day. Sometimes, I wouldn't see her for over a week, just hear her banging around out there in the night."

Freya's father was a powerful entertainment lawyer and a workaholic. He'd been a distant and distracted parent, but she'd

inherited her drive and work ethic from him. Her parents' marriage was tense and dysfunctional.

"My dad loved my mother, but she was a liability. He never
knew what she was going to say or what she was going to do.
Once, he took her to a film premiere and she made out with the
female lead."

I was tempted to laugh at the outrageousness but didn't know
if I would offend my teacher. Luckily, Freya chuckled.

"She was nuts, but she was never boring." She set down a scalpel-
like trimming. "And boring is the worst thing you can be."

I couldn't suppress my smile. I knew people considered me
odd, charmless, intense—but not boring. I was complicated. I was
complex.

After numerous affairs, her parents divorced. Freya's mom
moved to Topanga Canyon, but Freya stayed in the Palisades with
her dad. "I knew if I lived with my mom, I'd become her care-
giver. And my dad had a lot of useful connections in the entertainment industry."

Freya had started out as a model. "Commercial stuff," she
explained, as she demonstrated how to apply slip to a bowl with
a squeeze bottle. "I wasn't tall enough for editorial." She looked
at me then. "Have you considered modeling, Low? You've got the
height and a really unique look."

My response was a blank stare. In addition to the lack of a
modeling industry in our tiny community, I'd never thought of
my lanky body and pointed features as positives.

"Actually, don't do it," Freya continued. "You'll end up with
low self-esteem and an eating disorder."

It had been a throwaway compliment, but I clung to it for
days. Unlike every other person on our island, Freya saw something different when she looked at me. She saw someone inter-

esting, fashion-forward, maybe even elegant. I swear my posture improved in the afterglow.

Freya had been an actress, too, a career she called *soul-crushing*.

"I did a teen sitcom pilot that never got picked up. And a sappy Christmas movie that was just embarrassing. My character's name was Trixie Gains. Do I look like a Trixie fucking Gains to you?"

I laughed. "No."

"We filmed it in LA with fake snow. I had to wear angora sweaters in every scene, and it was ninety degrees. LA is a cesspool," she informed me, "but I miss the weather."

In more recent years, she'd been a social media influencer. "It was the best gig ever," she said, her eyes sparkling with remembrance. "I'd get paid twenty grand for a post. Up to thirty for a live story. I got invited to clubs and restaurants and concerts. And I got so much swag! Beauty products, electronics, even vacations."

I avoided social media like a root canal, but I said, "Sounds amazing."

She put down the sponge she'd been using to wipe the wheel. "I had half a million Instagram followers. I'd get over a hundred thousand likes on my posts. Sixty thousand views of my stories. It was addictive—all the attention, all the adoration, and positive reinforcement."

I smiled and nodded, though I was unfamiliar with the feeling of public validation.

"But then . . . all those people turned against me." She dropped her sponge into a bucket of water and stood. "It was never real. They never cared about me." She moved toward the back sink, leaving me to ponder her bitterness.

Other than some superficial chitchat—*What's your favorite class at school?* Photography. *What kind of music do you like?*

Eighties and nineties alternative—Freya talked exclusively about herself. This worked well for me. I wasn't ready to open up to her, didn't want to dispel the illusion that I was just a regular girl. I couldn't risk her judging me as a freak and cutting me off. She was the most interesting, extraordinary person I had ever met. I was already addicted to her.

Since her marriage, Freya had lived in Montreal, Las Vegas, and New York. "I loved it there," she told me. "In my heart, I'm a New Yorker."

"You've lived in a lot of places."

"My husband was a professional hockey player. When he got traded, we moved."

My family did not watch sports. Our motto was: *Cooperation, not competition.* (Yes, my family had a motto that was embroidered, framed, and hung in our entryway.) Hockey, in particular, was too violent and pugilistic . . . though I'm sure my spaz of a brother, Leonard, would have loved it. But I knew enough about pro sports to be impressed. By the money, the fame, the athletic prowess.

"Has he retired now?" I asked.

"Sort of," she said, eyes on the perfect cylinder forming under her expert touch. "He was forced to leave a couple of years ago. After he killed someone."

Abruptly, I pulled my hands from the tower of clay, my precarious structure caving in on itself. "Oh my god."

Freya's voice was nonchalant. "It was an illegal hit. Broke the guy's neck. He was paralyzed from the waist down. And then . . ." She finally released her vase and looked up. "He overdosed on his pain meds."

It was wrong to be relieved—it was still terrible, a man was still dead—but Freya had made it sound like cold-blooded murder.

"So, it wasn't your husband's fault," I said.

"Tell that to the dead guy's family," she snapped, and her face darkened. "They sued us for millions. It wasn't enough that Max's career was ruined. That he pled guilty to assault charges. We've been harassed online and in real life. We've had to move to the middle of fucking nowhere and still . . . they had to make us pay."

Freya hated these people who had lost their son, their brother, their uncle; she had no compassion, no empathy for them. Perhaps I should have taken note. But I didn't. Instead, I stammered, "I-I'm sorry."

"Thank you, Low." Freya looked at me for a long moment. "You know, if you want to come to the studio more often, you're welcome to. It's hard to get much done in just one session a week. Besides"—she smiled, and she looked ridiculously pretty—"I enjoy your company."

Something bloomed inside of me, spreading warmth to my stomach, my chest, and my throat. Her attention nourished me. It filled the empty place in my soul, cast light into the dark shadows of my psyche. Even if I had known then how it would all end, I wouldn't have walked away.

I couldn't.

3

I know what you're thinking: I was in love with her. And I was, in a way. But a *crush* is far too simplistic a term for what we shared. Romantic love doesn't even begin to convey our bond. Freya and I had a *soul connection*. I know that sounds like something I read in one of my parent's New Agey books (and it is), but it's also the truth. My friendship with Freya felt complex, profound, and eternal. She made me feel like a whole person, for the first time in my life.

My sexuality, at seventeen, remained undefined. I had, on occasion, had crushes on boys and, as often, on girls. These feelings had all gone unreciprocated, though, which prevented me from declaring a preference. And while I longed for a romantic relationship, it wasn't about sex for me. I wanted intimacy and connection but felt no need to get naked and swap bodily fluids. I might have been biromantic asexual. Or maybe I was a bisexual late bloomer. There was no pressure to label myself. I was raised in a progressive community, in an unconventional family. I was taught to have an open mind. My polyamorous parents led by example.

My mom and dad had a girlfriend named Gwen. They had been with her for most of my life. Gwen lived in a cottage at the edge of our property line. In the summers, Gwen's lover Janine moved in. Janine was not a poly so her relationship with my parents was strictly platonic. She was a teacher on the mainland but spent her summers with Gwen working on her short-story collection.

A few other lovers had come and gone, but the only other repeat offender was Vik. He kept a double-wide mobile home on the island's northern tip and traveled a lot, but he occasionally shared my mother's bed, and, when Janine was in the city, sometimes Gwen's. (My dad and Vik were close friends but not romantically involved.)

The thing was, it worked for everyone but me. My parents and their partners really loved one another. They were caring and considerate of everyone's feelings, warm and affectionate to us kids. My brothers had never known any different, so they loved Gwen, Janine, and Vik like stepparents. Or aunties and uncles. I was less enamored.

Perhaps it was because I was the eldest. I'd had loving, stable, *normal* parents until I was five. Then, they sat me down and told me things were about to change.

"You know how Mommy and Daddy love each other?" my mom began.

I nodded.

My dad picked it up. "We feel that we can love other people that way, too."

"Like Grandma?" I asked.

They'd exchanged an amused look. "We love Grandma but not in that way," my mom said. "We want to love other people in a mommy/daddy way."

My father clarified. "When mommies and daddies are only allowed to love each other, that's called monogamy. We feel that's unnatural. It's an outdated biblical construct that's been perpetuated by conservative elements in modern society."

I was *five*. Lost in their incomprehensible explanation, I had given them my blessing.

It wasn't uncommon for couples to swap partners on the island. Locals called it the "Hawking Shuffle" or "the island way." But this behavior was strictly sexual, a party favor even. My parents and their partners considered themselves a family. I didn't realize it was weird to have three to five adults attend a recorder concert or a school play until the third grade. That's when I noticed the whispers and sidelong glances of the other parents. That was the first time Evan Wilcox called me a *hippie*.

After my eighth birthday party, when my guests' parents came to retrieve them, our fate was sealed. They looked at our chickens and goats and the shelves full of my mom's canning with a wary eye. They spotted Vik rubbing my mom's shoulders while my dad, Gwen, and Janine served the birthday cake, and soon we were proclaimed a freaky free-love, hippie commune. I was mortified.

My parents were not ashamed of who they were. "We all love each other so much. It's a beautiful thing," my mom said.

"Sex and physical affection are an expression of that love," my dad tried, but I wasn't listening.

Perhaps my apathy toward sex stemmed from growing up with parents who so exuberantly enjoyed it. It wasn't like they *did it* in front of me, but nor did they pretend, like all parents should, that they never did it at all.

Shortly before I met Freya, my mom had announced that she was three months pregnant with her fourth child.

"I can't wait to be a big brother," Wayne said. But he was just nine, too young to understand the optics of this new addition. I was too old to be a big sister, yet again. I was too self-conscious to welcome another human into our large family. And I was resentful. A baby would take up more room, more time, more love. My parents' affection was already spread too thin.

At home, I was an afterthought. At school, I was a pariah. At Freya's studio, I was everything. Freya was a best friend, a parent, and a crush all wrapped up in one worldly, glamorous package. Later, people would say I was obsessed with her, but I wasn't.

With Freya, I was home.

4

After about a month, Freya invited me up to the main house. "I need a glass of wine," she said, after a particularly arduous session with a set of eight matching dinner plates that had been commissioned for the new gift shop in town. "Want one?"

I was seventeen. I rarely drank alcohol. Booze was a social beverage, so I had few instances to indulge. I also had to drive home after. But I couldn't turn down the opportunity to explore the stunning cliffside house. To see where Freya and her husband lived. To gain more insight into her life.

The house had floor-to-ceiling windows on all sides, providing ocean views, abundant natural light, and a significant lack of privacy. Given its isolated location, this was a nonissue. When I parked my car, I was allowed a glimpse into the home through the glass. It looked like something out of a magazine, so tidy, so serene. Once, I'd caught a brief glimpse of a man passing by with a cup of coffee in his hand, and my interest was piqued. I wanted in. I wanted more.

"Sounds good."

Despite its scenic location, its awe-inspiring exterior, its jaw-dropping price tag, the house was warm and homey. The floors, cupboards and closets were a soft golden wood that seemed to glow in the afternoon light streaming through the walls of glass. Everything else was white: the walls, the furniture, the quartz countertops. The decor was distinctly Scandinavian—sleek, unfussy—obviously a nod to Freya's maternal heritage. It was so different from my own cluttered, chaotic, colorful home with its abundance of noises and scents. I felt an almost overwhelming sense of peace and belonging. I wanted to spend time here. A lot of time. I wanted to live here.

I followed Freya to the pristine kitchen that had a distinctly unused feel. She expertly opened a bottle of red wine and poured us two large glasses. Handing one to me, she led us to a sunken living room that afforded us views of the dark blue Pacific. I chose a Danish-style leather-upholstered chair; Freya curled up on the white sofa, pulling a white blanket across her lap. She was the kind of person who could drink red wine on white furniture. I was not.

"This house is amazing," I said.

"Thanks," she said, looking around her as if seeing it for the first time. "Too bad it's not in New York or LA. Or anywhere that's civilized. But then we wouldn't be able to afford it, since we settled the lawsuit."

"Yeah," I mumbled, unsure of an appropriate response.

Freya looked at me intently. "Does this feel strange to you?"

"What?"

"Us. Our friendship."

"It feels great to me." I covered. "I mean, it feels *normal*."

Freya sipped her wine. "I'm so much older than you, but I feel so close to you. I was lonely. Maybe even depressed. And then you came along and now . . . I just feel lighter and happier."

My voice came out a croak. "Me too."

"I thought I had friends before, but I didn't. I had fans and followers. I had acquaintances. When the shit hit the fan, they disappeared. Poof."

"I-I'm sorry."

"But now I have you. And I know you'd never let me down like that."

I was about to say that I wouldn't. No matter how many people her husband killed, I would have her back. But she kept talking.

"I'm grateful for the stuff I've been through. I can read people now. I can tell who's a shallow hanger-on, and who's a true, quality friend." She drank more wine. "I'm more complicated and interesting now. Strife builds character, you know. People who have never experienced hardship just don't get it."

I was so desperate to grow our connection, to show her that I was complicated and interesting, too, that I decided to share the details about my unconventional family.

"My parents are polyamorous," I blurted. "They have a girl-friend who lives on our property."

Freya stared at me for a beat, and then her face lit up. "Oh my god . . . Do you live in a sex cult?"

"No, it's not like that."

"But your parents are swingers."

"Poly is different. They have multiple relationships, but everyone is in love. And they just have a normal amount of sex, I think. At least now that they're middle-aged."

Just then, a man walked into the room. He was tall—much taller than I was—and muscular. He was all right angles: square jaw, square shoulders, big strong arms and legs. . . . He was wear-ing sweats (but expensive sweats) and a fitted black T-shirt. A few curls of dark hair peeped out from under a black knitted hat. His eyes were brown, almost black, and his skin tone was warm. (The next day, when I googled him, I found out that he was Métis, a descendant of Indigenous peoples and French settlers.) He had a bit of dark stubble above his lip and on his chin. He was serious, unsmiling . . . and ridiculously attractive. So this was Freya's husband.

"Hey, Max," Freya said. "This is Low. She lives in a sex cult."

I blushed to my ankles. "No, I don't!"

"Hi," Max muttered, as if living in a sex cult was like living in a duplex.

"N-nice to meet you," I managed, my heart thudding audibly in his presence.

Freya asked him. "How was your run?"

I noticed that he was sweaty and breathing heavily. My heart began to flutter. My romantic feelings may have been ambiguous, but at that moment, in the presence of this aggressively masculine specimen, I was decidedly hetero.

"Good," he said, pulling off his hat, revealing thick black waves of hair. Jesus Christ.

"Join us for a drink?" Freya suggested.

His face darkened. "I'm going take a shower."

"You're no fun," she said to his departing back. And then to me: "He says he's quit drinking, but I'm not buying it. Anyway . . ." She stood, picking up my glass, which, to my surprise, was empty. "More for us."

"No, thanks," I said, but she was already in the kitchen, already refilling both of our glasses.

"You can't let me drink alone, Low."

Freya returned and handed me the glass. She'd brought the bottle with her, which I instinctively knew was a bad sign. Or was it a good sign? I felt giddy and relaxed and happy, and I didn't want it to end. So I went with it.

"So . . . ," Freya said, continuing her inquiry, "are you excited for your graduation?"

"Yes," I said quickly. "School sucks."

"I hated it, too."

"Really?"

Freya was so pretty, so charismatic. She had to have been popular.

"I couldn't wait to get out into the world and start my life for real. Are you going away to college? Traveling?"

"I'm taking a gap year," I said, my practiced answer. "I'll hang out here and figure out what I want to do with my life."

My teachers and counselors had pressured me to apply to colleges. I'd focused on general arts programs at West Coast schools and been accepted by all of them. I'd even been offered scholarships to a few, but I had deferred, citing a need for a break. My parents thought I should travel for a year—preferably to Eastern locales that would open my mind and prompt a spiritual awakening. But I was too intimidated. I had never been accepted by my peers. Why would I think that a world full of strangers would embrace me? And now, I had Freya. For the first time, I felt warm and welcome and accepted.

"I'm glad," she said, draining the bottle into both of our glasses. "I like having you around."

"I like being around."

I wanted to grab the words out of the air and swallow them back down. Freya's proclamation had sounded casual and breezy; mine sounded creepy and obsessive. And needy and gross. So I changed the subject.

"I have a joint."

I didn't smoke a lot of pot. Or maybe I just didn't smoke a lot of pot compared to my dad and the cool kids at my school. But I usually had a joint in my wallet, just in case. A few tokes could enhance a sunset or take the edge off a stressful social situation.

"Fun," Freya said, standing up. "I'll get a lighter and an ashtray. And another bottle of wine."

Though I was a novice drinker, I knew that cross-fading (combining pot and alcohol) was a bad idea. No way would I be able to drive home now. But I had set something in motion that I couldn't stop. Didn't want to stop. So I reached for my wallet and extracted the blunt.

I'd worry about getting home later.

5

maxime beausoleil

I didn't know the tall, gangly teen drinking wine in our living room, but I didn't want her there. Freya shouldn't have been serving alcohol to a kid. And she shouldn't have been smoking pot with one, either. (I could smell it, even from the second floor.) We'd had enough trouble and controversy. We couldn't handle any more without coming apart. But Freya had always liked to be adored, craved it even.

When I first met her, I didn't know she was famous. She was beautiful and *effervescent*, like expensive champagne. Back when I drank, I was a beer guy, but no one can turn down really good bubbly. She was a social media celebrity, an *influencer*. I wasn't on social media, didn't even know that you could make money that way. But Freya had turned posting about nightclubs and clothes, workouts and makeup into a lucrative career.

We met at a charity fundraiser in Beverly Hills. I was with the LA Kings then, and the whole team was there. I believed in giving back, in using my celebrity to raise money and awareness for important causes, but I was never comfortable at these events. I grew up in a small town in the Yukon with a population under fifteen hundred; LA was like another planet. And people acted weird around me. Grown men turned into excited little boys. Women fawned and flirted. That fundraiser was for a children's hospice, so I pushed my unease aside. I like kids, and the thought of them getting sick, even dying, hurt my heart. So I was standing on the lawn of this mansion, soaking my lips in a sickly signature cocktail, when she approached me.

"You're obviously one of the Kings," she said. "You any good?"

This was early in my career, before I was written off as the team enforcer, the muscle, the vigilante. I was a physical player, but also a strong face-off man with a powerful slap shot, so I said, "Yep."

"I'd better get a photo with you then."

I obliged, letting her nestle under my arm, holding her phone out as instructed. She curled herself into me, smiling coyly at the camera. She was transformed on the screen; polished and pouty and perfect. I thought she was more beautiful in real life, when she was animated and real. After I snapped a couple of photos, she took back her phone.

She looked at the images. "We look good together." She didn't seem to require a response, so I didn't give her one. Her eyes were on the screen, her fingers tapping on the keyboard. "What's your name?"

"Maxime Beausoleil. My friends call me Max."

"Are you on Insta, Max?

"No."

She looked up then. "Are you a caveman or something?"

She was condescending, borderline rude. I don't know what's wrong with me, but I found it attractive.

"I get enough attention," I said.

Her eyes roved over me. "I'll bet you do."

She tapped away at the device again and then proffered it to me. I looked at the photo of the two of us. I was smiling, ever so slightly. I hadn't even realized it. And then I read the caption:

Just met my future husband.

And that was it. We were together.

Women have always been attracted to me. I'm tall and fit. My face is handsome, except for the long scar that now slices across my upper lip, a constant reminder of the stick to the face that changed everything. Freya used to say it was sexy, it made me look like a warrior. But it's been a long time since she's said that. And, of course, I have money. Not as much as I used to, but still . . . a lot. When I first started playing, I gave in to the attention. I thought it was harmless. But I learned the hard way, how much trouble a one-night stand can cause.

So I was ready for a relationship, tired of flings and hook-ups. Freya and I were good together. We looked the part. We had physical chemistry and common interests (like fitness and nutrition). And we complemented each other. I was quiet; Freya was talkative. I was big; she was tiny. I was organized; she was flighty.

But there was a darkness inside of me, a violence that I'd always struggled to contain. The steroids made it worse, but there were plenty of guys in the league who took them and didn't maim anyone. During that fateful game, Ryan Klassen hit me in the mouth with an intentional high stick, and I saw red. I wanted to hurt him. Maybe I even wanted to kill him, just for a moment.

When I went back on the ice, I slammed him headfirst into the boards. I thought I'd get a penalty, maybe a game misconduct. I didn't know I'd ruin his life. And my life. And Freya's.

She would never forgive me, and rightly so. I didn't deserve it. But that didn't mean I'd stop trying to make it up to her.

Freya knew that. And she used it.

6

low

I woke up sometime during the night. Or maybe it was early morning. It was dark outside the window, a crescent sliver of moon and an abundance of stars visible from where I lay. My mouth was dry and cottony and tasted liked I'd eaten a bale of that pink fiberglass insulation that people use in their attics. (Not that I've ever done such a gross thing, but I can assume that's how it would taste.) It took a few seconds for the evening's events to come back to me: Freya inviting me into her house; pouring me many glasses of red wine; introducing me to her big, hot, surly husband. I'd gotten drunk. And then I'd gotten stoned. I probably was *still* drunk and stoned, judging by my clouded brain and my queasy stomach.

My eyes grew accustomed to the light, and I took in my surroundings. I was in a tastefully furnished guest room, on the lower level of the house. How had I gotten there? Had I been able to stumble down the stairs of my own volition? Or had Max carried me down there? Had he held me in his strong arms like a long, limp spaghetti noodle? At that moment I realized that my jeans and flannel had been removed. I wore only a yellowing bra and a matronly pair of cotton underpants. Who had undressed me? Shame burned my cheeks and throat. I wanted to get up and leave, but I couldn't drive in my condition. Rolling over, I decided to sleep for another hour or two, then make my escape.

As my eyes closed, I heard a bang. And then another. It didn't alarm me. It could have been the wind or a wild animal knocking about outside. Living in the woods came with a nighttime soundtrack. It was the noise that followed that made me sit bolt upright in bed. A scream, almost a roar—agonized, enraged, in pain. It was a woman. It was Freya.

I had to go to her, had to do what I could to help her, protect her, save her. I clambered out of bed, but the room tilted, and my stomach flipped. Oh God. I was going to be sick. I couldn't puke in this pristine guest room with its seagrass rug, its snow-white duvet, its Wedgwood-blue accent pillows. But if Freya was in physical or emotional pain, she needed me. I didn't know if Max was there, if he was hurting her or helping her. I sat back down and dropped my head between my knees, just for a moment, until I regained my equilibrium.

But when I raised my head, a few second later, the noise had stopped. No more banging or wailing . . . just silence. Had I dreamed it all? Were auditory hallucinations a side effect of the red wine–pot combo? I didn't usually drink, and I rarely smoked the stimulating sativa strain at night. Perhaps it had all been a vivid, disturbing dream? I didn't want to go prowling through the dark and silent house, searching for a scream that may not have happened. I lay down again, and soon, I was asleep.

When I awoke, the sun was high in the sky. I had overslept bigtime. There would be no clean getaway; I would have to face

Freya and Max. Finding my pants and shirt folded neatly on a wooden chair, I dressed and slipped into a nearby bathroom. I peed, splashed water on my face, and patted at my unruly hair. There was a green tinge to my complexion, but I knew it would soon be obliterated by the pink of embarrassment. Freya had offered me a glass of wine, and somehow, I'd ended up in a coma. It was humiliating. And would highlight the fact that I was too young, too childish, too inexperienced to be Freya's friend.

She was at the kitchen window, wearing oversize sweats, her hair sexily unkempt. Her hands gripped a steaming mug of coffee as she stared out at the sparkling ocean view. She was so still, mesmerized by the beauty or just lost in thought. I wondered if I could sneak past her and leave without a word.

And then she turned. " 'Morning, party girl." There was an amused, mocking tone to her voice.

"'Morning," I muttered, inching toward the front door. "I'm sorry about last night. I don't normally drink. And I shouldn't have smoked up."

"Don't worry, hon. We've all been there." She walked toward the fancy espresso machine. "Coffee?"

My stomach churned. "No, thanks. I should go."

"Okay," she said breezily.

"Apologize to Max for me."

"He's out in the kayak. You have nothing to apologize for, but I'll tell him when he gets back."

I nodded and moved toward the door but stopped. There was something I had to ask.

"Last night . . . I thought I heard you scream."

"Really?" she said, with a smirk. "You must have dreamed it. That pot was strong. I had crazy dreams all night."

I had no choice but to believe her. And so I did.

7

For a few days, I was too ashamed to go to the pottery studio. I'd made a fool of myself, shown how immature and inexperienced I was. As I drove home after school one afternoon, not long after that crazy night, I felt a distinct sense of melancholy. My time with Freya had been the highlight of my mundane existence, and I'd ruined it. When I got home, I noticed the text messages. From her.

Are you coming today?

Is everything okay?

And then:

I miss you

A warmth spread through me as I read her words. I wasn't used to being missed. When I'd spent the night in Freya's guest room, my parents hadn't even bothered to call me. Even though staying out all night was highly out of character, they had not panicked that I'd been in a car crash, mauled by a cougar, abducted by a pervert. That morning, when I'd finally shuffled into the house in my bedraggled state, my mom, my dad, and Gwen were having coffee in the kitchen.

"Look what the cat dragged in," my mom said teasingly.

Gwen chimed in. "Uh-oh. The grad parties have begun!"

"Want some eggs?" my dad offered. "The amino acids will help your hangover." He was a plumber by trade but considered himself something of an expert on the healing power of food.

My stomach churned. "No, thanks," I grumbled. For my parents to think that my classmates would suddenly embrace me because the end of school was imminent just showed how clueless they were about my life. I hurried to my room.

But now, Freya was worrying about me, asking after my well-being, missing me. I was tempted to run out to my truck and drive directly to her studio, but it was getting late. So I texted back.

> Got tied up at school. Can I come tomorrow?

Within a minute, she replied.

> Of course! You can come anytime.

And then, three heart emojis. *Three.*
With a small smile on my face, I turned off my phone.

When I arrived at the studio the next day, Freya didn't mention my drunken performance, or the scream I had heard (or dreamed). She acted like the night had never happened, chatting breezily about a movie she'd watched recently, and a fish pie Max had made for their dinner. Since our cocktail party, she seemed to take an interest in me. Or, more accurately, an interest in my living situation.

"I'm so glad you opened up to me about your family," she began, as we pulled our works-in-progress from the drying shelves. "I think polyamory is really modern and evolved. Monogamy isn't easy. In fact, it's impossible for some of us."

For some of *us*?

"My parents cheated on each other constantly," she continued. "And they'd get so fucking jealous. Once," she said, moving to the open door to sand a vase in preparation for glazing, "my mom tried to run my dad's mistress down with her car."

"Jesus."

"She missed her, thank God. Drove into the side of the restaurant." She set down the sandpaper. "You're lucky that your parents are mature enough, and self-confident enough to have sex without all the possessiveness and ego."

She had a point. The free-loving adults in my life never tried to run each other over. So, I said, "I guess."

Freya resumed her vigorous sanding. "How do you know which guy is your dad?"

"My parents were monogamous when I was born." I was at the wheel attempting to trim the bottom of a vase. The clay was too dry, causing it to flake and chip under my tool. "Vik and Gwen joined the family when I was about five. Plus, Vik's Indian. If he were my dad, my complexion wouldn't look like skim milk."

"Your skin is *alabaster*," Freya said, causing me to flush with delight.

"I wouldn't be surprised if my dad wasn't actually my dad," she continued. "I was going to do one of those DNA tests, but if he found out I wasn't his, he'd be angry. And what if my real dad was the pool boy or something? Or worse . . . an *agent*!"

I chuckled, though I knew nothing about agents.

"Besides, if things with Max and me don't work out, I'm going to need my rich daddy."

My carving tool gouged the clay, and I stopped the wheel. Were there problems in Freya's marriage? Was there a possibility that she and her husband would separate? They looked so perfect together. I couldn't imagine why anyone would ever leave a man like Max. Or a woman like Freya.

She didn't seem to notice my physical reaction. "When you get older, will you have an open relationship?"

My response was instant. "No."

She looked up from her project.

"I want to be treasured," I said. "I want to be someone's one and only."

Freya seemed taken aback by my vehement response. I couldn't blame her. Given my lack of romantic experience and prospects, it was surprising that I'd given the question previous thought. But I had. I'd given it a lot of thought.

Despite my lack of partners and sexual interest, I was still consumed by romantic notions. I'll admit I fantasized about Freya. And, sometimes, about Max. My attraction was aesthetic (I wanted to drink in their beauty) and sensual (I longed to cuddle and hold Freya; to be held and cuddled by Max). One day, I might develop sexual arousal, but what I wanted, now, was a significant other, someone who would adore me, worship me, and possess me.

I'd had to share all my life. I was done with it.

8

In June, I graduated from high school. The ceremony was held in the school gym, decorated with crepe paper streamers and rosettes in our school colors, navy and gold. My entire family was in attendance. From my vantage point on the stage, I could see them: my pregnant mother; my dad; Gwen and her lover Janine; Vik; and my brothers, Leonard and Wayne, filling an entire row of folding chairs. My heart pounded with dread as I waited to receive my diploma. When my turn came, I would have to walk across the stage, shake hands with Principal Graph and pose for a photo. I hoped my entourage wouldn't clap too loudly, whistle, or cheer, thus drawing attention to their numbers. I felt guilty for being ashamed of them, but I was.

And then there was the issue of my name. My *full* name that would be announced as I crossed the stage to receive my diploma. As the story goes, the precise moment I slid from my mother's womb into the tepid paddling pool set up in our cluttered living room, a tiny blue bird had alighted on the windowsill.

"Look." My mom pointed at it with a trembling hand.

My father saw it, too. "Is it a robin? A sparrow?"

If only.

The doula placed my slippery, squirming body on my mother's chest.

"It's a swallow," she said. "I've never seen one perch on a windowsill before. They usually prefer wires or fences."

Oh, the poignancy! They knew. *They just knew.* My parents considered themselves artistic, spiritual beings. They convinced themselves that calling me after this little bird was poetic, when really, it was just literal. And kind of lazy.

As a kid, I liked my name. Being named for a bird was *unique*. I read up on swallows, focusing on their positive attributes like their streamlined shape and their ability to fly all the way to Mexico in the winters. I ignored less-appealing factoids like the property damage caused by their habit of pooping off the edge of the mud nests they built on the side of homes and barns. (Really, this was a sign of a very clean bird, but I still didn't like to focus on it.) Bird imagery became a personal theme, its form appliquéd onto my lunch box, my backpack, and the sleeve of my denim jacket.

And then came middle school.

It was about four days into seventh grade when Kai Boyd, a short, sporty boy with a smattering of freckles across his nose (they gave his face a misleading innocence), approached me.

"Hey, Swallow."

"Hey."

"So . . . do you?"

"Do I what?"

"Swallow?"

Unfortunately, my naivete resulted in an honest answer. "Uh . . . yeah. Of course. Everyone does."

"She does!" he shrieked. "She swallows!"

Maple Dunn was kind enough to explain my answer in a detailed, sexualized context. That's when I shortened my name to *Low* (and, possibly, lost interest in sex). My parents were hurt by my rejection of the highly meaningful moniker they had chosen for me.

"Swallows are tiny little birds capable of great feats," my father said. "Just like you."

"You can't change to please other people," my mom added. "Do you want to live your life as a conformist?"

But I wasn't tiny or capable of greatness. And I certainly wasn't a conformist. (If I had been, I would have had more friends.) In the end, my parents understood my decision, but insisted on calling me Swallow when we were at home. I grudgingly allowed it. Nikki Minty was now crossing the stage to a chorus of cheers from her popular friends and polite, supportive applause from her parents and brother. With the alphabetical roll call, I knew I would be next. I was prepared for the snickers and whispers. While the kids who had grown up with me already knew my full name, the others didn't.

"Swallow Morrison."

As I stood, a male voice rang out from behind me.

"And she does!"

There was a chorus of gasps and titters, stern looks from the school administrators on the stage. My face burned with anger and embarrassment as I moved toward our principal. All I needed now was for my multitude of parental figures to make a show of themselves, and my humiliation would be complete.

I heard a whistle—the shrill, two-fingers-in-the-mouth kind. To my knowledge, no one in my family possessed that skill. Looking into the crowd, I saw her. Freya was standing, smiling, clapping. Everyone saw her—beautiful in a summer dress topped with a jeans jacket, her blond hair gleaming in the faint glow of overhead pot lights. This cool, beautiful, stylish woman was cheering for *me*: tall, friendless Swallow Morrison.

"Go, Low!" she cried, and I couldn't help but smile. I felt special, cool . . . chosen. (A month later, when we received the photo of Mr. Graph handing me my diploma, I was beaming.)

Eventually, we got through the roll and our principal announced that we were all high school graduates. My classmates tossed their mortarboards into the air. I abstained because my ceremonial cap had to be pinned securely to my bushel of hair with barrettes and bobby pins. As my peers gathered their headpieces, I hurried off the stage and out of the gymnasium.

Outside, parents and guests milled about in the parking lot, huddling together in the June downpour. In the Pacific Northwest, it was not uncommon for May to offer beautiful warm weather, only to be followed by an unseasonable blast of winter in June. *Juneuary*, people called it, like it was clever and not just ripped off from some corny weatherman. It was difficult to find my family amid the sea of umbrellas, but I spotted them clustered under an overhang. My mom was deep in conversation with Freya.

My stomach flipped over. What were they talking about? Me, of course. They had nothing else in common. What was my mom telling her? I had been presenting a carefully curated image of myself to Freya, revealing personal information only as I saw fit. My mother could blow this for me.

I hurried up to them. "Hey."

My mom swept me into a hug. "Congratulations, honey!"

I turned to Freya who hugged me quickly. "I'm so proud of you."

"Thanks."

"Freya says you're an excellent potter," my mom said.

"I wouldn't go that far." But I was pleased.

"Low's my favorite student," Freya added.

Other than a group of seniors Freya taught on Sunday after-noons, I knew I didn't have a lot of competition. But still, I was warmed by the compliment.

"That's so nice," my mom said. "Can you join us for dinner, Freya?"

While I wanted to celebrate with Freya, the thought of bring-ing her back to our home filled me with anxiety. What would she think of our clutter and chaos? The plethora of parents bustling around the kitchen, playfully teasing and tickling each other. Our chickens, goats, and the pig? Would she judge us like so many others had?

"I'd love to," Freya said, squeezing my mom's hand, "but I'm meeting a friend."

A friend?

Something dark and ugly filled my stomach, worked its way up to my chest and throat. It was jealousy. I'd experienced it years earlier with a brief middle school friendship. But this was deeper, more powerful. Because Freya had made me feel special, treasured, unique. She was mine and I was hers. And now I was finding out that she had a *friend*? Who was she? How had Freya found her? And could this mystery person offer Freya something that I could not?

She turned to me. "I've got to run, but I wanted to see you on your special day." Standing on her toes, she pecked my cheek and then left.

I watched her hurry through the rain, as did my mom, Vik, Leonard, and a number of others intrigued by her beauty and presence. It could have been an excuse, I realized. The thought of eating lentil stew with my motley family may have provoked the invention of an imaginary friend. As Freya climbed into her white Range Rover, my mom spoke.

"She seems nice."

"She is."

"And she's very pretty."

"She's beautiful."

I could feel my mom's eyes on me then: curious . . . even suspicious. But she must have pushed her innate protectiveness aside, because she smiled. "Let's get you home. I made a big pot of dal. Your favorite."

But dal wasn't my favorite. A bacon double cheeseburger was my favorite. My own mother didn't even know me.

"I'll join you guys in a bit," I said. "I want to stop by one of the grad parties."

My dad approached us then. "I've got some homegrown in the glove box. Do you want to take it?"

"I'm good."

Gwen said, "Don't be late. I've made baba ganoush for an appetizer."

My family scurried through the rain, toward the two vehicles required to transport them home. I skulked to my truck parked on an adjacent street, the rain wetting my mortarboard and blue synthetic graduation gown. Freya had come to see me receive my diploma. She had stood up and cheered my walk across the stage. I was grateful . . . I was.

So why did I feel so betrayed?

9

I drove directly to Freya and Max's waterfront house. If the white Range Rover was in the driveway, I would know that Freya had fabricated this friend. I'd know that she had no one but me to confide in, to laugh with, to support her . . . and I would be happy. If the white Range Rover was there, I could cheerfully go home to my family celebrations, to baba ganoush, and my eighth favorite meal. But if it wasn't there . . . I wasn't sure what I would do.

From the road, I could peek through the trees into Freya and Max's yard. The house had a two-car garage, but I'd never known them to park their cars in it. Freya had casually mentioned that it housed Max's motorcycle (the image of him on a Harley prompted a feeling that bordered on sexual arousal), and a bunch of boating equipment. I spotted Max's black Range Rover, but Freya's white model was missing.

My face burned, and my pulse pounded as I turned the car around and drove back toward town. It wouldn't be difficult to find her. There were three restaurants in Hawking that would be up to Freya's health, taste, and cleanliness standards. Only one had an ocean view, so I drove there first. Pulling up across the street from the boutique hotel that housed the eatery, I parked my truck. From there, I could see the hotel's tiny parking lot, and Freya's big white SUV. I had guessed correctly.

I was trembling by then, sweat beading my forehead and upper lip. I'd experienced intense jealousy only once before. Her name was Topaz. She had shown up at my school in ninth grade. She'd been shy and awkward, and I was sure I'd found my person. But after a month, she began to settle in, to come out of her shell. Soon, she was shrugging me off like an itchy sweater, easing her way into more popular circles. I'd felt hurt and angry, but I had let her go. Now, when I saw her laughing and smoking with her popular friends, I felt nothing.

But this was different. Freya had lied to me. She had told me that she had no one else. That she was bullied and taunted and I was her only friend in the world. Without me, she would be depressed and alone. She had let me feel important and needed. And now, she was out for dinner with some random bitch.

I got out of the truck and loped toward the waterfront board-walk. The restaurant abutted it, offering views of the Pacific, the boats, and, on a clear day, the mountains off in the distance. Even in the rain, Freya and her *friend* would be drawn to the outlook, their eyes darting from their salads to the spectacular scenery. If I brazenly walked by the window, they would see me. A six-foot-tall woman in a royal-blue cap and gown wouldn't exactly blend in. Would Freya feel like she had been caught cheating? Would she drop her fork? Spill her wine? Run after me and beg my forgiveness?

But I wasn't ready to make a scene, not yet anyway. I stopped several yards away, a vantage point that allowed me to see into the dining area without being spotted. The mortarboard still tenuously affixed to my head acted as a mini-umbrella, keeping the rain out of my eyes. If Freya wasn't in a window seat, I would have to rethink my strategy. But I knew she would be. Only the best seat in the house would do for Freya. As predicted, I spotted her light blond hair at a table for two.

Freya's back was to me, allowing me to examine her companion unobserved. The woman had a dark bob, tawny skin, a pretty face. She wasn't stunning like Freya was, but she was undeniably attractive. She looked to be about Freya's age, give or take a couple of years. Their body language was casual and familiar, like they had been friends for months. They were chatting and laughing, drinking white wine and noshing on bowls filled with healthy grains and roasted vegetables. They looked so right together, like a pair of matching salt and pepper shakers. It hurt me. Even when I wasn't drenched, wearing a drooping cap and massive gown, I would never look like I fit with Freya.

The summer storm did nothing to cool my roiling emotions. As I watched this woman spear a piece of avocado and put it in her mouth, her eyes suddenly met mine. Her brow furrowed, ever so slightly, at the sight of the sopping graduate lurking on the boardwalk. But her gaze quickly returned to Freya. She was enamored with the beautiful blonde, just like I was. And then, I realized I had seen her before. I knew who she was. And I knew how to get to her.

I turned and hurried away, my gown billowing out behind me like a Dickensian villain.

summer 2019

10

jamie vincent

On a Wednesday afternoon at the end of June, Low Morrison came into my gift shop with her résumé. She'd been there before, browsing through the items, paying particular attention to the pottery section. She was hard not to notice—over six feet tall with a mop of dark red hair and pale, almost translucent skin. There was something familiar about her, but I couldn't place her. I observed her with my nerves on edge, afraid she'd break something. She just seemed so gangly and awkward. But then I saw her pick up one of Freya's cerulean-blue dishes. She handled the piece delicately, almost lovingly.

On this visit, she strode directly to the counter. "Hi. I'm Low Morrison. I'd like to apply for a summer job," she said.

I hadn't advertised for a shop assistant, but I hoped I was going to need one. I'd opened my store last fall, when the tourist season was in decline. Retail was new to me, and I was nervous. Opening off-season gave me a chance to ease into the business before the summer's tourist boom. Covering rent over the slow winter months was not ideal, but thanks to our savings and my husband's recent book advance, it was possible. And I knew the shop would be a success. I had carefully curated my merchandise, supporting local artisans and other Pacific Northwest designers. My price point was high-end but within reason for the clientele I was sure to attract. I'd done my research into the tourist market.

But, something about Low made me uneasy. She was so intense, so direct, so . . . *looming*. Maybe it was discriminatory hiring practices, but I was afraid she would scare away customers.

"I'm not actually hiring at the moment," I said sheepishly. "But I'll keep your résumé on file and give you a call if things pick up."

The girl just stood there, blinking at me for several seconds. "You'll be overrun by tourists come July, and you're going to need help."

"I hope you're right," I replied with a smile. "I'll give you a call then."

She stood for a beat longer and then stalked out.

Hopefully, I'd get a few more applicants before the summer rush. I'd envisioned a salesclerk who was bubbly, warm, and gregarious. Low was the opposite. Perhaps she'd be fine with customers, but I wasn't sure I wanted to spend so much time with this odd girl in close quarters. I was vulnerable then, still shaky from what I'd endured. I was healing, but slowly. Very slowly.

The move to the island was supposed to be a fresh start. I was leaving behind a stressful career in marketing, manifesting my dream of owning my own gift shop. My husband, Brian, had recently sold a series of young-adult fantasy novels and was eager to leave his teaching job to write full-time. If we sold our Seattle house (thanks to Amazon, real-estate prices had skyrocketed), our stock portfolio, and most of our furniture, we could just afford to pursue our dreams on this relatively affordable island.

"And we won't talk about the baby," Brian said. "We'll put all that pain and ugliness behind us."

"Okay," I said.

But I couldn't. While my husband was able to immerse himself in a dystopian universe filled with heroic teenagers, my mind still drifted to our loss. The store—Hawking Mercantile—was demanding, time-consuming, energy sucking, but it was not mentally taxing enough to distract me from what we had endured: the crushing disappointment as all our efforts to become parents failed.

I had always wanted to be a mom. Despite my devotion to my career, I didn't take my fertility for granted. When I turned twenty-eight, I suggested we start trying to get pregnant. Brian wanted to wait. He wanted to save more money, buy a bigger home, get a better car. "If we wait until everything's perfect, we'll never have a child," I cajoled him. He acquiesced and we pulled the goalie. After a year of fruitless unprotected sex, we saw a fertility doctor.

Thus began three years of acupuncturist visits, funky herbs, hormone injections, expensive in vitro treatments, and tears. Endless tears. *I* was the problem. Tests confirmed that Brian's sperm were swift and healthy, but I had a *hostile vagina*. That's the term my (male) doctor used to describe the bacteria in my cervical mucus that was attacking Brian's sperm. My husband's healthy, well-intentioned swimmers were being murdered by the evil guardians of my barren womb. I envisioned a horror-movie scenario where stalwart explorers were taken out by a giant vulva with snapping shark teeth. It was a wonder Brian could bear to touch me.

Eventually, we decided to adopt. We didn't need a biological connection to love a child and make it ours. After diligent research, we found a reputable agency to help facilitate an identified adoption. This meant that a birth mother would select us. Brian was uncomfortable with some of the tactics the agency recommended. In addition to posting a "sparkling" profile on their site, they suggested we create our own website and Facebook page, sharing photos of our home, our travels, our pets, and our hobbies.

"I feel like we're trying to sell our apartment or our car. But we're selling ourselves," he said.

"There are a lot more people who want to be parents than there are babies," I countered. "We need a pregnant mom to choose us over everyone else." So we smiled for the camera; we poured our hearts out on video; we showed off our tidy home, our outdoorsy lifestyle, our devotion to each other. (I wanted to adopt a rescue dog, but Brian's allergies precluded it.)

And it worked! We were chosen! A seventeen-year-old girl named Mia selected us. She had wide-set eyes, a bow of a mouth, and long dark hair. She lived in a suburb of Chicago, was five months along when we were introduced via Skype. Her bump was clearly visible. We were meeting our baby, too.

I liked her. Mia was cute and bubbly and bright. We messaged often, Skyped once a week. She sent us her twenty-two-week ultrasound photo on time, our baby the size of a small banana.

"It's a girl," Mia told us, and Brian and I burst into happy tears.

My chats with Mia went beyond the pregnancy. She told me about the baby's father, a cute, sporty boy whom she had thought she loved, until she realized he was selfish and immature. There was drama in her friend group, some related to her condition, some typical mean-girl stuff. Her parents were supportive, she said, but they didn't want to engage with Brian and me. It was hard for them to give away their grandchild, but they knew it was for the best.

"It might make them feel better if they spoke to us," I suggested.

"One day," she assured me.

Mia said the things I needed to hear. "My baby is so lucky to have parents like you." And "One day, I'll be a great mom, too. I'm just not ready yet." I felt altruistic. We were giving a baby a loving home; we were giving her mother a chance to grow up.

The agency insisted that all financial help be funneled through lawyers. Mia's family had not arranged counsel yet, so we would have to reimburse her for the doctor's bills, the prenatal vitamins, and the maternity wear. But I sent her gifts: a rich buttery lotion that would prevent stretch marks; a diffuser and several calming essential-oil blends; tickets to a concert she wanted to see. She was moved and grateful. Our bond developed.

But I needed more. I needed to meet her in person, to share a meal with her, to hug her. "We should go to Chicago," I said to Brian. "I don't want our first meeting with Mia to be when we take her baby away."

He agreed, so I shared the news with Mia on a video call.

Her brow furrowed. "I've got a big exam coming up," she explained.

"We'll work around your schedule," I offered. "We'll come whenever it works for you." She smiled then and relaxed. So we set a date and flew to O'Hare. Mia wanted to meet us at her favorite restaurant in Wilmette. Her parents would have us over for dinner the following evening, but we would meet alone first. It made sense to me. This would be an overwhelming encounter. As I settled myself into the booth of the Italian joint, I was jittery, emotional, on the verge of tears. I had brought Mia a gift—a necklace with two heart pendants. It had been expensive, but I wanted her to have it. I loved her and what she was doing for us.

We waited for an hour. And then for two. I sent her an e-mail, but it bounced back. My Skype insisted there was no such address. We went back to the hotel, where I fell on the bed and wept. Brian paced the room, muttering incredulities to himself. In the morning, I called the agency.

"What's going on? Did she change her mind?"

"She may have," the woman said. "Or . . . it's possible there's no baby."

"*What?*"

"Some girls like the attention. The gifts and the messages."

"But we saw her bump! She sent us the ultrasound photo!"

I heard the woman sigh. "There are websites devoted to faking a pregnancy."

"Are you kidding me?"

"These sites offer fake test results, sonogram images, latex bumps and breasts. We try to do our due diligence, but sometimes they slip through the cracks. I'm sorry."

Our baby had never existed, but to me, she had died. I took a leave from work to grieve in private. In addition to our loss, I was humiliated by our gullibility. We had wanted a baby so badly that we'd ignored the red flags. Friends, relatives, and colleagues would be talking about us. How could we not have seen that Mia was a liar? That her bump was fake? That her parents would have been involved if she was legitimately pregnant? And then, Brian suggested the move.

I needed counseling; I can see that now. But starting a new life seemed more important. I could seek help when we were settled . . . except that Hawking was sorely lacking in mental-health services. Even if there had been a psychologist, residents would have been too embarrassed to visit. Everyone knows everything in a town this size. So I had suffered in silence. And then, one day, Freya walked into my shop. She charmed me, lifted me out of my funk, convinced me that I could be happy again.

Freya's friendship was my lifeline.

11

Most people were wowed by Freya's beauty, style, and charisma, but there was more to her than that. She was creative, visionary, a truly talented artist. She had come into my store carrying a large cardboard box. She'd set it on the countertop and extracted several pottery pieces. The bowls, vases, and platters were somehow rugged and delicate at the same time, the glazes evoking the sea and the sky and the beach. They fit perfectly into my aesthetic, and I knew I had to stock them.

I'd suggested we discuss terms over coffee, so we moved to a cozy café across the street. At a tiny table, with two steaming lattes (Freya's was a beet latte with almond milk), we discovered we had much in common. In addition to sharing a passion for art and design, we were the same age, married without children, and struggling to adapt to our new environment. And though we didn't articulate it then, we were both lonely. I think we recognized that in each other.

Soon, we were seeing each other on a regular basis: for coffee, lunch, or wine. We had dinner with our husbands twice—

once at Freya's magnificent waterfront home, once at our modest
bungalow. I'd been ashamed of our slightly run-down cottage set
back in the woods, but Freya and Max pronounced it "homey and
cozy." Despite their differences, the guys had hit it off, too. Brian
and I had never really had "couple" friends. In the past, I would
become friendly with a woman only to discover her partner was
a pompous ass. Brian would introduce me to his buddy's wife,
who'd turn out to be competitive and snarky. But we liked Max
and Freya in equal measure.

One night at dinner, when Freya bemoaned the island's lack
of a SoulCycle, we planned more vigorous visits. On Tuesday and
Thursday mornings, before I opened the store, we went for a forest hike. It was a walk, really, the path meandering gently through
the woods and along the coastline. The rain forest felt magical,
almost prehistoric with its massive cedars, abundant ferns, cur-
tains of moss. It was on these walks, our environment so private,
isolated, almost confessional, that our friendship grew and deepened.

Our standing date was weather dependent, of course. The
island got a lot of rain, which Freya struggled with. It can be
depressing for people who come from sunnier climes, but I was
used to it. I'd spent my entire life in the Pacific Northwest—or
as we Canadians call it, the South Coast. I was born and raised in
Vancouver, moved to Seattle when I married Brian. I had spent
my life in the gray and the gloom. It wasn't the weather that
caused my malaise.

It was a bright but mild morning, perfect walking weather,
when Freya mentioned her connection to Low. "I hear my favorite student applied for a job at the store."

I knew Freya taught pottery classes to a group of seniors. I
couldn't recall anyone from that demographic looking for work.

"Her name is Low Morrison," Freya elaborated, over the crunch of her expensive hiking boots on the pine needles underfoot. "She's tall."

"Oh. Right." The unique name and stature of the girl instantly sprang to mind. Her résumé still sat alone in my drawer. I'd expected to receive more applications, but the summer hiring pool was small on the sparsely populated island. And I was competing with higher-paying, more dynamic employers like the marina, the kayak rental shop, several restaurants, and two ice cream stores. Apparently, teens were not that keen to stand behind a counter helping gray-haired tourists pick out a soap dish.

"She's kind of . . . intense," I said. "I'm not sure a gift shop is the right fit for her."

"I know she seems odd, but she's sweet," Freya said. "And she *really* wants to work for you."

"But why?" I had to ask. Low Morrison seemed more suited to a solitary profession—like, working after hours at a grocery store stocking very high shelves.

"She loves ceramics and art in general. And she's a talented potter," Freya explained. "And once you get to know her, she's quite fascinating."

"Really?" My curiosity was piqued.

"She lives in a sex cult."

I stopped walking. "Pardon me?"

Freya laughed. "It's true. We had a few drinks one night and she told me all about it. Her parents are polyamorous. They live on a commune with their lovers and a bunch of goats and chickens."

In the onslaught of information, I didn't register Freya's mention of drinking alcohol with the taciturn teen. "Wow. No wonder she's so . . . *different*."

"She's not, though," Freya said. "She's shy. And she's been ostracized by the other kids because of her family and her looks. But she's smart and creative, and she'll work hard for you. I really think you should give her a chance."

Freya's championing of the unusual girl was effective. I felt for Low. And I wanted Freya to see my compassionate side. But I had a business to run. "I'll think about it," I promised.

"I actually respect her family's lifestyle," Freya continued, as the trail afforded us views of the slate blue ocean. "Sex and love without possessiveness or jealousy? I think it's admirable."

"Really?" I prompted. Some would have dismissed Freya's opinions because of her beauty, her California accent, the fact that she was hiking through the forest wearing overpriced, designer athleisure wear. But she had hidden depths. I loved our philosophical discussions.

"Everyone swaps partners on this island, and then they judge Low's family for making it official. They're a bunch of hypocrites."

The island's free-love culture was well-known. Brian and I had discussed it before we moved, speculating on how much was real and how much was legend. But it wouldn't impact us, we knew. We were committed. Solid. Traditional even.

"True," I mumbled.

"Monogamy is completely unrealistic for some people," Freya expanded. "I should know. I'm married to a professional athlete who's hot as fuck."

Those precise words had run through my mind the first time I met Max Beausoleil. And every time after that. *Hot as fuck.* It wasn't just his dark good looks enhanced by a sexy scar running across his lip; or his tall, muscular, athlete's body. It wasn't his fame and notoriety. When I met him, he'd been pleasant and engaged, but there was a darkness, a broodiness, a profound sense of tragedy about him. The combination was ridiculously attractive. Even Brian seemed enamored with him. (My husband's overt fawning was significantly less hot.)

Freya kept going. "Women throw themselves at Max constantly. I'd be naive to think that he never slept with anyone when he was on the road."

"That must have been hard for you."

"I honestly didn't care, as long as he used protection," she said. "I didn't want an STD. Or worse, a *baby*."

Her comment stung. We had been so desperate for a child and Freya was comparing a baby to a case of herpes. But I hadn't yet told her about our fertility struggles, or the evaporation of our adoptive child. I was sure she wasn't being insensitive.

"But Max and I never talked about it," she continued. "We never said, *I love you, but I'm lonely. We're apart so much, and I have needs*."

"Did you . . . ?" I didn't want to articulate it, didn't want it to sound like a judgment or an accusation.

She looked over and met my gaze. "Sex and love are not the same thing. Sex is physical. Sex is fun." She ducked under a heavy cedar bough. "The people on this island get that. Everybody cheats. At least they're open about it."

"Not *everybody* cheats."

"Really? You've never?"

"No . . . And I don't think Brian has, either."

"How can you be so sure?"

"My husband is a straight arrow. He's just monogamous by nature. We've been together since college. I know him."

"Wow. And you've never wanted to be with anyone else, either?"

"I didn't say *that*." My face was warm as I continued. "I guess I've thought about it. When I started college, I thought I would date and fool around and have fun. But I met Brian early on and he was so sweet and solid and . . . there. He was always there. . . ."

"Do you worry that you missed out on things?"

"Sometimes. At one stage, I actually brought up doing the hall-pass thing. But Brian couldn't. He said the thought of me with someone else made him sick. And I wasn't going to risk a great relationship just so I could have sex with someone other than my husband."

Freya stopped short. "So you've only ever had sex with Brian?"

I was used to being judged for our sexual exclusivity. People seemed to think we were old-fashioned or prudish. They acted as if screwing a bunch of strangers was a rite of passage like going to prom or learning to drive. "Yeah."

"Oh, honey." She looked at me with such pity. "We need to fix that."

"I love my husband," I insisted. "He's a good man. And . . . we have great sex." I felt awkward sharing this intimate detail, but I wanted Freya to understand me, understand what I had with Brian.

Freya held her palms up in front of her chest. "I was kidding, babe. I think it's beautiful that you found the right person when you were a kid."

"We were in college, not kindergarten," I quipped, as we began to walk again.

"I totally get it," Freya chirped. "Brian is smart and witty. They say that's the most attractive trait to females. A sense of humor. And bonus—he's super cute, too." She looked over and smiled. "And, of course, he wouldn't want to share a gorgeous woman like you."

"Thanks." I felt myself warm in the onslaught of compliments.

"But now that you live on this hippie island, maybe you can have your cake and eat it, too?"

"What?" I chuckled, bemused.

"I'm kidding." Freya waved the comment away. "You and Brian fit together perfectly. You don't need anyone else. You just make sense."

"You and Max seem like a great pair, too." They did. Visually at least. His dark masculinity was a perfect complement to her delicate blond perfection.

"Our relationship is complicated. We've been through a lot."

She was referring to the hit, the death, the lawsuit. I knew all about it. Everyone did. It had been in the news, off and on, for over three years. I gave her an understanding smile. "I know. I'm sorry."

"It's been so hard. Sometimes, I'm not sure it's all worth it."

"If you love him, it's worth it," I said.

"I do." Freya smiled. "And he's hung like a stallion."

I laughed, enjoying my friend's wit.

When I went home to shower and get ready for work, I replayed our conversation in my mind. I'd never been one of those women who chatted about orgasms and vibrators and blow jobs over brunch. But Freya was so comfortable with the subject, so open about sex and desire and freedom. I was fascinated. And titillated. And I loved having a girlfriend with whom I could discuss even the most intimate subjects.

Later that morning, when I opened the store, I pulled Low's résumé out of the drawer. Freya had gone to bat for this girl, had assured me that she was a good kid who deserved a break. Freya's word was enough for me. And I wanted to please my new friend. I called the number at the top of the page.

12

low

Even though Freya had personally vouched for me, it took almost ten days for Jamie to offer me a job. She was probably too busy—walking through the forest with Freya, going for coffee with Freya, having dinner with their husbands—to think about her business. On the other hand, she may have been waiting for more applicants, but that wasn't going to happen. A rumor had circulated through my peer group that Jamie would be a tyrant to work for. She'd told a previous applicant that he wouldn't be allowed a lunch break, would have to clean the toilet twice a day, and she would dock his pay by the minute if he turned up late. I'm not sure who started it. . . .

My first day on the job was a Tuesday. We were into July now, and the tourist season was in full swing, but weekdays were relatively quiet—perfect for training purposes. Not that there was much to learn. It was a gift shop, not an ER. But Jamie took me painstakingly through my duties: dusting merchandise, gift wrapping on request, using the till and the credit card machine. Had Freya not mentioned that I was intellectually superior to most seventeen-year-olds? I could have figured out these mundane tasks on my own.

I would work a couple of days a week and most weekends. Jamie chuckled as she gave me my schedule. "So I can have a bit of a social life."

With Freya. I tasted the acid of jealousy, but I forced a smile. "Works for me. I don't have a social life."

"If you ever have plans with your friends or family, just let me know. We can always work something out."

"I never have plans."

"Well, you might one day."

"I doubt it."

Jamie gave me a quizzical look before changing the subject. "Let me show you the kitchen. It's tiny, but it has a kettle and a microwave." She smiled. "And I always keep cookies in the cupboard, so help yourself."

The job was meant to be a reconnaissance mission, an opportunity to monitor Jamie and Freya's friendship, but I kind of enjoyed it, too. The store was a visually pleasing space with whitewashed plank floors, high ceilings, natural wood countertops. Even when it was full of customers, it still felt serene somehow. Jamie had curated a great selection of products, I had to give her that. I spent a lot of time dusting or wiping shelves. It gave me a chance to handle these beautiful objects.

On my third shift, Freya came into the store. "Hey!" she said, her face lighting up to see me there. "How's it going?"

"It's good." I smiled at her. "Thanks for telling Jamie to hire me."

"I didn't *tell* her to hire you. I told her that you're smart and creative and a hard worker. She made the decision all by herself."

Jamie emerged from the bathroom then, her purse in hand. Her expression was dour, but she brightened when she saw Freya. "Hi, you."

"I see your shop assistant is working out well."

"She's been great," Jamie said, and I blushed a little.

"Do you want to grab some lunch?" Freya asked.

"Sure," I said at the precise moment Jamie said, "Sounds great."

No one spoke for an awkward moment. And then, Jamie turned to me.

"Do you mind if I go this time? I've been eating hummus sandwiches behind the counter since I opened. I'm dying to sit down and eat a proper lunch."

Bitch. She was possessive of Freya. Already. But I had known Freya longer, I knew her better. I had saved her from loneliness and depression. All the time we spent together in the studio, the night when we drank red wine and smoked a joint together, she hadn't even mentioned Jamie.

"I fired some of your pieces," Freya said to me. "Come by the studio later and you can glaze them. I'd love to hear about your first week on the job."

After they left the store together, I returned to my dusting, picking up one of Freya's bud vases. It was a simple design but deceivingly hard to produce. It had a narrow base, a tall sleek neck and a delicate opening like the petals of a flower. She'd used two glazes—one sage, one denim—to re-create the color of a stormy sea. It was exquisite. And then, somehow, it was on the floor, smashed into five clean pieces.

Oops.

13

jamie

Freya and I liked the restaurant in the Blue Heron hotel. It offered harbor views and a good-size menu, though the food never quite lived up to the scenery. On weekends, the eatery was packed with tourists, but the midweek-lunch trade was sparse. Only three other tables were occupied; Freya and I easily got our favorite spot by the window.

When we'd ordered salads and iced tea, I said, "I hope Low isn't angry with me."

"It's my fault," Freya said. "We've spent so much time together over the last few months, that she thinks we're BFFs. I enjoy her, but she's just a kid."

"She's barely said a word since she's been working for me. I'm not sure how to make her feel more comfortable."

"She'll open up," Freya said as our drinks arrived. "But you can tell her anything. She's a great listener."

Suddenly, there was a crash behind us, a plate and cutlery falling to the floor. I turned in my seat to see a child, about six months old, perched on its mother's lap. The baby had a fuzzy

blond head, a pale green onesie, and a wide toothless smile—
evidence of its delight in the noise and mess it had created. The
mother, in a loose-fitting dress and Birkenstocks, looked weary
as the father, his long brown hair threaded with silver, bent to
retrieve the carnage.

"Why do people think it's okay to bring babies into restaurants?" Freya sniped. "If you're going to procreate, you have to
stay home. There should be a law."

I turned back to her. "Cute kid, though."

Freya looked over at the child. "It looks like it needs a bath.
And some vaccines."

To my embarrassment, my eyes moistened. I blinked franti-
cally, but my companion noticed.

"What's wrong? Was it the vaccine comment? Did I cross the
line?"

I grabbed my napkin, dabbing at the tears that threatened to
spill over. "It's not that. I just . . . I just got my period."

"I used to get really bad PMS when I was younger," Freya
said. "Have you tried going on the pill? It can ease the symp-
toms."

"It's not PMS." I dropped the napkin from my face. "I was a
bit late and I thought . . . I hoped . . ."

Freya leaned forward. "Are you trying to get pregnant?"

And then it all came out. The months of crushing disappointment, the costly and uncomfortable treatments, the humiliating
and painful adoption scam. I knew everything about Freya's fall
from social media grace, the bullying and abuse, the trial and the
civil lawsuit, but I hadn't wanted our friendship to be tainted
by my sad backstory. And yet, the words flowed out of me like
a burst dam. Somewhere in the middle of my monologue, our
salads arrived, but they sat untouched. Freya didn't pick up her

fork. She let me talk about my desperate, unfulfilled need for a child, our greens wilting before us.

"Brian says we can be happy without a baby," I finished. "I promised to try but . . . I just don't know if I can be." Tears leaked from my eyes.

"I know. It's hard." Freya patted my hand. "Society expects women of a certain age to become mothers. If you're not, everyone thinks there's something wrong with you."

I nodded.

"When people learn I don't want kids, they think I have some mental or emotional defect. They feel sorry for Max. He doesn't care if he has kids, but they just think the *cold bitch* he married won't give him any. I've stopped talking to his mother. And I've had to drop all my friends who've become moms because they're so annoying."

"People come right out and ask, don't they?" I inserted. "*Why don't you have kids?*"

"Like it's any of their fucking business." Freya picked up her fork then. "I'm tired of being treated like I'm less of a woman because I'm not a mom."

I watched her stab a cherry tomato, pop it in her mouth, and chew aggressively. Freya understood. We had completely opposite desires—I yearned for a child, and she disdained the idea of having one—but we had one thing in common: we were both made to feel incomplete.

"Let's do something fun," she said, "something only we *unfruitful* women can do."

I tucked into my salad. "Like what?"

"Come over tonight, you and Brian. We'll get drunk." She lowered her voice. "We'll take Molly."

"Molly?"

"MDMA. The love drug. The four of us will have a blast on that shit."

"No," I said, "no chemicals." Coming from Vancouver, the fentanyl crisis was top of mind for me. Street drugs were being cut with the potent synthetic opioid, and people were dying. The lethal drug did not discern between addicts and dabblers.

"'Shrooms, then. Completely natural."

"Where would you even get them?"

"Low's a teenager. She'll know someone who can hook us up."

"I can't buy magic mushrooms from my shop assistant!"

"I'll buy them. I won't tell her you're involved."

"I don't know. . . ."

"We'll put on some music and dance and laugh." She took a sip of iced tea. "It'll be cool. It'll be mind-expanding."

I wanted to be Freya's fun, wild, adventurous friend, but I had a bad track record with the persona. In college, I'd tried 'shrooms, pot, even ecstasy once. My dabbling inevitably ended in paranoia, vomiting, and/or diarrhea. I might have had the will, but I didn't have the constitution to be wild and adventurous. But for Freya . . . maybe I could try?

"They're perfectly safe," she insisted. "Max and I have done them a few times." She bit her lip coyly. "Have you ever had sex on psychedelics? It's amazing."

I had not. But maybe drugs were the answer to the sexual lull my husband and I were in? Not on a regular basis, but perhaps a night on magic mushrooms would allow us to recapture the passion we'd once had for each other.

"And it'll make us appreciate our freedom," Freya nudged. She lifted her chin toward the parents behind me. "Those two won't be having any fun tonight. They'll be hand-washing their kid's shitty diapers."

I giggled a little. The baby *was* cute, but Freya had a point. "By the looks of them, they'll be weaving the diapers themselves on their loom."

"From thread they spun themselves. From their pet lamb."

"The baby needs to be changed!" I joked. "Quick! Shear the sheep!"

Freya chuckled. "See how lucky we are? You have to come over tonight."

"I'll see if Brian's into it." He would be. His man-crush on Max aside, he was the fun-loving half of our partnership. While his asthma precluded him from smoking dope, he was always up for a beer and a laugh. A night on magic mushrooms would be up his alley.

"Awesome," Freya said, then she peered past me to the baby and its family. She pointed with her fork. "Look at that."

I turned to see a waitress making goo-goo eyes at the child while she wiped food from the table. Next to her, the middle-aged manager was cheerfully sweeping up the broken crockery.

"If we yelled and threw food and broke dishes, we'd get kicked out," Freya said. "People will forgive anything if you have a baby."

14

low

I had finished my shift at the store in tense silence. After Jamie had hijacked my lunch date with Freya, I was not in the mood for chitchat. Given my taciturn nature, she may not have noticed that I was giving her the cold shoulder, but I was. When I left at five thirty, she called after me, "Have a nice night, Low."

"Yep," I muttered, adding, "You too," as the door closed behind me. I couldn't lose this job, but I was pissed at my boss. She was so desperate for a friend that she'd pulled rank on me, jumped at the chance to share a meal with Freya. It was pathetic. I had just reached my truck when Freya's text came in.

Are you coming to the studio?

As usual, Freya's message lifted my spirits. When she had gone for lunch with Jamie instead of me, I'd felt angry and excluded. But her text validated that it had been me she'd wanted to eat with, me she had wanted to see.

On my way, I responded.

Her reply was instant.

Can you get me some shrooms? Enough for four people.
I'll pay you when you get here.

Of course I could get some 'shrooms. They grew wild in the
island's northern forests and several kids at school collected and
sold them. But Freya's request hurt. She was treating me like
a drug dealer. And 'shrooms for *four*? If she'd said 'shrooms for
three, or even five, I would have assumed she was inviting me to
join in. Although I didn't care for hallucinogens, I would have
made an exception for Freya and Max. But she'd said four. *Four*.
Who was she planning to trip with?

It had to be Jamie and Brian. While my straitlaced employer
did not seem the type, four months of careful observation over
the course of my friendship with Freya had convinced me that
she had no other friends. She was *friendly* with a few people,
like the seniors who took her pottery classes, but they weren't
friends. Definitely not friends who did 'shrooms together. Max
didn't seem to have any pals, probably because he spent most of
his time alone in a kayak, or on a motorcycle, or exercising.

But disappointing Freya was not an option, so I drove to the
taxi company where a former classmate worked in the office and
sold drugs out the back door. I bought five grams of magic mushrooms for fifty bucks. Freya was thrilled when I delivered the packet
to her.

"You're a doll," she said, handing me a bill. And then:
"Umm . . . Were you still planning to glaze your pieces tonight?"

"I was."

"It's just . . . Jamie doesn't want you to know she's doing
'shrooms."

So, it *was* Jamie. I liked that Freya was betraying her confidence for me. "Why would *I* care? I've done 'shrooms plenty of times." This was an outright lie—I had done 'shrooms only once, and I'd thought my lamp was laughing at me—but I hoped it might prompt an invitation.

"You know how Jamie is," Freya said. "She's kind of uptight."

Her disparaging comments about Jamie made me feel deliciously warm. "Just a bit," I joked.

"I don't want her to be paranoid and have a bad trip. Come back tomorrow."

The glow of satisfaction evaporated. Freya was dismissing me, like a delivery person. Like a mule.

"Sure."

"Thanks for being so cool," she said. She stood on her tiptoes then and kissed my cheek. It was an odd thing to do, but she must have sensed my feelings of betrayal and rejection, must have thought she could assuage her guilt with this pathetic show of affection.

"No big deal."

But it was. A big fucking deal.

15

brian vincent

I was supposed to be working on my novel, but at some point that afternoon, I'd fallen down a social media rabbit hole. When Jamie walked through the front door at six fifteen, I was startled to realize I'd squandered hours of writing time. Feeling guilty, I jumped out of my seat.

"Hey, babe." I hurried over and kissed her cheek. "You surprised me. I was *in the zone*."

"Were you?" She gave me a wry smile. "Or were you on Facebook?"

"Twitter," I admitted. "But there's a plagiarism scandal going on with this huge YA author. Technically, it was research."

"Or schadenfreude."

I held up two fingers about an inch a part. A bit.

We moved into the kitchen, where lunch dishes and coffee cups still littered the counters. I began stuffing them into the dishwasher, as I asked, "Are you hungry? I bought a piece of fish at the docks. I could make some risotto to go with it."

"Freya invited us over tonight."

"Oh." I stopped. "For dinner?"

"For magic mushrooms."

"Seriously?"

Jamie went to the cupboard and pulled out a glass. "Apparently Low can hook her up."

"Are you into it?"

Jamie and I had taken 'shrooms in college. I'd had a decent trip, though I'd spent most of the night rubbing her back while she vomited into a garbage can.

"I don't know." Her pretty face looked troubled as she poured water from the Brita. "I had a hard day today."

"Did something happen at the store?"

"No." She turned away, grabbed a cloth, and busied herself wiping mustard from the counter. "I got my period, that's all."

"Jamie"—my voice was gentle—"you can't get sad every month."

"I know that," she replied, still vigorously cleaning. "I wouldn't have, but I was late. I got my hopes up a bit."

"How late?"

She hesitated before answering. "Two days. But my period is like clockwork. I thought . . . maybe . . . I've got an assistant, my stress levels are down. . . ."

I moved toward her, tried to draw her into a hug, but she pecked my cheek and stepped away.

"I'm fine now. Really." She rinsed the cloth under the faucet. "Freya and I had lunch. We talked about how society expects women to become moms. Everyone thinks I'm defective because I can't have a baby. Freya doesn't want kids and people think she's a heartless monster."

"And then you decided to get high on psychedelics?"

"Basically, yeah." She smiled as she wrung out the cloth. "She thought a night of friends and music and tripping would make us appreciate our childlessness. I'll probably just have some wine, but the rest of you can take mushrooms, if you want."

"Sounds kind of fun."

"I knew you wouldn't want to miss a chance to see your *boyfriend*."

I rolled up a dish towel and whipped it at her butt as she laughingly skittered from the room.

"My boyfriend," I muttered to myself as I pulled the fish from the fridge. Of course there was nothing romantic about my feelings toward Max Beausoleil, but I liked the guy. He was a small-town boy who hadn't let fame and fortune go to his head. Or, maybe it had gone to his head, but then the fallout from the illegal hit, the lawsuit, Ryan Klassen's overdose, had brought him crashing back down to earth. Like everyone with a TV, I'd watched the replay of Klassen's incendiary stick in the face, and Beausoleil's retaliatory check. I saw the anger and aggression on Max's face in slow motion. I also saw his tears as he apologized to the Klassen family in an emotional press conference outside the courthouse. It was hard to muster pity for the rich, handsome athlete with his sexy blond wife hanging off his arm. He'd pled guilty to assault to "spare them the ugliness of a trial," but many thought it was a PR move, that he was crying crocodile tears. I'd been one of them.

Growing up, I'd hated his type. The scene at my Seattle high school was straight out of *The Breakfast Club*: jocks, stoners, Goths, rich kids, nerds . . . I was firmly, and quite happily, entrenched in the nerd clique. In fact, I was a member of a nerd subset known as the creative nerds. We were the Dungeons & Dragons players, the Warhammer fans. My group was held in even lower esteem because of our lack of earning potential. The computer geeks and gamers would end up with lucrative careers as programmers and coders. We were destined to work in comic-book shops or toy stores.

No one looked down on us more than the jocks. When we contributed to class discussions, they snickered, coughed into their hands and said, "Dork!" They pushed us into lockers and knocked us down in noncontact games of soccer and baseball. They even broke into the resource room we'd commandeered for our lunch-time D&D sessions and messed with our laborious setup. My smaller friends bore the brunt of it. I was just under six feet tall, quick and agile, so less of a target. But I wasn't big, strong, or competitive. And I was intelligent and inquisitive. To those sports-obsessed assholes, that made me a loser.

When Jamie told me that her new friend was married to Maxime Beausoleil, I knew I'd hate the guy. He was a jock, a bully, a killer. Still, I was glad Jamie had found Freya. My wife was happier, lighter, laughing more. When she came in from a walk or a wine date with her friend, she looked placid and content. I hadn't seen that look since before she realized that her life with me was incomplete. That she and I were not enough. I wouldn't begrudge her that friendship, but I would steer clear. Jamie knew me well enough not to suggest we become "couple friends." And then one day, I bumped into Freya at Hawking Mercantile.

I was prepared to dislike the California blonde in her impec-cable makeup and pricey yoga pants, but she won me over. In a brief, ten-minute introduction, she found a way to compliment my wife, her shop, me, my career, my past career ("teaching is the noblest profession"), and my marriage. I was powerless in the face of her beauty and charm. So when she said, "Why don't you two come over for dinner? Max will love you." I agreed.

Max Beausoleil was nothing like I expected. Well, he was huge like I expected, but he was also soft-spoken, humble, and interested in *me*. He asked me about my books, said they sounded great and promised to buy them for his nephew (the sure-fire way to win over any writer). When I complimented their stunning home, he brushed it away, gave credit to the architect, the builder, and his wife. Our next get-together was at our house. Jamie was embarrassed by our humble abode, but Freya kicked off her shoes and curled up on the sofa. "I *love* this place. I feel so cozy and at home here." Over the salmon steaks I'd barbecued, Max and I discovered that we both liked kayaking, canoeing, and fishing. I told him about two summers spent working on a commercial crabber, and he talked wistfully about fly-fishing as a kid in the North. The amount I liked the guy was in direct proportion to the amount I'd expected to dislike him.

Even though Jamie and I were grown up, confident, and self-assured, it still felt like the prom king and queen wanted to be our friends. So we couldn't turn down an invitation to blow off some steam, let our hair down, and take some recreational drugs in a safe environment. Why would we? We all had the luxury of setting our own schedules, except Jamie, but the store didn't open until ten. She was planning to stick with wine, anyway. Max didn't drink, so I wasn't sure if he'd partake in the 'shrooms, but we were all adults; we all knew what we were getting into.

At least we thought we did.

16

jamie

I was jittery when we entered our friends' cliffside home, a combination of nerves and anticipation. On the ride over, I had reconsidered my wine-only stance. It wouldn't hurt to get high with some good friends. True, the last time I'd done 'shrooms I'd vomited vociferously, but I was in college then. I was older, stronger, wiser now. I'd take it slow, go with the flow, enjoy the change in perspective. The opening of my mind . . .

My lunch conversation with Freya had looped through my head until it became a sort of epiphany. Maybe I *could* have a great life without a child. A life of fun, adventure, and hedonism. It wasn't what I had imagined for Brian and me, but I could change the channel. Psychedelic drugs on a Tuesday was only the beginning. With our cool new friends, I could envision travel and adventure: zip-lining in Thailand, swimming with manta rays in Australia, a safari in Africa. And it could all start tonight, with a different sort of trip.

Freya welcomed me with a hug, though I'd seen her only a few hours ago. When Max kissed my cheek, my stomach fluttered. I wasn't lusting after my best friend's husband—I want to be clear about that—but he had a physical effect on me. He was so large, so rugged, so aggressively masculine. My female body simply reacted. I handed Freya a bottle of chilled white wine.

"Thanks, hon. But we're having tea tonight."

I was momentarily confused until I saw the twinkle in her eye. Mushroom tea. I followed Freya into the kitchen, where she reached for a wineglass and then paused. "It's not a good idea to mix alcohol and 'shrooms. You'll have tea with us, won't you?"

It was the moment of truth: wine or 'shrooms. Conservative or wild. The usual or the unique. "Yeah, I'll have tea."

"That's my girl."

We moved to the sunken living room, where a pottery teapot sat steeping on the low coffee table. Freya placed four handleless mugs next to it, and Max filled them carefully. We each took one and leaned back on the gleaming white sofas. I sipped the earthy concoction slowly, gingerly, as we chatted. Freya was entertaining us with the story of a high school friend who had taken mushrooms and went into a 7-Eleven to buy Doritos stark naked. While funny, it did nothing to quell my anxiety. I'd been afraid of puking; now, I could add public indecency to my list of fears. I looked at my husband. His face was alight as he listened to Freya's story and casually drank his tea. He felt my gaze and met it.

You okay? his eyes asked.

I smiled and gave a slight nod of affirmation. I was fine. I was *fun*. This was the new me.

As Max talked about a music festival he'd attended while on 'shrooms, my mind drifted to Freya's earlier proclamation. Sex on psychedelics was amazing, she'd said. Later, Brian and I would put that to the test. When the frivolity here had died down, we'd call a taxi (the island had a fleet of four cabs), go home, and make love while high on mushrooms. We needed a night of wild, uninhibited pleasure. Our fruitless efforts to conceive had taken a toll on our sex life. A renewed lust for each other was another perk of the indulgent life I was embracing.

"Are you feeling anything?" Freya was addressing me.

"I don't know," I said, and then I giggled. It just bubbled out of me. I looked down and found my mug empty.

"They're kicking in," Brian said, but I was too busy noticing how white the sofas were. So white they were almost blue. Like snow in sunshine.

Freya stood. "We're going to need water. Jamie, come help me."

Obediently, I got up and followed her to the kitchen.

It was brighter in there, but everything had soft, blurry edges. Freya ran the filtered water tap and filled four tumblers with the cold liquid. I stood by and watched, mesmerized by the sight of the water burbling from the faucet, filling the frosted glasses. When she'd filled the last one, she turned toward me.

"How are you feeling?"

"Good." I smiled and found I couldn't stop. "*Really* good."

Freya smiled back. "Me too. I'm so glad you guys were into this."

"I wasn't sure at first, but you're right. I should be more fun. And adventurous."

Freya reached out and rested her hand on my shoulder. "You deserve this, babe. There's no need to feel guilty."

Guilty? I may have been more conservative than Freya, but I didn't feel guilty about taking magic mushrooms with friends. "I don't," I said with a bleary smile.

"You've been such an amazing friend to me." Her teeth were so white, as white as her couches. "I don't know what I'd do without you."

"I feel the same," I said, perma-smile still in place.

"Let's get back to the boys." She turned and picked up two of the glasses. I grabbed the other two and trailed her back to the living room.

The men were lolling on the sofa, their pupils huge, their smiles wide. Freya handed a glass of water to my husband and sat beside him. I took her previous seat next to Max, placing both our glasses on the coffee table.

"Thanks," he said, and smiled at me.

Glancing at Brian, I saw the same wide grin affixed to his face. We were all tripping by then.

"Music!" Freya said. "I made a playlist. Max, get my phone."

My seatmate got up, towering over me for a moment on his way to find his wife's device. I sank into the firm sofa. It felt like I was floating on a raft in a calm sea. I closed my eyes, my smile still in place.

The music came on—something cool and modern, vaguely South American. My eyes fluttered open, and I saw Freya get up and dance across the room toward Max. Her body moved fluidly, her arms above her head, her eyes closed. On her face, a beatific smile. Max was smiling, too, his eyes on his wife's undulating form. Should Brian and I get up and dance? Was that part of *letting loose* on psychedelics? I didn't want to. I wanted to stay put on my floating couch. I looked at my husband, but he was watching our hosts, seemingly rapt by the two beautiful people before him.

"Come dance," Freya called, and Brian stood up. He held his hand out to me, but I shook my head. I didn't want to move; wasn't sure I *could* move. So Brian went without me.

The music washed over me in a wave of vibration and color. I turned my head to watch my husband and our two closest friends swaying, giggling sporadically. Max and Freya were focused on each other, their bodies moving in time with the beat. Brian looked awkward, shifting side to side like a seventh grader at a sock hop, but he was smiling, going with it. He caught my gaze and beckoned me to join him, but I shook my head. I felt extremely high, but safe, warm, comfortable on the sofa.

And then, something shifted. The pleasant fog turned into something darker, colder. I found myself shivering, my teeth almost chattering. My jaw was tense, and my stomach had turned sour. Oh shit. . . . It was happening again. I'd been an idiot to think the 'shrooms would affect me differently this time. I didn't have the stomach for drugs. And I couldn't barf on this pristine white sofa. I staggered to my feet.

"I need to lie down somewhere."

I hadn't meant to yell, but I must have. Freya stopped dancing, and all eyes turned toward me. But no one spoke. No one moved. And then, I crumpled to the floor.

Somehow, they got me to the guest room in the basement. I was unable to take in the magazine-worthy decor, but I appreciated the serene palate, the cool, quiet air. I was aware of Brian in the doorway, but it was Freya who sat next to me, pulled a blanket up over me.

"You'll be fine, babe. You just need a little time-out."

"I might puke," I said, glancing at the creamy blanket. So much white. White everywhere.

"Max is getting a bucket. You might feel better if you throw up."

"I don't want to," I moaned.

Max must have delivered the bucket to Brian, because my husband set it beside the bed. He kissed my forehead. "I'll check on you in a bit. Get some rest."

I wanted him to stay. I wanted him to *want* to stay. When we'd done 'shrooms in college, he'd sat on the kitchen floor of my apartment for hours, rubbing my back as I heaved uncontrollably. Now, years later, he was abandoning me to dance and have fun with Max and Freya. But I couldn't say that. For one, I didn't want to be a buzzkill, the reason the night of fun was ruined. For two, my mouth was too dry to speak.

So I let him go.

17

low

I tried to put their antics out of my mind. I ate dinner with my mom and my brothers, but the roasted yams were tasteless, and the chickpeas turned to dust in my mouth. In my room, I tried to read a memoir about a survivalist family in the wilds of Alaska, but I couldn't concentrate. I wasn't jealous exactly. I was angry at being used, at being sent away like an errand girl. It should have been *me* getting fucked up with Freya and Max, not boring-ass Jamie and her nerd husband. So maybe I was a *bit* jealous.

Around eleven, I gave up on the memoir and went out to my truck. I told myself I was just going for a drive, just trying to cool off so I could get some sleep. But I went through town, past the school, along the coastal road on autopilot. When I reached the secluded pullout, I parked the truck and got out.

I crept down Max and Freya's tree-lined driveway. My pulse was pounding in my ears, adrenaline surging through my body. If they caught me—lurking, watching, spying—I would lose everything: my job, access to the pottery studio, and worse . . . my friendship with Freya. I had an excuse at the ready—I'd say I dropped my house key earlier and had come back to find it. That I'd parked on the road so I didn't disturb their mushroom trip. But I wasn't going to get caught, not this time.

Walking past Jamie's Mazda sedan, I moved to the east side of the house. Massive windows were designed to let morning light into the living room and bedrooms, but in the darkness, they afforded me unobstructed views inside. I planted myself in the dense brush and I watched them. They were dancing . . . though the guys weren't really dancing, they were more like *swaying*, their eyes on Freya. She was beautiful, sensually moving to the music. But where was Jamie? Peering into the bedroom on the lower floor, I detected a motionless lump under the covers. That would be her.

Abruptly, Freya stopped dancing. She moved to the speaker system and must have turned off the music. When she returned to the men, she spoke solemnly, seriously. There was some back and forth between Brian and Freya . . . perhaps he was reluctant for the night to end. But clearly, the party was over. And then, they disbursed.

I leaned back against a birch tree, and I watched.

18

jamie

I didn't puke. Nor did I sleep. When I closed my eyes, colors danced behind my eyelids. When I opened them, the furniture swayed and moved. It wasn't a terrible experience, but it wasn't enjoyable, either. It just was, and I had to ride it out. And then, when I felt some semblance of my normal self, I could return to the party.

I could have been alone in the darkened guest room for a few hours or a few minutes—time had lost all meaning. Above me, Freya's carefully curated music continued, the bass thudding through the floor. Other than that, I heard nothing but the occasional tinkle of her laughter. That's when I wanted to get up and join the fun, but my body had other plans. It wanted to lie on the soft bed, the cozy blanket over me, and let the psilocybin work its way through my system.

Perhaps I dozed off, I can't be sure, but when Brian entered the room, the music had stopped. The house was dark and silent as my husband moved tentatively through the blackness. I felt grateful and relieved; he had promised to check on me, and now he was. But as he got closer something about his presence was unfamiliar. When he stood next to the bed, I realized . . . that was not my husband. It was Freya's.

"How are you feeling?" Max asked.

"I'm okay," I said, propping myself up on my elbows. "Ummm . . . where are Brian and Freya?"

He perched, tentatively, on the edge of the bed before answering. "They're upstairs. In the bedroom."

The words didn't compute. I was still high—very high. Why would my husband be in the bedroom with my new best friend?

"Freya said you talked about it," Max said. "She said you wanted this."

I sat up fully. "Wanted what? What's going on?" My head was spinning, my heart racing. Freya and I had had a frank discussion about sex and monogamy, but had we talked about sleeping with each other's husbands? No, we had not.

"It's okay," he said softly. "We don't have to do anything you don't want to." He stroked my cheek with the back of his fingers. They were slightly rough, a man's hands. Brian's hands were always soft from typing and washing dishes. I found Max's eyes in the darkened room and felt the pull of attraction. I swallowed audibly.

"I can't. Brian would never."

"Freya is very persuasive."

I knew this to be true. Was Freya seducing my husband right now? Was Brian high enough to forget his moral code? Hot enough for my beautiful blond friend to break our vows?

"Forget about them." Max's fingers trailed down my neck. "What do *you* want?"

My hand moved of its own accord to his chest. When I felt his muscles through his shirt, the heat of his skin, my breath caught in my throat. Oh shit . . . I did want this. I wanted it badly.

"Can I kiss you?"

I should have said no. I should have thrown off the blanket, gotten up, hurried upstairs. I should have called for Brian, phoned a taxi, gone home. But I didn't. I let Max kiss me. I let his rough hands roam through my hair and over my body. Lust surged through me, and suddenly I was tearing at his clothes, yanking his shirt over his head. My hands ran over his broad shoulders, his strong arms, his powerful chest. I loved Brian's body, it was lithe, furry, warm. It felt like home. Max's felt like an adventure.

My fingertips felt the wound first, sliding over the puckered flesh on his impressive pec. Pulling away from his kiss, I peered at the damage. In the dark, I could make out four evenly spaced puncture marks, already turning to scar tissue.

"What happened?"

He moved my hand away from the lesion. "Long story." He kissed me again and lay me back on the bed. And then, he moved over me.

I could blame the drugs, or the toll infertility had taken on my sex life with my husband. I could put it on my lack of sexual partners, or my recent epiphany about living an indulgent, hedonistic life. But there is no excuse for what I did that night with Freya's husband. I told myself we were all consenting adults, mature enough to handle this. I told myself it would all be okay.

But I was wrong.

19

It took me several seconds to get my bearings when I woke up in Freya's spare room. The sun was low in the sky, indicating the early hour. I was alone in bed, and I was naked. The night came back to me in a rush: the 'shrooms, the music, the colors, the visions. And Max. His strong body over me, on me, in me.

Perhaps I had hallucinated the whole encounter? Maybe it was just an incredibly vivid psychedelic trip? God, I wanted it to be. But the warmth of Max's skin, the taste of his mouth, the sensation of his muscles under my hands was so real. A bubble of guilt rose in my throat . . . guilt mixed with a heavy dose of jealousy. Because, if I had made love to Freya's husband, that meant she had made love to mine.

Feeling fragile and shaky, I found my clothes on the floor beside me and quickly dressed. I slipped into the bathroom to pee and wash my face. Taking in my reflection in the mirror above the sink, I saw that my skin was pale, my eyes puffy, my lips dry. My pupils were still dilated, making my eyes look dark and haunted. Jesus Christ.

My heart hammered in my chest as I climbed the stairs to the main floor. I didn't know what to expect after our night of debauchery. Would we talk about what happened, or pretend it never had? Would we act as if everything was fine, or would Freya say: *Morning, hon. Your husband was great last night. How was mine?* I couldn't bear it. I needed to find Brian, get in our car, and drive home to our cozy cottage. I needed to shower away the memory of last night, to make coffee, and talk to him about what happened. We needed to reaffirm our love and commitment, we needed to put this incident behind us.

The smell of food hit me then. Fried eggs and toast. It should have been appetizing, I should have been hungry, but my stomach churned as I entered the kitchen. Freya was seated at the dining table wearing an oversize gray sweater and flannel pajama pants. She looked sleepy but pretty. I looked like an ogre.

"'Morning, gorgeous," Freya said, through a mouthful of gluten-free toast. "How are you feeling?"

"I'm okay." My voice was raspy. "How are you?"

"Starving," she said, forking up some fluffy omelet. "That was quite a night."

I moved closer, tentatively sitting across from her. "It was."

"Can I make you some eggs?"

"No, thanks. I'm not hungry."

"I guess I burned off more calories than you did."

An image of Freya riding my husband like a racehorse flashed through my mind. My face flushed, and I felt hot and nauseated.

"I danced my ass off," Freya said, crunching her toast. "But I crashed not long after you did. Those 'shrooms were potent."

"They were," I croaked. "I was really messed up."

"I noticed," she teased. "They hit me hard, too. Sometimes, I can party all night on mushrooms. But these ones put me right to sleep."

My brow furrowed slightly. "What about the guys?"

"They stayed up for a while, I think. When Max came to bed, he said Brian was passed out on the sofa."

I tried to slot the puzzle pieces into place, but my brain was spinning. If Freya had gone straight to sleep not long after I had, did that mean she *hadn't* made love to my husband? Had Max come to my room while Brian snoozed on the couch? Had he told me we were having a couples' swap to trick me into having sex with him? He seemed earnest and authentic, but not long ago he had broken a man's neck. Manipulating a woman into sex was nothing compared to that. Not that I had presented much of a challenge. I'd been so hot for him, I'd been eager to believe his story.

I looked at my friend shoveling eggs into her mouth like she didn't have a care in the world. "Where are the guys now?" I asked.

"They took the canoe out. They'll be back in a half hour."

I couldn't sit there for half an hour smelling Freya's breakfast and pretending everything was normal. I needed to see my husband. I needed to go home. I needed to salvage my marriage. To tell him that I had made a terrible mistake. Unless . . . unless he had made the same mistake. But would Brian and Max take the boat out together if they had swapped wives last night? I felt sweaty, dizzy, and off-kilter. I stood.

"I need coffee."

"God, I'm a terrible host." Freya jumped up. "Latte? I have oat milk or regular milk."

"Finish your breakfast. I can make it."

But she was already hurrying to the kitchen, already digging in the fridge. "I'm full. And the coffee machine is a pain in the ass."

"I'll have regular milk with it, please."

As Freya fiddled with the coffee maker, my confusion increased. My friend was completely comfortable, entirely casual. If she had slept with Brian, if she knew I'd slept with Max, wouldn't there be some residual awkwardness? A modicum of guilt? But there was none.

"Regular latte for Janey," Freya said, imitating a Starbucks barista.

"Thanks." I smiled despite myself and sipped the milky coffee, hoping to clear my head. I was still unclear on the nights' events, but I knew one thing: I would never take magic mushrooms again. They had messed with my judgment, skewed my moral compass, and left me in a haze of confusion and regret.

"Let's have our coffee on the deck," Freya said. "The sun is gorgeous."

I followed her onto the expanse of cedar where a large, white (of course) outdoor sofa was covered with dusky blue throw pillows. We settled into our seats, sipping our lattes and watching the morning sun sparkle off the bright blue water. Freya closed her eyes, held her face up to bask in the rays. She was smiling slightly, at peace, content.

"Freya," I began, my voice strangled by the thickness in my throat. But I had to know what we had done last night.

She opened her blue eyes. "There they are!" she said, pointing to the canoe in the distance. She stood up and waved. The two figures in the boat waved back, then resumed their paddling. As they glided toward us, I studied my husband's expression. Max and Freya may have been untroubled by a sexual swap, but I knew my partner. If Brian had slept with Freya, if he knew I'd had sex with Max, he would have felt even worse than I did.

But Brian appeared to be immersed in the rugged beauty around him. He looked placid and content, not upset, jealous, or angry. Max's expression was blank, harder to read. He seemed singularly focused on the physical action of propelling them to shore. I was the only one among us experiencing confusion and turmoil.

Freya sat back down and smiled at me. "I'm so glad we met you guys."

"Me too," I said, and my voice shook. Because I meant it, with all my heart. Freya was my salvation, my new life, my fresh start. She and Max were our best friends. Whatever I had done the night before—whatever *we* had done—didn't matter. We couldn't lose them.

"What were you going to say before?"

I forced a smile and shrugged. "I don't remember."

20

Letting go of that night was easier said than done. My guilt consumed me, destroying my appetite and my sleep. At work, I was groggy and out of sorts. I would catch Low watching me, her eyes narrowed, mouth in a grim line, like she knew what we had done. But she couldn't have. *I* didn't even know for sure. At night, I woke in a pool of sweat, confused and aroused by vivid dreams of Maxime Beausoleil. I googled *magic mushrooms flashback* and found out it was a thing. Was I destined to be tortured by memories of making love to my best friend's husband?

Meanwhile, Brian seemed relatively normal. If he had been unfaithful to me, it would have shown on his face, manifested itself in his behavior. I was on high alert for any changes in his actions or mood, but he seemed his usual cheerful self. One day, he popped into the shop to say hi.

"Did you get your hair cut?" I asked.

"Yeah." He touched his exposed ears. "I needed a trim."

"It looked fine before," I said, feeling a stab of jealousy. Who was he trying to impress—Freya? Was she a sucker for a tidy haircut? Max's hair was quite long, but maybe she wanted something different on her side guy.

Brian looked puzzled. "I didn't realize I needed your permission to go to the barber."

"You don't." I smiled and tried to cover. "I just like it a little longer."

Low skulked by us then. I thought I saw a flicker of amusement on her face, but I must have imagined it.

I'd canceled my forest walks with Freya that week, claiming I had to do inventory. I wasn't ready to be alone with her in such a private setting, wasn't ready to have the conversation that needed to be had. I had slept with her husband, and I needed to know if she had slept with mine. But I was a mess: jealous, confused, riddled with regret. . . . I needed clarity. The only person who could give it to me, without risking a relationship, was Max. But how could I get to him alone?

And then, eight days after that fateful night, I saw my opportunity. It was a Wednesday, often our slowest day of the week. Low and I were puttering around the shop when I saw Freya's white Range Rover pass by. I moved to the window and watched her pull into a parking space in front of the day spa. She got out of the car, in her ball cap and sunglasses, and headed inside.

"Low, I need to run an errand," I said, adrenaline surging through my body. "Can you hold down the fort for an hour or so?"

"Sure."

I practically ran to my car. If Freya was having a facial, I had an hour-and-a-half window. If she was having a pedi, it was more like forty-five minutes. I raced toward her home, knowing this was my chance to catch Max alone. He could tell me what really happened that night. If Brian had slept with Freya it would be painful to hear. If he hadn't, my guilt would be compounded. But anything was preferable to my current muddled state.

Pulling up behind Max's black SUV, I scurried to the house. I was shaky, sweating, and I stumbled on the concrete steps, but that didn't slow me down. Clambering to the door, I rang the bell and waited, my heart hammering in my ears. I would finally know the truth about that night, one way or another. When Max didn't answer, I rang again, and again, stabbing the button repeatedly. Still, no one came.

Fuck . . . Fuck, fuck, fuck. Max's car was there, so he couldn't be far. Maybe he was in the shower. Or out in the kayak, or windsurfing. I would go down to the beach and look for him, wave him to shore. If he wasn't too far out, we'd still have time to talk before Freya returned. As I was making my way toward the water, I remembered Freya mentioning Max's motorcycle. If he'd gone for a ride, he might not be back for hours. Damn it.

The sound of a door closing behind me stopped me in my tracks. I turned to see Max exiting the garage wearing a wet suit. Well, half a wet suit. The top of the neoprene garment hung around his waist, leaving his massive chest and shoulders bare. His hair was wet, slicked back from his face. He was a ridiculously attractive man, but I felt no lust, no attraction as I hurried toward him. All I wanted from him was the truth about what happened that night.

"Jamie," he said, clearly surprised to see me. "Freya's not here."

"I know that," I said. "I wanted to talk to you."

"Are you okay?"

I was about to say that no, I wasn't okay. I was troubled, stressed, confused . . . And then I saw them. Those four precise puncture marks above his right nipple. I had felt them as I ran my hands over his body, as I kissed him, as I made love to him. It all came flooding back to me in a rush of heat and remorse.

"What happened that night?" I said, my voice barely a whisper, my face burning.

He let a heavy breath out through his nose, his handsome face troubled. "I'm sorry. I thought—" But he didn't finish his sentence because we both heard it; a vehicle was approaching. Seconds later, Freya's white SUV pulled up and stopped beside his dark model.

"Hey, you," she chirped to me, hopping out of the Range Rover. "What are you doing here?" In her hand was a small bag from the day spa.

"Finally finished inventory," I said. "I thought I'd sneak away for a quick cup of tea with you."

"Great. Come on in."

But I couldn't. Because I knew what I had done with her husband, and yet, I was still wondering what she had done with mine. I needed clarity . . . But not from Freya.

"Low just texted," I lied, already moving to my car. "The burglar alarm is going off and she put in the wrong code. It's locked up. I've got to help her."

"Oh no," Freya said. "Let's get together soon. We can all have dinner."

"Yes. Definitely." A quick wave to Max, then I backed up and peeled out of the driveway.

My husband was in his office, working on his manuscript . . . if staring at the screen while he stretched his arms overhead could be considered working on it.

"I'm *plotting*," he always said, when I caught him staring at the floor or the ceiling or even his phone. He swiveled in his chair when I walked in.

"Hey, babe. What are you doing home?"

I hurried toward him and knelt beside him. "You know I love you. No matter what."

He gave me a bemused smile. "I love you, too."

"I'm going to ask you something. And I want you to be honest with me."

"Okay."

"The other night . . ." My voice faltered. "Did anything happen between you and Freya?"

"Anything like what?" Brian rolled his chair back a few inches. "What are you getting at?"

I cleared the knot from my throat. "I went to bed so early. I just wondered . . . if . . . you guys . . ."

"God, Jamie. We were on mushrooms not ecstasy." He rolled forward and took me by the shoulders. "You know I have never wanted to be with anyone else. Since the day I met you . . . you're the only one for me."

Looking into his warm hazel eyes, I saw his sincerity. And I hated myself. "Sorry." I sat back on my heels. "I guess the drugs made me paranoid."

He kissed my forehead. "You don't need to worry about me." Then he swiveled back to face his manuscript.

So now I knew the truth. I had not participated in a consensual couples' swap; I had betrayed my husband and my best friend. I should have spun Brian's chair around to face me, should have told him what Max and I had done, but I was a coward. Instead, I got up, went to the kitchen, and poured a glass of water. I gulped it down, hoping to dilute my regret and self-loathing, but it didn't work. Setting the empty glass on the counter, I gazed out the window at the waxy leaves of our camelia bush, its early pink blooms already dead and decomposing at its feet.

Max Beausoleil had lied to me. He had tricked me and manipulated me. I should have been enraged, but I couldn't blame this
all on him. I knew how much I'd wanted him that night, how
eager I'd been to believe what he told me. If I confronted him and
accused him, it could damage his marriage to Freya. She claimed
to be open-minded and sexually adventurous, but those were just
words. There was no way she'd be chill about her husband bed-
ding her best friend while she slept upstairs. She would hate Max.
She would hate *me*. The thought filled me with dread.

And Brian . . . Oh God, poor Brian. The thought of hurting
him made my stomach ache.

I made a decision, then. What Max and I had done was over.
It did not need to be discussed, dissected, or analyzed. Dragging
it into the light was not worth jeopardizing my marriage or my
friendship. I loved Brian too much. I loved Freya too much. So, I
buried it.

Like a body.

autumn 2019

21

low

On October 5, I came home to find Gwen, Janine, my dad, and a midwife wearing a white turban helping my mother give birth in a wading pool. I turned around and walked back out, drove into town, ate three slices of pepperoni at the pizza joint, got an ice cream cone, and savored it in my truck parked at the boat launch, then went to the convenience store for a slushie. Finally, when a couple of hours had passed, I drove home.

"Meet your new baby brother," my mom said, cuddling a mint-green bundle to her chest. "This is Eckhart."

"After Tolle," my dad elaborated. Like there were other Eckharts the poor little bugger might be named after.

He was very small and practically fuchsia and shriveled like a prune. I touched his soft cheek and his tiny hand. He grabbed my finger in his little fist and brought it to his mouth. He was cute. I might like this kid more than my other brothers. And then he started screaming. I didn't realize then that he wouldn't stop for four months.

"It's colic," my mom said, as she bounced and jiggled the angry purple creature that was my brother. "He'll grow out of it."

"When?"

"Don't start, Swallow! Don't fucking start." And then she burst into tears.

I'd really misjudged my new sibling. I liked him even less than the other ones. What did he have to be so miserable about? He had my mom, my dad, and Gwen at his beck and call. They spent every moment of the day trying to make him comfortable: feeding him, burping him, changing him, swaddling him, swinging him, singing to him, and taking him for walks and car rides, even boat rides. Nothing pleased Eckhart. He was an asshole. An infant King Joffrey.

To remove myself from the noise and chaos, I spent more and more time at the pottery studio. I had nowhere else to go. The tourist trade had dwindled with the summer and so had my employment. Jamie had apologized profusely, but she couldn't afford to keep me on full-time. I only worked weekends now, or the occasional mid-week shift if she had plans or was away. It was virtually impossible to find off-season employment on the island, but I had a plan.

I had been working in the studio several days a week for seven months. My wheel work was passable, but I didn't have Freya's delicate touch, I couldn't replicate her unique creations. But I'd discovered a talent for handwork, pinch pots to be precise. I had made a perfect little cup and then decided to add an oversize lid that made it look like a toadstool. It was a decorative, whimsical piece, but when you removed the cap, it was a perfect container for earrings, pills, or paper clips.

"That is so adorable," Freya had gushed. "If you make a few of these, I bet Jamie would sell them."

"Really?"

"I'll talk to her," she said, with a wink. "I got you the job, didn't I?"

I let myself imagine a lucrative toadstool pinch-pot business. Jamie would sell them at her store, and eventually, I'd take a trip to the mainland and find some retailers there. Photography had been my favorite class at school, and I'd excelled at it. With those skills and Freya's social media expertise, we would build the brand online. They would take off, become a trend. I'd continue to make them by hand, each one unique, expensive, a collector's item. I'd taken to adding intricate embellishments—a butterfly, a bumblebee, a caterpillar—so each piece was one-of-a-kind. I envisioned toadstool pinch-pot world domination.

No one would work harder or longer than I would—24-7 if necessary. The studio was already my favorite place to be, and now, it had become my refuge. Unbeknownst to my hosts, I had been sleeping in the unfinished attic space. It was accessible through a trapdoor in the ceiling that had a drop-down ladder. The room was only about five feet high at its center, and I had to share it with a few dusty cardboard boxes, some bits of lumber, and a length of ductwork. But they made better roommates than Eckhart. (Since I no longer had to get up for school in the morning, my parents had decided I should share a room with my constantly wailing brother. They probably hoped it was the kick I needed to leave the nest.)

I didn't tell Freya and Max that I was spending most of my nights on their property. On some level, I must have known that setting up my sleeping bag and pillow in her studio space without permission was crossing boundaries. They might resent the lack of privacy, might think that spending my entire day at the studio and then the entire night in the attic justified them asking for some sort of rent. Part of me thought they'd be fine with it, might even offer me a piece of foam to sleep on or a bedside lamp. But I couldn't risk it. So, around seven o'clock each evening, I went home for dinner and a shower. And then, at around eleven, when Eckhart's nightly screamfest was well underway, I parked my truck on the side of the main road and slipped silently into my newfound attic bedroom. In the mornings, I rose early, ate a bagel or a doughnut or a croissant from a stash of breakfast food I'd left there, and cleaned up in the studio bathroom. Then I went straight to work building my pinch-pot empire.

Freya usually joined me around ten, after her yoga class or power walk with Jamie. We puttered around the studio, throwing, firing, glazing, trimming . . . Now that she was so comfortable with me, Freya didn't keep up her constant stream of chatter. In fact, some days, she barely said a word, seeming morose, or introspective. On others, she was crabby, stomping around, slamming down pieces, then cursing aloud when they chipped or broke. Seeing her vulnerability, her anger, her realness, didn't make me adore her any less.

One morning, her disposition seemed darker than usual. There were circles under her eyes and her shiny hair was dull and lank. She muttered hey and then disappeared into the kiln room. I was getting used to her moods by now. It was best to stay quiet, keep my head down, and let her work through her emotions. Eventually, my lovely, charming Freya would return. But that day, as I was staining the veins on a butterfly's wings, she stormed toward me.

"You got glaze all over the kiln shelves, you moron! Your stupid fucking pots are fused to them!"

Freya had been cranky and snappish toward me, but she had never verbally assaulted me before. I was shocked by the intensity of her anger. Setting down my brush, I managed to croak out a response. "They can't be. I waxed the bottoms."

"Oh, okay . . ." Sarcasm dripped off her words. "I guess I just imagined the fucking mess in there."

"I-I'll take care of it," I stammered. "I'll buy you a new shelf."

"This is a specialized gas kiln! Where are you going to buy a shelf for it on this godforsaken island?" She was falling apart, and it wasn't over a kiln shelf. Something else was wrong. Very wrong.

"Are you okay?" I asked.

"No! No, I'm fucking not." She turned away and dropped her head into her hands.

I stayed frozen on my stool, unsure whether I should go to her or give her space. My heart was pounding, and my throat was thick with dread.

"I'm sorry, Low," she said through her hands. "This isn't about you." Then she lifted her beautiful face. "Can I tell you something?"

"Of course."

She took a deep breath. "I'm pregnant."

There was no joy in her voice, so I didn't have to fake any. Because I was not joyful, not joyful at all. I didn't want to share Freya with some needy, clingy, sniveling infant. I'd just been run out of my home by one baby; now another was threatening my territory.

"Oh no," I said softly.

Freya sighed. "I don't know how it happened. I didn't think I could conceive."

Silence hung heavy between us. I was at a loss for words, stunned by her news. Maybe I shouldn't have been; Freya was a married woman of childbearing age, but she didn't have a maternal bone in her body. When I'd told her that Eckhart had been born, she'd wrinkled her nose in distaste before muttering, "Congrats, I guess." On more than one occasion, she had commented on my mother's mental health for having four children. And for having another baby at forty-two. She said things like:

"Is your mom trying to fill some emotional void by having all those kids?"

And:

"Is your mom on crack?"

She'd told me about her crazy mother and their fraught, on-again, off-again (mostly off-again) relationship. I simply couldn't imagine Freya as a parent.

She moved to the small paned window and stared out into her driveway. "My periods have always been sporadic," she explained. "I just thought I was getting fat." She turned back toward me. "I don't even know if I'm going to keep it. But I'm already in my second trimester."

I should have said something to make her feel better about this terrible mistake; that was my role as her friend and confidante. But all I wanted to say was: *Get rid of it. Make it go away before it ruins your life and mine!* I couldn't be so callous, of course, but the words of support would not come.

Then she said, "Promise me you won't tell Jamie."

"Jamie?"

"She wants a baby so badly, and she can't have one. This will devastate her."

My employer had never mentioned her desire to be a mother, but I guess it made sense. Whenever an infant or toddler came into the store, she was all over it. After, she'd seem wistful, lost in thought, even tearful. During our hours together, Jamie often tried to engage me in conversation. When I remained uncommunicative, she'd babble on about her former marketing career, her husband's fantasy trilogy, her college experiences at the University of British Columbia. But my boss had never admitted she wanted a family.

"I won't tell her."

"Thanks," Freya muttered, heading for the door. "I'm going to lie down. Clean up the mess in the kiln."

When she left, I looked down at the intricate butterfly wings I'd been working on. Somehow, I had snapped them in two.

22

I didn't sleep well that night. Normally, I went out like a light, even on the hard attic floor. But that night, I stared at the rafters for hours. Freya was pregnant. If she had the baby, it would usurp my space in her life. She wouldn't come to the studio anymore, wouldn't have time to do pottery with me. I knew firsthand how demanding babies were, how noisy, smelly, and needy. Freya might allow me to continue my work, but did I want to without her? Was my pinch-pot plan as fulfilling without her involvement?

And I didn't want to go back to my parents' house. Even if my mom's assurances that Eckhart would grow out of his monster phase were true, I didn't want to be there. My youngest brother had tipped the scales. We had gone from being a large, noisy, loving family to a chaotic shit show. The last few months had shown me that I needed space and calm and quiet.

If it had been a normal night, if I had been asleep, I wouldn't have heard them. The screams were too far away, weren't loud enough to wake me from a typically deep teenage slumber. Later, I would wonder if the cacophony was a regular occurrence. When I'd slept in Freya's spare bedroom, I had thought I'd heard similar shrieks, but I'd been too drunk and high to know for sure. But this time, I was stone-cold sober. And I could hear Freya screeching.

Panic sent me scrambling out of bed, down the ladder, and out into the night. Luckily, I'd been sleeping in a T-shirt and a pair of sweatpants, so I wasn't streaking across their lawn in pajamas or less. As I hurtled toward the house, I didn't consider how my appearance at their door in the middle of the night would look. My sole focus was Freya's anguish. I had to save her from what was clearly an awful fate.

The front door was locked, so I ran up onto the deck where double doors connected it to the kitchen and dining room. Residents of the island were lax about security, but Freya and Max were from the city. They would be in the habit of locking their doors to bar intruders. Had they fallen into complacency? Had a burglar gained access through an open door? A murderer or rapist? As I reached for the handle, I saw them through the glass.

Freya and Max were facing each other in the kitchen. She wore a silky pink robe; he was in a pair of boxer shorts. I watched as Freya smacked her husband across the head. Hard.

"You stupid piece of shit!" she growled. "I fucking hate you!"

She smacked him again. And then again. Max just stood there, accepting her blows, flinching only slightly under the assault. Blood trickled from an angry scratch on his left cheek.

"You ruined everything for me!" Freya screeched. She moved backward, picked up a pottery mug off the counter, and hurled it at her husband with a guttural roar. Her arm was impressive, but Max was quick and agile despite his size. He ducked, and the mug missed him by mere inches. Instead, it hit the cupboard behind him and fell to the floor with a crash.

"You're a stupid fucking animal!" Freya screamed, grabbing a two-pronged barbecue fork. She drew her arm back, and I didn't know if she was going to rush at Max and stab him or throw the weapon and impale him. Either way, I couldn't stand there and watch it happen. I turned the door handle and it gave way.

"Stop!" I shrieked, as I burst into the room.

They both turned toward me, and I saw the shock on their faces. It was quickly replaced by fury on Freya's, something like shame on Max's.

"What are you doing here?" Freya growled. I had seen her annoyed, irritable, even angry, but this was different. This was unadulterated rage. She was still holding the fork and a frisson of fear ran through me.

"Put the fork down," I said, keeping my distance.

Freya slammed the utensil down on the counter. "Why are you here?"

Max added, "This is none of your business, Low."

Suddenly, I realized that *I* was the intruder, that my help, my interference, was unwanted.

"I—I was working late," I stammered. "I guess I dozed off. I heard screaming. I came to help."

"Get out, you psycho." Freya's voice was cold.

I looked at Max.

"Go home," he said softly.

As I slinked across the deck and down the stairs, I heard Freya's voice. "And don't come back!"

She didn't mean it, I told myself. She was angry and overwrought and would regret her words in the morning. What had Max done to warrant her fury? This had to be about the baby. Maybe he was making her keep it? Or making her get rid of it? It had to be something really bad to make her want to fork him like a steak.

When I reached the studio, I grabbed my keys and hurried to my truck. Climbing in, my fingers fumbled with the ignition, my key stabbing blindly in the darkened cab. My breath was coming rapid and shallow. I was on the verge of hyperventilating, on the precipice of a full-blown panic attack. I was in no state to drive, but I had to leave. I had to put distance between myself and the scene at the luxurious home.

As I drove the dark and deserted road up the island, I breathed deeply through my nose, trying to calm myself. Tomorrow, Freya would text me to explain. It was a lovers' quarrel heightened by the unfortunate pregnancy news. The hormones had made her crazy; she wouldn't really have hurt Max. She'd thank me for diffusing the situation, apologize for her harsh words, beg me to come back to the studio. She'd promise to have an abortion as soon as possible and then things would go back to normal.

Even after what I had seen, I was still desperate to be a part of their lives.

23

When I got home, my dad was lying on the sofa with Eckhart on his chest. He didn't question my entrance at 2:40 A.M., didn't ask where I'd been spending my nights for the past few weeks.

"Be quiet," he whispered, and pointed at my brother, who was still sniveling even in his sleep. And I *was* quiet. I tiptoed up to my room, which now had a crib in one corner, and climbed silently into my bed. As soon as my head hit the pillow, Eckhart began to wail.

It was almost noon when I woke to a silent house. Leonard and Wayne had gone to school, and my parents must have taken Eckhart for a soothing walk or a drive. I rolled over and retrieved my cell phone from beside the bed. I knew Freya would have texted me, would have made everything right.

But there were no messages—not from Freya or anyone. My stomach plummeted with disappointment. And with dread. What if last night's incident would not simply blow over? What if my interference in Freya and Max's domestic drama was a deal breaker? The thought that Freya could have meant those words—*and don't come back*—made me nauseous.

I got up and padded down the creaking stairs to the kitchen, where I found a cold pot of coffee. I turned the machine back on to warm it, indifferent to how long it had been sitting there. Caffeine would make me see things more clearly. It would make me see that Freya was not going to destroy our pure and perfect friendship just because I had witnessed her tantrum. She couldn't. It meant too much to both of us.

The disastrous state of my family home did nothing to soothe my angst. Cloth diapers hung from a drying rack set up near the extinguished wood fireplace. Baby paraphernalia—blankets, burp cloths, toys, and rattles—covered every surface, interspersed with my school-aged brothers' books and balls and hoodies and left-over snack plates. A disturbing odor permeated the air, either a bucket of soaking diapers, or a bucket of fermenting sauerkraut. Either was a possibility.

The coffeepot was warm by now, and I poured myself a cup. It tasted like shit, so I added some honey and milk. I gulped the lukewarm concoction, waiting for the caffeine to hit my system, to wake me up and give me clarity. Taking my mug out to the back patio (a few paving stones with a couple of wrought iron chairs), I breathed in the crisp autumn air, let the chill awaken my senses. And it worked. Soon, I could see that I really had no reason to be upset about last night.

As far as Freya and Max knew, I had done nothing wrong. They had no idea I'd been squatting on their property. My excuse of having worked late and dozing off in the studio was completely plausible. And they couldn't have known I'd spied on their magic mushroom party. They were all high at the time, and otherwise occupied. So, for all intents and purposes, I was the innocent party here. The reason Freya hadn't contacted me was her own embarrassment. I had seen her at her worst . . . violent, ugly, mean. She was ashamed of herself, and so she should be. But I still worshipped her. She needed to know that.

Setting my mug on the ground, I texted her.

Don't worry about last night. I still think you're awesome.

After I hit SEND, I went in and refilled my coffee. It was properly hot now, and the taste was improved. I decided to take it up to my bedroom, where I'd left a half-finished novel I'd abandoned when I moved into the studio's attic. Crawling into my soft bed, away from the mess and the smell of the main floor, I could feel myself relaxing. It was all going to be okay.

The sound of car doors slamming, wailing, and tense voices announced my family's return. I snuggled deeper into my bed, not in the mood to deal with the sights, sounds, and smells that accompanied my new brother. I was pretty sure my parents were too exhausted to remember how many kids they had, so I'd be able to read my novel, drink my coffee, and wait for Freya's response in peace.

"Low?" It was my dad's voice, calling up the stairs. Dammit.

"Yeah?" I hollered back.

"Stop yelling," I heard my mom admonish. "You're upsetting Eckhart." Sure enough, Eckhart's cries had turned into frantic, hiccupping sobs. He was such a spaz. Dragging myself up, I went downstairs.

"What?" I asked, standing on the bottom step.

"This was on the front porch," my dad said, pointing to a pile of stuff on the floor behind him. As my dad moved to the kitchen, I saw my sleeping bag, my pillow, half a package of cinnamon raisin bagels, and a white plastic garbage bag. I jumped off the step and opened the red drawstring top. Inside were my handmade pinch pots, smashed to smithereens.

I felt the color drain from my face (not that it ever had much color). Freya had found my camp and it had so enraged her that she'd destroyed months of painstaking work. I could visualize her tossing my tiny pots into the garbage bag and then smashing the whole thing on the ground. Or she might have thrown each of my handmade creations across the room, then swept the refuse into the sack. My legs trembled as I heard in my head her angry scream, heard the bisque clay breaking. In that moment, I hated her more than I'd hated anyone.

Gathering my belongings, I hurried back upstairs. My parents, absorbed by my malcontent brother, didn't sense the hurt, anger, and betrayal consuming their eldest child. Alone in my room, those emotions gave way to another, more powerful one: fear. Freya hated me. She was cutting me out. My phone buzzed then, and I picked it up off the floor.

Stay away from me, stalker

It was from Freya.

24

jamie

Autumn is not as spectacular in the temperate rain forests of the West Coast as it is in the deciduous forests in the east. Most of the trees here are conifers, but the few maple, beech, and birch trees seemed determined to make up for their small numbers with a display of colorful leaves. As Freya and I strode along the packed-earth path, my eyes darted to the vibrant reds, yellows, and oranges above us. Soon, the leaves would fall to the ground and winter rains would turn them into a brown, sodden carpet, but for now, they clung to their hosts, dazzling me with their beauty.

Freya didn't seem to notice nature's pageantry. She was subdued that morning, her hair pulled back, her designer tights replaced with baggy sweats and an oversize jacket. I'd noticed a subtle change in her disposition over the past couple of months. She was a little less bubbly, a little less vivacious. When I asked after her well-being, she was dismissive, saying she hadn't been sleeping well. She yawned a lot, which seemed to back up her story. But she wasn't yawning today. And her face looked troubled.

"I have something I need to tell you," she said.

She didn't look at me, didn't slow her pace, but her delivery was ominous. I felt my jaw clench. Our friendship had pretty much returned to normal since the night I had betrayed her. We saw each other regularly for walks, salads, or wine. But we hadn't socialized as couples; Brian was struggling with finishing his book, going back and forth with his editor. And I didn't want to see Max.

Our night together had been consensual. Max had asked if he could touch and kiss me, assured me that we didn't have to do anything I wasn't comfortable with. I had given him my exuberant permission. But I still felt tricked, duped, and ashamed of myself. I didn't know what to say or how to act around him, and so I avoided him. But I had worked hard to return normalcy to my friendship with Freya. Things felt fine between us. At least I thought so. . . .

"Okay." My voice sounded strangled.

"It's about Low."

Relief flooded through me. "What about her?"

"I caught her spying on Max and me."

"What?"

"We were up late the other night talking in the kitchen. It was past midnight. Suddenly, we saw Low watching us through the glass patio doors."

"Jesus. What was she doing there?"

"She said she was working late in the studio and she fell asleep." Freya looked at me then and her tone became pointed. "Turns out, she'd been living in the attic above the studio."

"Oh my god."

"She had a sleeping bag, a pillow . . . She even had breakfast food."

"And she didn't ask you if she could stay there?"

"Of course not." Freya gave a derisive snort. "If we had known she was there, she wouldn't have been able to creep around outside watching us like a stalker."

I was not close to Low, not like Freya had been, but the girl seemed harmless. She was unusual, awkward, even aloof. But she was just a kid. It couldn't have been easy growing up feeling different, being ostracized by her peers.

"Could there be another explanation?" I asked. "Maybe something's going on at home?"

"An explanation for squatting on my property? For staring into my windows in the middle of the fucking night?"

Freya was angry. She felt violated, and I would have, too. Of course, if Low had been staring into my windows in the wee hours, she'd have nodded off from boredom. Brian and I went to bed religiously at eleven. We made love on Sunday mornings. The most exciting thing a Peeping Tom would see at our house would be a late-night trip to the toilet.

"And I have no idea how long she's been spying on us." Freya paused then, just for a breath. "Who knows what she's seen. . . ."

It twigged on me then. Low could have been there the night we took the magic mushrooms. She could have seen Max and me having sex in the guest room with its massive, uncovered windows. I glanced at Freya, but her eyes remained on the trail ahead of us. I'd tried to let that night go, convinced myself that it couldn't hurt me. But my heart palpitated with dread.

"I'm not telling you to fire her," Freya continued. "I'm just saying be careful. Don't trust her."

"I can't fire her without cause," I replied. "Besides, she's only working weekends right now."

"It's your call," Freya said, feigning indifference, but she was clearly annoyed.

We'd reached the parking lot by this time, Freya's gleaming white SUV waiting with my shabby Mazda. There were two cars parked between us, their passengers nowhere in sight. Freya escorted me to my vehicle.

"Low might tell you things," she said. "About me. About Max. Don't believe her. She's obsessed with us. She'll say anything to hurt us."

"Do you really think she's that sick?" My voice was tight with concern—for Freya, for myself, even for Low. She might need psychological help, which was hard to find in our small community.

"She's fucking crazy." Freya was adamant. "I just hope she doesn't hurt anyone."

With those ominous words, she kissed my cheek and moved to her car.

25

low

No word could have hurt me more . . . *stalker*. It was the same term thrown in my face when Topaz had ditched me in ninth grade. I had wanted to speak to the girl alone, to see if we could salvage our friendship, but she was constantly surrounded by a gaggle of popular assholes. Tapping on her bedroom window in the middle of the night had seemed a good strategy. I'd done a couple of practice runs, hiding in the shrubbery, working up my nerve. And then, I finally made my approach. How was I to know that Lara Wittman and Kyra Ma were sleeping over? That my looming presence in the night would send them into frightened hysterics? That I would theretofore be labeled a stalker—or more precisely a *lesbo* stalker—even though I had never been attracted to Topaz in that way.

It was like Freya had known the best way to wound me. While I'd never shared the exact details of my ninth-grade friendship gone wrong, Freya knew I was sensitive about my loner status. She knew I was afraid to put myself out there socially and have my desperation thrown back in my face. She had carefully chosen her words to cut me. She was cruel and heartless. Why didn't that make me stop loving her?

All I wanted was to talk to her, but I couldn't, not without perpetuating the myth of my obsession. I couldn't risk driving down her street, walking past her yoga studio, eating at her favorite restaurant. I had to observe her from a safe distance. In fact, I had to borrow a pair of binoculars from Vik. If Freya spotted me, it would make everything a million times worse.

My life had become empty and meaningless. I considered Virginia Woolf–ing myself—filling my pockets with rocks and walking into the freezing ocean. I would have done it, if I thought anyone would care. My family would be upset, of course, until they realized that Eckhart could have his own room, then they'd be secretly grateful for the space. Freya would be flattered. She'd tell people that I was so obsessed with her, that I'd offed myself when she'd sent me away. I'd become notorious in death, the tall friendless stalker whose ghost haunts the harbor.

At least I still worked at Jamie's shop on the weekends. I'd shown up for my first shift after the incident filled with trepidation. Freya might have told Jamie to fire me. She might have told her that I was creepy, even dangerous. If I lost my job on top of it all, I really would have drowned myself. Because Hawking Mercantile offered me the tranquility I craved. There were practically no customers from October to April. And I liked being around Freya's vases, bowls, and dishes. They made me feel close to her. And Jamie was my only link back to Freya.

My boss had been warned about me, that much was clear. She and I had never been especially close, but we'd become comfortable with each other. And she had trusted me. The point of my employment was to give her a break, allow her to take a day off, or go for a leisurely lunch. But now, I could see her watch me, hover over me. Was she afraid I'd steal from the till if she wasn't looking? Burn the place down if she went to grab a sandwich? What had Freya said about me?

On my second shift after the incident, I was dusting the merchandise when Jamie said, "You miss her, don't you?"

How had she known I'd been thinking about Freya? Had I murmured her name unconsciously? Then I looked down at the dish I was cradling, gently stroking it with the dust cloth. It was one of Freya's; she had made it with her own two hands. I'd been there when she glazed it. I set it down.

Jamie said, "I don't know the full story, but I'm sorry your friendship with Freya had to end. And I hope you won't feel awkward around me. Freya and I are close, but that won't affect your employment."

Her tone was sympathetic and her eyes full of warmth. But she wasn't fooling me. Jamie thought she had replaced me in Freya's affections. She thought she had won. I met her gaze and shrugged.

"I don't blame *her*," I said. "I blame the pregnancy hormones."

My boss's tawny face paled, evidence that she was unaware of Freya's condition. The news clearly pained her, but she deserved it for gloating about their friendship. Besides, Freya was almost four months pregnant now. She couldn't hide behind stretchy pants and flowing tops for much longer. If, in fact, she was still pregnant. Either way . . . now she'd have to explain why she'd kept her situation a secret from her supposed best friend. I suppressed a grin of satisfaction.

Jamie fussed around the till, but I could see her grappling with the news. Her brow was wrinkled with confusion, her jaw clenched with tension. But mostly, she just looked sad. When she felt my gaze on her, she looked up and her eyes were shiny with emotion.

"Hormones can be really powerful," she said weakly. "I just hope you two can sort things out one day."

"I don't know. She made some pretty crazy accusations."

"Do you want some tea?" her voice was strained. "I'm going to make some."

"Sure. Thanks."

Jamie scuttled to the kitchen. I picked up another one of Freya's creations and wiped it gently with the cloth.

26

jamie

Alone in the kitchen, I flicked the kettle on and paced the tiny space, waiting for the water to boil. My stomach was queasy, my forehead hot. Freya was pregnant. Why had she kept it from me? I thought we were friends . . . *best* friends. Her pretense disappointed me. But I had to admit the real source of my distress. I was jealous. Freya, who hated children, who had never wanted one, was pregnant. And I was not.

Of course, Low could be lying. Freya had warned me that the girl would say anything to hurt Freya and Max, the gorgeous couple in the glass house. But this pregnancy news didn't hurt Freya, it hurt *me*. Low had no reason to wound me like that. I had stood by her. I had kept her employed even after Freya had banished her. Why would she tell me my best friend was expecting if it wasn't true?

The electric kettle boiled then and automatically turned itself off. I reached for a mug but stopped. I couldn't stand there, drinking tea with Low, wondering if what she had told me was the truth. I had to know for sure. And there was only one way to find out. I hurried out of the kitchen.

"It's so dead today," I chirped. "Let's close early."

Low glanced at the clock on the wall. "But it's only four."

"I know. But we haven't had a customer in hours. There's not much point staying open."

"If you want to go, I can stay till five thirty," my assistant offered. "I'll cash out and lock up."

Low had worked alone before. She knew the closing procedures and was fully capable of handling them on her own. But Freya's words rang in my memory. *Don't trust her.* And Low may have just lied to my face, may have said those words just to crush me. Until I knew for sure, I couldn't leave her alone in my store.

"It's fine," I insisted. "You can go. I'll close up."

Low loped into the back room to grab her coat. Shooting me a resentful look, she left. I immediately texted Freya.

Closed early. Meet me for happy hour?

If she *were* pregnant, she wouldn't be drinking. *Shouldn't* be drinking, anyway. I tried to remember the last time we'd had alcohol together. Our recent visits had mostly been walks and coffee dates. She'd brought sandwiches to the store a couple of times and we'd had a picnic on the front counter. But I was almost certain that Freya had had a mimosa on a recent brunch date. Maybe she wasn't expecting?

Her text came back.

Busy in the studio. Coffee tomorrow morning?

Her refusal to meet for drinks meant that she *could* be pregnant. But I needed confirmation. And I couldn't wait until tomorrow.

I need to see you. It's about Low.

The message was read, but she didn't respond right away. My heart pounded as I waited for the shivering ellipsis that prefaced her reply. Finally, they came, followed closely by the words:

Come to the studio.

I'd been in Freya's pottery studio a couple of times. In contrast to her pristine home, it was a disaster: dust coating every surface, buckets full of muddy clay on the floor, filthy rags draped over the backs of chairs or the edge of the sink. But in the midst of it all were racks of Freya's creations at various stages of finish. They were all so beautiful that they compensated for the slovenliness of the space.

Freya wore a large smock, which did double duty in protecting her clothes and hiding her bump. If there was one. She wiped her hands on a cloth.

"Hey, hon." Freya kissed my cheek.

I decided to dive right in.

"Low says you're pregnant."

Freya's face darkened. "It wasn't her place to tell you."

"So it's true."

She reached for my hand then, her blue eyes soft. "I didn't want to hurt you. I knew it would be hard for you to hear."

"I'm your friend," I said, through the lump in my throat, "I'm happy for you."

"Are you sure? I know how much you wanted a baby and I never wanted to be a mom. It doesn't seem fair."

But maybe it was fair? I had betrayed my best friend and my husband when I slept with Max. Perhaps karma had played a hand in conception. "I'm thrilled for you. Honestly."

"Thank God." She gave my hand a squeeze, then released it.

"Because I'm going to need you. I have no idea what the hell I'm doing."

"We'll figure it out together." I would get over my envy, tamp it down inside of me. I would be there for Freya and her child. My infertility would not impact my support.

"I would have told you, but I was in shock," she said. "I wasn't even sure I could conceive. We'd always been kind of lax with birth control. I just assumed we couldn't get pregnant."

"How far along are you?"

"I'm at the end of the first trimester." She smiled then and smoothed the smock over her tummy. Her normally flat abdomen was slightly inflated, like she'd swallowed a small melon. "The baby's due in May. Spring is my favorite season."

She was delighted, glowing. Any reservations I'd had about her desire to be a parent evaporated in the face of her excitement.

"Max must be thrilled."

"He was surprised at first, but he came around. This feels like a positive new chapter for us."

"A baby is a gift," I said.

"It is." Freya's eyes were sparkling. "I even got back on Instagram. I took a photo of my belly. Just a simple shot, but the lighting was really beautiful, so I thought . . . what the heck. I'll reactivate my Instagram and post it. I just said: hashtag new beginnings. And I got fifteen thousand likes!"

"Wow," I said, through a twinge of discomfort. Freya wanting to share her baby news with her legions of fans was not all that unusual, but she'd told me many times how toxic and ugly social media was. Her followers had turned on her in the face of Max's trial, spewing vitriol and hatred. Freya had lashed back at them, and she'd received death threats, they'd had to hire security. Max's lawyer had instructed her to deactivate her account to avoid inflaming tensions. Now, she was sharing her most special, most intimate moment with all those strangers . . . but not with me.

"There's been so much pain and ugliness," Freya said, and she looked beatific, almost angelic. "And now, we can focus on a beautiful future as parents."

"It's wonderful news," I said, drawing her into a hug.

It *was* wonderful news, I told myself. Even if it wasn't *my* wonderful news.

27

After my meeting with Freya, I picked up some groceries for dinner and a couple of bottles of wine and drove home. I expected to find my husband writing—Brian's deadline was fast approaching—but his laptop was hibernating, and his chaotic mess of an office was empty. When he still wasn't home after I put the food and wine in the fridge, I texted him.

Where are you?

As soon as I hit SEND, I heard the rumble of feet on the front steps. Brian staggered in wearing running tights and a fleece jacket. He was sweaty and panting.

"Hey, I just texted you," I said.

"You're home early." He kicked off his sneakers and paced in a slow circle. "I went for a run."

"You've been running a lot lately."

"It's great for stress." Then he suddenly dropped to the floor and assumed plank position.

My husband had been blessed with a quick metabolism and a natural wiriness. Over the course of our years together, he'd worked out sporadically, usually staying fit with games of pickup basketball or bike rides with his buddies. As I watched him on the floor strengthening his core, I realized how isolated Brian had become. He'd left his sporty pals behind. On the island, he had no friends but Max, a professional athlete who worked out like a warrior. And they hadn't seen each other in months.

"I left work early to see Freya," I said, to the back of his head. "She had some news."

"What was it?" he asked, through gritted teeth.

"She's pregnant."

Brian held his position for a few more seconds, then lowered his knees. "Really?"

"I was surprised, too. And so was she. She didn't think they could conceive, but it just happened."

He didn't speak for a moment, absorbing the news. Then he said, "Are *you* okay?"

"Yeah," I said, my voice trembling slightly. "I felt jealous at first, but I'm happy for her. I think she really wants this baby."

My husband gave me a sympathetic smile and squeezed my arm. "I need water," he said, and moved to the kitchen.

"She'd always told me she didn't want kids," I said, trailing after him. "She sounded like she kind of hated them. But it'll be different with her own."

Brian filled a glass with water. "And Max?"

My one-time lover's name on my husband's lips elevated my pulse, but I affected a casual tone. "I haven't seen him, but Freya said he's happy. He was surprised, but they both feel like this is a new beginning for them. They've been through a lot of ugliness. A baby will bring so much joy."

Brian drained the glass and set it down. "It's hard to envision them as parents."

"I thought so, too, until I saw how excited Freya is."

"A baby will change their lifestyle. No more magic-mushroom parties, for one."

"Definitely not." I laughed awkwardly.

We had never talked about that night. My one attempt at a confession had been subverted, and I could see no reason to bring my dalliance with Max into the light now. So I changed the subject.

"Freya's feeling pretty overwhelmed. But I said I'd help her and support her."

"You're a good friend to her."

"We can have a role in this baby's life, Brian. We can be its auntie and uncle."

My husband almost smiled, but not quite. "I'm going to take a shower."

"I'll start dinner."

As he walked to the bathroom, I saw the tension in his posture. This was hard news for him to hear, too. He'd wanted a baby as much as I had, and our best friends—our only friends—on the island were expecting. But he would come around eventually. My acceptance had been expedited by a guilty conscience. Brian's would take more time.

I grabbed a bottle of pinot noir and poured myself a large glass.

28

low

Revealing Freya's pregnancy secret to Jamie had not turned out as I'd hoped. I thought Jamie would feel jealous and betrayed, that the ruse would blow up their friendship. I imagined Jamie calling Freya selfish and insensitive, a lying, duplicitous bitch. Her outrage would drive Freya back into my waiting arms. But somehow, Freya had explained away her deceit, had charmed Jamie and won her over. To my chagrin, their friendship seemed to have deepened with the baby news. Jamie acted like an excited aunt. And I was the one left feeling envy and betrayal.

I knew from my parking-lot surveillance at the Blue Heron that the two women met for lunch regularly. I'd also seen them walking into the coffee shop on a number of occasions when I just happened to be driving by. Freya had gone to a yoga retreat for a couple of weeks, but she spent most of her holiday texting with my employer. Jamie stood with her elbows on the counter, tapping away at her phone and giggling. When I joined her behind the till under the auspices of fetching a dustcloth, she hurriedly tucked her phone away, but not before I saw Freya's name on the screen. Upon Freya's return, Jamie asked me to man the shop for a couple of days so she and Freya could take the ferry to the mainland to buy baby paraphernalia.

Freya still hated me, perhaps more now than ever. On top of squatting on her property and sticking my nose into her dish-throwing business, I'd broken her trust by revealing her secret. There was no point trying to contact her. She would only reject me, hurt me, crush my fragile spirit. Sometimes, I was still angry over her cruel words and my smashed pinch pots, but mostly, I just wanted her to let me back in. My logical mind told me to let her go, to move on, but my heart pined for reconciliation.

In order to maintain both my distance and connection to Freya and Max, I spent most of my days at the library in town. Our family PC was in the kitchen, and I required privacy (or at least anonymity) for the internet research I was doing. In the afternoons, I sat at one of the library's four computers and googled Maxime Beausoleil and Freya Light. I didn't read the toxic news stories about Max's deadly hit, the contentious law-suit, Freya's fall from social media grace. They were all lies, Freya had told me, all skewed to make the gorgeous couple out to be villains. Instead, I selected "Images," and pored over numerous photos of the attractive pair at galas and fundraisers, at Trader Joe's or leaving the gym. I sifted through pictures of Max on the ice, of Freya's endorsement deal with a short-lived vitamin water company, my emotions rocketing from longing to loss, from ado-ration to misery.

The three to four hours I spent gazing at their images online each day makes it sound like an unhealthy fixation. But I was getting on with my own life, too. For my November birthday, my parents had given me a high-end digital camera. It was second-hand but still in great condition. Though I had never explained the demise of my potting career, my family recognized my need for a creative outlet. And they provided for me.

Vik had taken some professional concert photos. We talked about perspective and lighting and use of space. I was mildly enthusiastic. Maybe reigniting my love for photography would be a way forward for me. I was already thinking less about Freya, spending less time staring at her likeness at the library or on my phone. Photography was an excellent distraction. At least it was supposed to be.

How could I have known it would lead me back to her?

29

jamie

Over the next few weeks, I became Freya's personal assistant. We took a trip to Seattle to pick out baby furniture. We painted the walls of the planned nursery a pale buttery yellow. (I did most of the painting; Freya didn't want to breathe the paint fumes, and Max was away dealing with some business.) I bought Freya baby books, and when she wouldn't read them, I read them myself and provided a verbal summary. There were back rubs and foot massages; casseroles and spur-of-the-moment ice cream deliveries. I still felt the ache and longing for a child of my own, a child I would never have, but I wanted to be there for my friend in her delicate time. And doting on her distracted me from my envy, resentment, and guilt. Almost.

I'd been able to avoid Max for the most part. Despite the impending arrival of his son or daughter, he was spending long hours on the water. He'd been traveling, too—a golf weekend with old teammates in Arizona, a trip north to visit family, frequent jaunts to the mainland to deal with business or legal affairs. The timing seemed odd to me, but Freya pointed out that Max would be on house arrest once the baby arrived. When he and I did cross paths, we were cool and civil. It was almost like nothing had ever happened between us.

But at night, he still came to me in my dreams. Torrid, sexual dreams that left me sweaty and aroused and hating myself. What if I murmured Max's name in my sleep? Could Brian tell what imaginings caused me to toss and turn? I never fantasized about Maxime Beausoleil when I was awake. In fact, I disdained him. But my subconscious refused to let him go.

We still hadn't socialized as couples since that fateful night. Freya had suggested it a handful of times, but between their travel schedules, my responsibilities at the store, and Brian's writing deadline, it hadn't come to fruition. My husband had been working on his manuscript, the second in the series, all summer. He'd delivered it in October, on schedule, but a month later, his editor called.

"She says it *lacks the tension* of the first book," he complained. "She says the last half is fucking garbage."

"Really? She said it's 'fucking garbage'?"

"She may as well have," he grumbled.

"I could read it," I offered lamely. "Maybe a fresh pair of eyes would help."

"Yeah, like you're going to solve the problems my professional editor can't."

His ego was bruised, his confidence shaken. And he was worried about money. Brian's advance checks were metered out in installments: a percentage when he signed the contract, another on acceptance of the manuscript, more on publication. Hawking Mercantile had had a decent summer, and we'd budgeted our money to last until he received his next payment. We'd assumed that would be shortly after his delivery date. But that sum would now be delayed—weeks, months, even years. As long as it took for Brian to make the book good enough to publish. And from what I could see, he was barely writing.

Instead, he was working out. A lot. There was something almost manic about his need for exercise, and it didn't sit right with me. It had started slowly, shortly after we began spending time with Freya and Max. I'd noticed a general uptick in my husband's self-care: regular trips to the barber, green smoothies for breakfast, twenty-five push-ups each morning. But now he'd added trail running to his repertoire, spending an hour or more in the forest on rugged terrain. His favorite route was in Hyak Canyon, a twenty-five-minute drive from our cottage. By the time he drove there, ran for an hour, drove home, showered and changed, it was three hours he could have spent writing.

I was enduring financial anxiety myself, but I didn't have time to gallop around in the woods. When I wasn't at the store, I was working on the books, trying to keep the business in the black. Reduced winter hours helped. Hawking Mercantile was currently closed on Mondays and Tuesdays and had reduced operations for the rest of the week. Low worked only Saturdays, until business picked up. Brian had suggested that I lay her off until July, but I'd be able to give her more shifts during the Christmas shopping season. Low gave me the freedom to run business errands (to the bank, to the accountant, to the store to replenish the cookie cupboard), and to be available if Freya needed me.

A perk of my diminished schedule was more time with my husband. Between the store and his novel, we had been existing in separate orbits. These extra hours would close the gap between us, get us back on track. I envisioned lunch dates, walks, even some afternoon delight.

But it didn't turn out that way.

It was a Monday, early in December. Next week, I would open the store for Christmas shopping and would be spending more time away from home. I'd decided to make Brian his favorite lunch. It would be nice to share a midday meal together before I returned to extended retail hours. As I grated cheese onto a piece of bread and tuna, Brian entered in running gear.

"I'm going for a run in the canyon."

"But I'm making tuna melts."

"I'll eat later." He was already lacing up his shoes. "I need to burn off some steam."

The block of cheddar I'd been grating hit the counter with a thud. "I don't know how you're going to fix your book if you never spend any time writing." It came out snarkier than I'd intended, but I was hurt. I didn't even like tuna melts. This lunch was for him.

Brian righted himself and looked at me. I'd expected anger or defiance or a lecture on the creative process, but all he said was: "I need to do this."

He grabbed his car keys and hurried out the door.

I slammed the tray under the broiler. Something was up with my husband, beyond writer's block. He was pulling away from me, I could feel it. He was distant and distracted; didn't want to eat, talk, or connect with me. His rigorous exercise routine made it clear that he would rather work on his body than his marriage. We still had sex, on schedule. It was still good—hotter than it had been when we were trying to conceive. But despite his attentiveness and vigor, my lover seemed emotionally detached.

As I cleaned the kitchen, my anger eased to a simmer. We were both under immense stress, I reminded myself. When Brian fixed his manuscript, when business picked up at the store, we'd find our way back to each other. We always did. A relationship like ours was built for the long haul. I was making too big a deal over a shared sandwich. Washing the knife and cutting board, I let my resentment run down the drain with the soapy water.

The oven timer dinged and as I turned toward it, I spotted Brian's inhaler on the counter. My husband's mild case of asthma was made significantly less mild with strenuous exercise. He never worked out without his inhaler, but his distraction was so complete that he'd forgotten it. If he had an asthma attack alone, in the middle of the forest, an hour from home, it could be serious.

I flicked off the oven, picked up the inhaler, and hurried to my car.

30

My Mazda hurtled down the winding road toward Hyak Canyon. It was a forested stretch of highway, rarely used except by a few residents of homesteads set back in the woods and miles apart. I was slightly uneasy in this largely deserted swath of trees. There were rumors of meth labs on this part of the island, of illegal marijuana crops. The canyon and its running trails were in a national park, but the surrounding area had a dark, criminal energy.

Brian's inhaler rattled in the console. If I didn't catch him before he started his run, I'd be too late. My husband usually stretched his quads and hamstrings before he took off, a process that could take anywhere from five to fifteen minutes. My foot pressed down on the gas. I hoped Brian was doing an extra-long warm-up today.

As I rounded a bend, a vehicle flew past me. It was white, an SUV. I caught a glimpse of light blond hair as the driver passed, her eyes focused on the winding road ahead.

Freya.

What was she doing out here? The area was almost deserted, except for the rumored meth cookers and pot growers. Freya couldn't have been hiking the rugged canyon trails in her condition. She had no reason to be in this area. Unless . . .

My stomach churned. Was something going on between my husband and my best friend? If so, what? Did they know what Max and I had done? Were they plotting to destroy us? To abandon us? Or . . . had my husband lied to my face about that night? Had he and Freya slept together, too?

The thought of Brian making love to Freya made me sick. She was so beautiful, so small and blond and perfect. My husband would have been enraptured by her, like I had been with Max. I'd been excited by the newness, turned on by the differences. Brian would have felt the same way. He'd have compared me to Freya, and I would have fallen short. Were they in love now? Having an affair? My mind and stomach reeled with the possibilities.

About seven minutes later, I pulled into the gravel parking area. Brian's truck was alone in the lot, and he was beside it, pacing in a circle. He was decidedly not stretching his hamstrings. He looked up as my car approached, and our eyes met.

My husband was not happy to see me.

I got out of the car and marched toward him.

"What are you doing here?" He couldn't hide his dismay.

I'd left his inhaler in the console. I suddenly didn't care if he had an asthma attack. "What's going on with you, Brian? Why was Freya here?"

"Freya?"

"I passed her as I was driving. Is something going on between you two?"

"Are you serious?" He snorted. "You think I'm sleeping with your pregnant best friend?"

"It would explain a lot! You're distant and moody. You won't talk to me. You're always running. Or so you say. . . ."

"I was going to run, but I forgot my inhaler."

"I brought it. That's why I'm here. But now I'd like to know what the hell is going on with you."

He turned away from me, dragging his hands through his cropped hair. Then he whirled around, his face dark and angry.

"You want to know what's going on with me, Jamie? My book is a disaster, and I don't know how to fix it. If I lose this deal, we're fucked. Your store doesn't make enough money to support us, so I'll have to go back to teaching. There won't be any openings on the island, so we'll have to pack up and move. You'll have to sell the store. We'll both have to give up on our dreams. All because I'm a fucking failure."

I saw the pain on his handsome face. It was genuine. He was telling the truth.

"I run all the time because it's the only thing keeping me off antidepressants," he growled. "Would you rather I self-medicate with drugs or booze?"

"Of course not. And you're not a failure."

"You won't be saying that when we lose everything."

I closed the distance between us. "I didn't realize you were in such a dark place." I reached for his hand. "It's all going to be okay."

"I don't know that it is."

"We've struggled before, and we always get through it. Together."

He sighed. "I hope you're right."

"But . . . why was Freya out here?"

He pulled his hand from my grip. "How the hell would I know?" he snapped. "She's your friend, why don't you ask her instead of accusing me?"

Brian jumped into his truck and peeled out of the parking lot, all plans for his run abandoned.

Alone in my car, I felt chastened and ashamed. I was transferring my own adulterous behavior onto Brian. It had so consumed me that I couldn't see that my husband was hurting, that he needed my support. All my energy had been focused on Freya and the baby, in making up for what I'd done to them in some small way. But I had betrayed Brian, too. And he needed me now.

That quick, lightning glimpse of Freya flashed through my mind. It could have been a blond tourist in a white Range Rover, but I knew it was my friend. Her presence in the middle of the island was a coincidence, nothing more. Freya was probably visiting a pottery student on one of the properties in the area. Perhaps she'd gone for a scenic drive to clear her head. Or maybe she was buying some weed? No, not in her condition. She wouldn't. Would she? Freya was a risk-taker, a rule-breaker. But she had to know that pot was not good for her baby.

When I got home, I parked next to Brian's vehicle and entered the house. I heard the shower running. Instead of washing away his sweat, he was washing away his anger and disappointment. I'd reheat our lunch, maybe open a bottle of wine. We could sit and talk, and I would listen, really listen. From that moment on, I would be caring and supportive, there for my husband in his time of need. I hung my sweater on the hook next to Brian's running shell, and that's when I saw it.

A long, pale blond hair clung to the shoulder of my husband's black jacket.

31

brian

Jamie bought it, thank God. If she had found out that my trail run was just an excuse to meet Freya, it would have hurt her too much. And despite what I had done, I didn't want to cause my wife any pain. That's why I had to be so careful, so discreet. If Jamie found out what was going on, it would crush her. All the lying and sneaking around . . . it was meant to protect her and her feelings.

I turned off the shower and reached for a towel, drying myself vigorously. My body felt stronger than it had in a long time, harder and leaner. Still, it couldn't compare to Max Beausoleil's physique. He would always be bigger, tougher, more masculine than I was. But maybe she didn't want that. Maybe his perfection bored her. It was possible . . . doubtful, but possible.

My robe was on the back of the door, and I wrapped it around me. It was winter, and the old bungalow was drafty. If my books ever took off, I would buy a new house on the water. At the rate I was going, that wasn't going to happen. The book had structural problems that needed my full attention, but my mind was consumed with thoughts of Freya. It was her fault that the book was a mess in the first place. She had come into our lives and turned everything upside down.

I emerged into the hallway in a billow of steam. The air was chilled, almost icy. Jamie should have turned on the furnace. In bare feet, I moved to the living room thermostat, where the real source of the cold front sat on the sofa, her mouth set in a grim line.

"Stop lying to me, Brian." Jamie's voice trembled with hurt and anger. "I know you were with Freya at the canyon."

There was no point denying it. "It's not how it looks," I said quickly. "We were just talking."

An incredulous laugh erupted from Jamie's throat. "Do you really expect me to believe that? How long have you been fucking my best friend?" The vulgarity was out of character, but appropriate, given the circumstances. But I chose different words.

"I'm not . . . *sleeping* with her," I said. "I *slept* with her. The night you slept with Max."

My wife's olive face blanched as guilt, confusion, and shame flitted across her features. But I knew my own pallor was even paler, even sicker. Articulating what happened that night, saying the words out loud, made me want to puke.

Jamie swallowed audibly. "Why did you lie to me? I've been racked with guilt."

"Poor you." My sarcasm was cutting. "Freya told me how much you wanted Max. She told me you were bored with me, desperate to have sex with someone else. That you'd missed out on so much, because of *me*."

"No. . . ." But her voice was weak.

"Freya said the swap would make you happy. That no one would get hurt. But I got hurt, Jamie. The thought of you and . . . him." My throat clogged, and I couldn't continue.

"No." It was firm this time. She got off the couch and rushed toward me. "Freya twisted my words. I never wanted to be with Max. But he said you and Freya were already in bed together. I was high. And I was weak. So I just . . . I went along with it. But I've hated myself ever since."

She tried to hug me, but I folded my arms, backed away. I wasn't ready to forgive her. Or myself.

"I wanted to talk to you about it afterward," my wife continued. "I wanted you to know that I only want to be with you. Ever. But you went out in the boat with Max. You acted like everything was normal."

"I was in shock. Maybe I was still high. I don't know. . . ."

"And then later, when I asked you point-blank, you denied that anything happened with you and Freya."

"I didn't deny it. I just told you that you're the only woman I've ever wanted to be with. And that's the truth."

"But we could have talked it through."

"I didn't want to talk it through." I forced the words past the knot of emotion in my throat. "The thought of you with this rich, handsome fucking athlete eats me alive. I can't write. I can't sleep. I can't think. . . ."

I let her take me in her arms then, let her run her fingers through my hair, let her whisper words of love in my ear. My shoulders sagged with relief, the tension in my jaw relaxed. Jamie was right. We needed to bring this out into the open, to talk about it and heal from it. Then I felt her pull away from me.

"Why were you meeting Freya at the canyon?"

Here it was. The part that would hurt her most.

"That night . . . we didn't use protection. Freya said we didn't have to worry. She and Max had been tested for STDs and they'd been monogamous since they moved to the island. And"—my voice caught, but I forced the words out—"she told me she couldn't get pregnant. She said she couldn't conceive."

Jamie's voice was a whisper as she put the pieces together. "Oh my god."

"When you told me she was expecting, I didn't know what to think. I had to talk to her. I had to ask her if . . ."

My wife's strangled voice completed my sentence. "If Freya's baby could be yours."

"The timing's off," I assured her. "The baby isn't due until May. The night we . . . *had sex* was in July. So, if the baby were mine, it would be due early April."

"How do you know her due date? Are you taking her word for it?"

I was a step ahead of her. "I asked Freya to show me a dated ultrasound photo. She brought it to me today."

"Those things can be faked. You know that from the fiasco with the baby in Chicago."

"It wasn't like Mia's ultrasound. This one had the hospital information on it. It looked legit."

"Do you have it? I want to see it."

"Freya kept it," I said. And then, "She's your best friend. Do you really think she'd lie to us?"

My wife's brow furrowed as she considered her answer. "I think anyone is capable of lying under the right circumstances."

"And she lied about you wanting to sleep with Max," I said, a hopeful lilt in my voice.

"I think she just misread our conversation." Jamie's eyes wouldn't meet mine. "I don't think she's a blatant liar."

"Right. Well, that's it, then," I retorted. "We can close the door on this. Forget that night ever happened."

Jamie's smile was weak. "Happy to."

But we couldn't, of course. What happened that night would haunt us forever.

winter 2020

32

low

One day in late January, just as my mother had promised, Eckhart abruptly stopped screaming. He was really quite cute when his face wasn't beet red and covered in tears and snot. I began to warm to him. In contrast to his first months as a malcontent, he was now extremely chill and docile. And, as if to make up for his months of endless rage, he slept long and hard. I decided to photograph him.

It was bright and crisp that day, the sun high in a deep-blue cloudless sky. After Eckhart had his breast milk breakfast, I bundled him up, put him in the sling, and walked down a path to the beach-access road. By the time I hit the shoreline, Eckhart was sound asleep. I removed the comatose little parcel and positioned him on the sand as the tide nipped around him. I took a number of shots of my snoozing sibling, and I liked what I saw. It became our routine. After nursing, my mom would hand over my brother. I'd walk him to the beach or into the forest and then photograph him as he slept on a piece of driftwood, a bed of polished pebbles, or a nest of cedar boughs.

The photos were reminiscent of the ones taken by Anne Geddes, but without the silly costumes and flowers. Eckhart was wrapped in a thick, natural wool blanket and wore a simple knitted hat. He wasn't a tiny newborn, either, but four months old now. He was small for his age, though; his incessant wailing had burned a lot of calories. The images were natural, rustic, and appealing. I'd used Lightroom, a photo-editing program to make them crisp and luminous, the colors deep and saturated. I was proud of them. I decided to print and frame a couple for my parents. I sent the files to the only drugstore in town, and twenty-four hours later, went to retrieve them.

Behind the counter was Thompson Ingleby, a kid from my senior photography class. Like me, he had been persona non grata at Bayview High. He was stocky, about five foot six, with green eyes and dirty-blond hair. I'd thought he was cute once, back in ninth grade, but then I'd grown half a foot and lost interest. He'd spent the first years of high school smoking pot at the edge of the soccer field with the other burnouts, but he'd suddenly became more academically focused in twelfth grade and subsequently lost all his friends. His family lived on one of the remote homesteads in the center of the island. Rumors of drugs and guns and sex dungeons swirled around them. We could have been allies, but throwing my lot in with Thompson Ingleby would not have improved my popularity.

"Hey, Low," he said, as if he were genuinely glad to see me. Unlike me, Thompson wasn't broody and resentful, but chipper, happy-go-lucky. He clearly wasn't right in the head.

"Hey," I mumbled. "I'm picking up some prints. Under Morrison."

"Right," he chirped, pulling open a long drawer near his knees. He extracted a blue envelope and slid it across the counter toward me. "Your photos are awesome."

"You looked at my photos?" I snapped.

"Umm . . . that's my job. Cashier and quality control. I make sure the photos print out properly. You'd be surprised how often the printer will screw up. But yours came out great. You could sell them."

"Who would want pictures of my brother?"

"People like babies," he said. "They don't care who they are." He read the back of the envelope and punched some numbers into the till. "Four sixty-eight, please.

As I dug into my wallet, Thompson said, "Are you on Instagram?"

"No."

"You should set up a page for your photography. You never know what might happen."

I plunked a bill onto the counter. "Like what?"

"I don't know . . . Maybe someone would hire you to photograph their baby?"

"Gross."

"But what if they lived in New York? Or Paris? They might fly you out there."

That was more enticing.

"You might get a gallery showing. Or free camera equipment. Or baby swag."

"Why would I want baby swag?"

"For your brother," he said, as he made change. "I manage a page for my cousin's baking business. She's got over three thousand followers now. She's getting her brand out there and she's starting to get a few orders." He leaned toward me and I saw a few straggly whiskers under his bottom lip, an attempt at a soul patch. "Don't tell anyone, but her food looks better than it tastes."

He handed me some coins. "When you get your page up, let me know. I'll give you a shout-out in our stories."

I wasn't sure why Thompson Ingleby wanted to help me. I'd never been very nice to him. On the other hand, I'd never been overtly mean to him, either, and maybe, in Thompson's world, that was enough.

"Thanks." I grabbed my prints and left.

33

For an outcast like me, social media was a fresh kind of hell—somewhere between livestreaming your Brazilian wax and being disemboweled and having your entrails set on fire in front of you. By avoiding Facebook, Instagram, and Snapchat, I could almost enjoy my complete lack of a social life. During my previous sojourn onto social media, I had realized its sole purpose was to make me feel bad about all the fun and frivolity I was missing out on, all the typical teen experiences I would never have. Though I hated fun and frivolity, and didn't even want those clichéd experiences, seeing my peers drinking and partying and declaring their undying love for one another with hashtags—#BFF #timeofmylife #memories—made me want to hurl.

But this Instagram page would be faceless. It would be about my photography only. I might actually enjoy having a bunch of strangers fawn over my work. Freya said it was the best feeling in the world . . . until it became the worst. It was all fake, she had said, and the people who adored you one minute would turn on you the next. There were bullies out there, empowered by the anonymity of the internet. Depression, anxiety, and negative body image were just some of the side effects of a diet of social media. But that wouldn't happen to me. Because this wasn't about me. It was about sharing my art with the world.

The name I chose was "Hawkeye 61." (Actually, I had to use The_Hawkeye_61 because someone already had the other label.) The moniker was derived from the town of Hawking combined with my eye for photography, and the fact that I was six foot one. I had always related to hawks. They were loners, watching, circling, waiting to strike. Over the next few days, I uploaded some of my favorite photos—of Eckhart, of nature, of the pig and the goat. I DM'd Thompson Ingleby and he worked his magic. Within the first few days, I had over four hundred followers.

I had conditioned myself to view social media platforms as evil, but I was beginning to see the beauty in them. Instagram didn't care if you hadn't grown since the ninth grade like Thompson, or if you *had* grown to a near-freakish height like me. It only cared about the facade, the pretense you chose to share with the world. And that worked well for me. My talent was being appreciated without the distraction of my unfortunate physicality. My confidence bloomed.

Freya had taught me the tricks of the social media trade. How to build my following, when to post to receive maximum exposure. The photos of my sleeping brother were the most popular, with the goat a distant second. In fact, Eckhart's images garnered a lot of attention from other photographers, mommy blogger types, and baby-clothing companies. One morning I woke up to three hundred new followers. Another day, I gained over five hundred!

As soon as I set up my account, I searched for Freya Light. I was thrilled to find she had reactivated her Instagram page:

Frey_of_Light. So clever! Her account was public, so I followed her. She posted mostly selfies, all focused around her pregnancy. She and Max had spent much of the winter in Mexico—Sayulita, Nayarit, according to the geo tag. They were on a "babymoon" sponsored by a five-star resort. Free accommodation in exchange for posts of the photogenic mother-to-be in her high-end quarters and around the scenic property. One photo offered a view of Freya's tanned belly and shapely legs, the ocean in the background. There was a shot of her round tummy floating in an infinity pool; a pic of her in a white robe eating fresh papaya for breakfast in her suite; one of her maternal cleavage bursting out of her bikini top, with the caption: These babies are ready for baby! #breastfeed #mothersmilk #noboobjob

While I was thrilled when I got a hundred likes, Freya got thousands. Scrolling through the comments, I found them to be largely positive and supportive.

So beautiful!

That's going to be a gorgeous baby!

Enjoy this special time!

Only a handful were cruel.

Ryan Klassen is dead. But enjoy your holiday!

Will baby grow up to be a killer like daddy?

Superficial, shallow c**t.

Monitoring her page, I found that Freya posted roughly every other day. She was back in the game. And it was only a matter of time before her dabbling became a full-blown career again. Her photos were decent, she looked stunning, but they were amateurish. That's when I saw an opportunity to get back into Freya's life. But I needed Thompson Ingleby's help.

I texted him and asked him to meet me for a slice of pizza. He responded instantly and exuberantly.

Sounds great!!!

When I arrived at the restaurant, he was already there, seated at a red vinyl booth. He stood when I entered. "Can I buy you a slice?"

"My treat," I said. "What'll you have?"

"I insist," Thompson said. "Unless you think that's chauvinistic? I respect you as a woman and your ability to pay for your own food."

"It's fine." I slid into the booth. "I'll have a meat-lovers and a Coke."

Thompson hurried to the counter and soon returned with a slice and a drink for each of us. He set my meal in front of me with a flourish.

"M'lady."

Like he'd just slayed a dragon for me. Four years ago, I would have been charmed, but this was a business meeting only. I knew I had to start with some small talk.

"How's your cousin's bakery business going?"

"Not bad," Thompson said, then proceeded to regale me with tales of his cousin's photogenic petit fours that looked great but tasted like dirt sandwiches. I nodded along, though I was barely listening.

"How's the photography coming along?" Thompson asked. "Are you still working at the gift shop?"

Instead of responding to his two-part question, I said, "I have a favor to ask."

"Sure."

"I want you to DM someone for me on Instagram. I want you to tell her about my page."

"I could do another story. You'll get more followers that way."

"I don't care about more followers. I want to photograph *her*."

Thompson chewed for a moment. "Who is it?"

"Freya Light. She's an Insta celebrity. At least she used to be. She lives here now."

"Cool." He was already digging out his phone, already looking her up. "She's very pregnant. And she's gorgeous." He looked up at me. "If you like that petite, blond type."

Was he flirting with me? I had literally no experience, so I couldn't tell. If he *was*, I should say something flirtatious back. But what? *You're kind of cute, and I might be into you if you weren't a head shorter than I am.* That wasn't all that charming, I realized, so I said nothing.

Thompson turned his attention back to the phone. "What do you want me to say?"

"Tell her you love her page, but there's a local photographer who could take it to the next level. Her Insta photos should be taken and edited properly. Then direct her to my page."

He tapped away for a few seconds. "Done."

"Thanks." I stood up.

"Do you want to get some ice cream?" he said quickly. "Or we could have some drinks? My parents make their own grain alcohol."

"I have to go home and babysit my brother," I lied.

Thompson looked bummed as he slid out of the booth, then followed me to the parking lot. "We should do this again sometime," he said.

I looked down at him. "Sure."

"When's good for you? I work Friday nights, but I can do any other night."

"My schedule is erratic. I'll let you know."

He hovered for a beat, and I suddenly wondered if he was going to try to kiss me good night (*try* being the operative word, since he would need a stool to reach my lips). But then he said, "'Night, Low. I hope this Freya person messages you soon. I'm sure her baby will be really cute."

"It will be."

But I would still hate it.

34

jamie

Freya and Max were gone for most of December and January, giving me ample time to dwell on the fact, now irrefutable, that my best friend had slept with my husband. I had no right to be upset—I had done the same to her—and yet, I was. I knew Freya was highly sexual, adventurous, and a risk-taker. And Max seemed to go along with whatever made his hedonistic wife happy. Swapping partners was probably no big deal for them. But that night had rattled my husband and me, shaken our foundation. And Freya had orchestrated the whole thing.

Shortly before their return, Brian announced that he didn't want to see them. "I feel awkward around Freya, and insecure around Max. Maybe I'll get over it in time, but for now . . . I'm not interested in being friends with them."

Freya had planted a toxic seed in my husband's psyche, and I resented her for it. She had made him think he wasn't enough for me, and I had my work cut out for me proving her wrong. I considered editing Freya out of my life, too. It was what Brian wanted—not that he'd said so specifically. But I had to agree that ending my friendship with my husband's lover, who was also my lover's wife, would make things a hell of a lot simpler. But I couldn't let Freya go.

What I had realized the most during her absence was that I missed her. Despite the toxic stew of emotions surrounding that night, Freya was the most vibrant, exciting person I had ever met. Without her, my life whittled down to Brian, whose mind was preoccupied with his novel; the store, which was struggling; and Low, who was . . . Low.

And I couldn't walk away from Freya's baby. The poor little thing needed me. Freya knew nothing about infants or children, seemed remarkably naive and uninformed about the process of birthing and rearing a child. While she was fun, stylish, and cool, she was also self-absorbed, flighty, and irresponsible. She had told me, numerous times, that she was out of her depth and would need my help with the baby. And I believed her.

I'd had several texts from her while she was in Mexico— breezy notes wishing I was there, wishing she could have a margarita, wishing she didn't look like a "beached whale" in her bikini. She sent photos, too—belly shots mostly. She was also posting them on Instagram. Though I wasn't very active on the platform, I'd noticed her photos and the outpouring of admiration they prompted. There were nasty comments, too, but the majority were supportive, adoring, worshipful. . . .

My responses to Freya's texts had been brief and ambiguous as I grappled with my feelings. I'd been too upset to confront her before she left, but as the date of her return approached, I found emotional clarity. I wanted Freya and the baby in my life, but there could be no more secrets, no more deception. We had to face our issues head-on.

She texted me the day after they got home.

I'm baaaaaaack. Coffee? Lunch? Drink?

We needed privacy for this conversation; a place where we could be completely and utterly alone.

Could you come by the store?

Late January was a retail no-man's land. Freya responded instantly.

Will Low be there?

My only employee had minimized the incident that led to her fallout with Freya. Her baby brother had been keeping her up at night, she'd told me, so she'd temporarily camped at the studio. A noise had woken her, and she'd rushed to the main house in concern only to find Freya and Max in the kitchen. A pottery bowl had broken, Freya had cried out in dismay. It sounded so benign, but Freya had been incensed by the invasion of privacy. Low had to have seen more than she was letting on.

I was certain that Low had caught Freya and Max in flagrante in the kitchen. My friend may have been sexually provocative, but she was not an exhibitionist. And she was pregnant. That would have made her feel more vulnerable. Freya was vain about her appearance. She must have been mortified and embarrassed, so she had cut Low off. What else could it have been?

I texted her back.

We're closed Tuesdays. I want to talk to you. Alone.

As I hit SEND, a frisson of foreboding traveled through me. If Freya could excise Low from her life over a misunderstanding, she could do the same to me.

* * *

Freya arrived at the store dressed in white to set off her tan. Her bump had grown in the six weeks since I'd seen her. It rode on her tiny frame like a perky basketball. Her hair looked even blonder; her eyes even bluer. On her arm was a bulging canvas bag that she set on the counter before sweeping me into a long, genuine hug.

"God, I missed you." She had a way of expressing intense, even intimate sentiments in a casual, offhand way. "And the baby missed you, too."

She placed my hand on her taut belly. There was nothing for a moment, and then I felt it move. Freya's child was rolling over, shifting position, letting me know he or she was there. A host of tangled emotions filled my chest. I already loved this baby.

"Wow," I whispered.

"I brought you something." From the bag, she extracted a bundle of newspapers. Inside was nestled an exquisite piece of hand-painted Mexican pottery.

"It's beautiful."

"I saw it and thought of you right away," she said. "I was terrified it would break, so I brought it as extra carry-on luggage. I had to charm the flight attendant to let me keep it in my lap."

I was touched by her thoughtfulness. "Thanks," I said, my voice husky. But I couldn't forget that she had manipulated my husband into her bed. "Have a seat." I indicated the stool behind the counter. "We need to talk."

"Sure." She perched, like a little pregnant bird, on the edge of it. "What's up?"

I took a deep breath. "I know you slept with Brian."

"And you slept with Max."

My cheeks burned with humiliation. "Yes, but you told Brian that I was bored with him. And desperate to have sex with someone else."

"That's what you told me, Jamie. That day when we were walking in the forest."

"No, I didn't."

"You said you had wanted to be with other people and have other sexual experiences, but you and Brian got together so young."

"That didn't mean I wanted to swap husbands!"

"So you didn't enjoy it?"

My face was practically on fire now. "I—I didn't say that. But my husband is hurt and upset."

"He seemed to be having a good time to me."

Jesus, she could be mean. My voice wavered as I continued. "And then you got pregnant. Brian was . . . concerned."

"The baby's not his," she snapped, hopping off the stool. "I showed him a dated ultrasound photo."

"Why wouldn't you tell me? Why sneak around behind my back?"

"That was Brian's idea," she said darkly. "He said it would hurt you too much if he got *me* pregnant, and not you."

My chest constricted and my throat closed. Even the suggestion of it hurt.

"Look," Freya retorted, "I was trying to do something nice for you. I don't appreciate being treated like some kind of villain for spicing up your stale marriage."

"It wasn't stale," I said, but my words wobbled.

"If you and Brian are too uptight to handle what we did, or if you're too jealous that I'm having a baby, we don't have to be friends."

"I *want* to be friends," I said quickly. "Brian's just . . . still feeling raw about what happened that night. But he'll get over it. He just needs a little break from you guys."

It felt like a betrayal of my husband, but it was also true. Freya's friendship was so valuable to me, that I would deal with my issues immediately. Brian would take more time.

But Freya was angry. "I think we could *all* use a break." She snatched up the empty canvas bag. "Enjoy your new vase."

I watched my only friend storm out of my store and out of my life, the emptiness already making my stomach ache.

35

low

Thompson had fulfilled his mission. He had reached out to Freya, and she had contacted me. I took a sip of kombucha, leaned back on my bed, and read Freya's message for the twelfth time.

Love your photos @The_Hawkeye_61. I'm a local influencer looking to take my page to the next level. Interested in a partnership?

Partnership. I didn't know what that meant exactly, but I liked the sound of it. Freya and I would be a team. I'd portray her as a wholesome, maternal beauty; rebuild her brand as a pure, angelic Madonna. No one would care about the dead hockey player, the illegal hit, the ugly lawsuit. Freya would get more money and swag, bigger and better sponsorships. And in return, I'd get . . . what? More followers? A free camera? I didn't care about any of that. I just wanted to be close to her again. I wrote back.

Would love to discuss. Can we meet?

Within seconds she had invited me to her home.

I debated whether I should reveal my identity before I turned up at her house. What would she do when she saw me on her doorstep? She was capable of extreme anger, even violence. But Freya wouldn't physically attack me. I'd spent months analyzing the scene I'd witnessed in her kitchen that night and concluded that Max must have deserved her wrath. He must have done something cruel and horrible, may have even hit her. Freya wouldn't throw crockery at me or chase me with a barbecue fork. But there were other ways she could hurt me . . . with her words and disdain.

But if I revealed myself through a message, she might shut me down instantly. She could block me from her Instagram page, and I would lose all access to her. It wasn't a risk I was willing to take. With my heart in my throat, I drove to her house. I parked my truck behind her Range Rover and walked, on spaghetti legs, to the front door.

Freya answered the bell seconds after I rang it. She looked gorgeous with her tanned skin and white-blond hair, her face fuller from the pregnancy. It made her appear softer and sweeter. But the smile flew from her lips, and her blue eyes narrowed at me. She looked like a very pretty, very pregnant viper, ready to strike.

"What are you doing here, *stalker?*"

"I-I'm the photographer," I stammered, "I'm Hawkeye Sixty-one. It's me."

There was a brief pause where I could almost see her slotting the pieces into place. "Oh my god," she said with a disdainful sneer.

"You've seen my page," I said quickly. "I'm good. Really good. I'm the best photographer on this island." I didn't know if this was true, but then neither did Freya. "And I want to help you."

Her expression remained stony, but she didn't slam the door

in my face, so I kept going. "I've created some Instagram presets just for you. And I've gotten really good at using Lightroom. I can turn you into a work of art, Freya. I can make your page cohesive and professional and mind-blowing. You'll get a million followers. Even more."

There was a spark of interest in her eyes, but they remained wary. I knew what I had to do, what I had to say. Swallowing my fear, I apologized.

"I'm sorry about before. I should never have slept in the studio without your permission. And I shouldn't have . . . *spied* on you and Max. On your . . . *argument*."

Freya folded her arms. "No, you shouldn't have."

"I screwed up. I know that. I will never cross your boundaries again. I'll totally respect your privacy."

Her eyes were like ice, but my cheeks burned under her gaze. I could feel sweat on my forehead and upper lip, as I wrapped up my pitch.

"I want us to be creative partners. I don't need money or credit. I just want to take beautiful photographs of you and make your Instagram amazing. Together, we can take you to the next level. Everyone will forget all the bad stuff that happened, and you'll be a huge star."

She inhaled through her nose, her swollen chest and belly rising as she deliberated. I stood before her, my pulse pounding in my ears. If Freya turned me down, that would be it. There would be no more chances.

Then she dropped her arms and took a step back. "Come in."

And just like that, I was back where I had longed to be for three months.

36

Februarys are long and wet in our part of the world, so we took a lot of photos indoors. This served double duty in showing off the beauty of Freya and her magnificent home. My subject hoped she'd capture the attention of some interior-design magazines. She was keen for a feature on her stunning abode. Freya had already received a new sofa in exchange for three tagged photos featuring it. I photographed her curled up on it, in pajamas, reading a Deepak Chopra book I'd borrowed from Gwen. (Freya had requested a prop that would make her look "deep"). In another, she featured the stain-resistant technology by holding a large bowl of chocolate ice cream that I ended up eating. In the third, I shot her naked, a blanket strategically covering all but her shoulders, legs, and belly. (This also satisfied the requirements of the pricey skin-care company sending her boxes of body lotion.)

Though I was the photographer, Freya was the art director. "Move closer. I don't want my feet in the photo," she instructed me. Or "Stand on my left. I have a zit on my right cheek." She inspected the photos as we went, insisting I delete or edit any unflattering shots. "Why would you shoot me from that angle?" she'd gripe. "I look morbidly obese." She didn't, of course, but perhaps my infatuation was messing with my critical eye. To me, she was perfection in every image.

She wasn't always bossy and demanding. She could be inquisitive and considerate, too. One day, as I shot her at the breakfast table eating plant-based protein patties couriered to her in a portable cooler (the same kind used to transport donated organs), she asked after Eckhart.

"How's your baby brother doing?" Her lips barely moved as she held a forkful of patty to her glossy mouth.

"He's good. Now that he's finally over his colic."

"What's colic?"

Jesus. She was in for a rude awakening. I lowered the camera. "It's when a baby screams its head off for weeks, or in Eckhart's case, months, for no apparent reason."

Freya made a face like she'd actually eaten the unpleasant patty. "Does every baby get that?"

"No. My other brothers were pretty happy. I think Leonard had it for a couple of weeks, which was pretty manageable."

"How do you make it stop?"

"Sometimes swaddling helps. Or a walk or a car ride. But I think you just have to let it pass."

"You know a lot about babies, don't you?"

Enough to know I don't want any, I was about to say, but then thought better of it. Freya was in too deep, and there was only one way out now. She was going to give birth to a baby who would poop and scream and puke and whine and keep her up all night. I didn't want to scare her. Or scare her *more*. So I said, "With three younger siblings, I guess I've picked up a few tips."

Freya dropped the fork, signaling that our shoot was over. "I'm really going to need you after the baby's born."

My jaw clenched as she took the plate and dumped the patties into the trash. I'd spent my life around the stinking little creatures, but that didn't mean I liked them. Especially this one. Freya's baby was sure to be adorable, wrapping both its parents around its teeny finger. It would turn them into pathetic, lovestruck sycophants, responding to its every whimper, indulging its every whim. Like some prehistoric giant squid, it would suck up all its parents' time and energy. I already resented the thing.

But I liked the thought of Freya needing me. So I said nothing.

37

jamie

Freya had said we needed a break. But how long did that mean? It had been almost three weeks since I'd confronted her about the couples' swap. Freya had to be missing me, too. Like me, she had no other friends on the island, only acquaintances. She had to be craving my companionship as much as I craved hers. Didn't she?

I would wait another week before I reached out. A month would have passed then; enough time to let all anger, resentments, and jealousies go. My reason for contacting Freya was twofold. I missed her. But I also needed to order more of her pieces for the store. Business would pick up in a few months, and Freya's pottery was among my bestselling items. With the baby coming, she wouldn't have much time at the wheel.

But mostly, I just missed her.

Freya needed me, too. Her due date was rapidly approaching, and I felt she was woefully unprepared for the birth and the baby. If she'd read the baby books I'd given her, she'd have known what to expect, but she'd pronounced them both "gross" and "boring." It was almost like she was in denial about what was to come.

About a month after she'd shared her pregnancy news with me, she'd asked me to be present at the birth. "I don't have a sister. And my mom is a lunatic. I want you there with me."

"I'd be honored," I said, touched.

"Besides," she chirped, "I'm going to be knocked out on drugs. You can tell me what happened."

I'd laughed, but I wasn't sure she was joking. Could the island's small hospital provide the level of sedation Freya was anticipating? Did they even have an anesthesiologist on staff? I had suggested that Freya and I sit down with her doctor and prepare a birthing plan. She'd promised we would after she returned from Mexico. But shortly after, she'd cut me off. For her sake, I hoped she'd done one without me.

While I felt lonely and blue, my husband's outlook had improved. His exercise had become less manic, and, between marathon phone calls with his editor, he was writing again. Brian was happy that Freya and I had fallen out. He didn't say so outright, but it was obvious in his chipper mood. And in his suggestions that I replace her with a new friend.

"Why don't you join a running club? Or take a watercolor class? It would be good for you to meet some new people."

"I don't have time for running and painting," I retorted. "I've got to do my ordering and scheduling before business picks up at spring break."

It was an excuse. I had plenty of time to take up a new hobby, but I didn't want to act on my husband's suggestions. On some level, I blamed him for the loss of my best friend. It was Brian's jealousy and insecurity that had severed my relationship with Freya. I appreciated his devotion to me. I was grateful for his loyalty. But Freya, Max, and I might have been able to close the door on the whole swapping incident and put it behind us. Brian was the one who couldn't get over it.

So, I bided my time, working at the store, going for long solo walks in the forest, reading. I had little human contact other than Brian. Of course, I had to respond to the artisans who contacted me, asking, in vain, if any of their products had sold. I dealt with the sprinkling of customers who dropped in for a birthday or housewarming gift. And Low worked with me every Saturday, although my introverted employee did little to assuage my loneliness.

One Saturday, she seemed marginally more upbeat. "Can I leave a bit early today?" she asked, as she was wiping a shelf of scented candles in mason jars. "I want to get some backlit photos of Freya for her Insta."

"Oh . . ." I cleared the frog in my throat. "I didn't know you two were friends again."

"Yep," she said, her tone breezy. "It was all a misunderstanding."

"Great."

"We're building Freya's brand. I've been taking some amazing shots of her. She's going to be more popular than she ever was."

Maybe Freya didn't miss me? Maybe she was consumed by her Instagram celebrity, her days filled with photo shoots and sponsorship deals and swag deliveries?

"So can I go?" Low asked. "The sun sets so early this time of year. If I leave here at five thirty, I'll miss the light."

"Yeah, of course." I forced a smile. "Unless it gets too busy, but I'm sure it won't. I can handle things alone. And close up alone. It's no problem. You go and get your sunset photos of Freya."

A small, triumphant smile twitched Low's lips, but she pulled it back. "Thanks." She returned to her dusting.

As soon as Low left at five, I got out my phone and tapped the Instagram app. I hadn't looked at Freya's page since she returned from Mexico. To my surprise, she'd been posting daily. The photos—Low's photos—were stunning, showing off Freya's fecund beauty. My former bestie had been photographed in a kayak, against a backdrop of fir trees, lounging on a pebbled beach. She was promoting everything from sofas to breakfast food to skin-care products. Freya was back in the game that had turned on her and tossed her out.

It was childish to feel jealous of my teenaged assistant, but I did. Low was in, and I was out; we had effectively traded places. It was Low who gave Freya what she needed now, who answered to her beck and call. Had Freya asked Low to help her with a birthing plan? To hold her hand and coach her through delivery? Would Low be there with her camera, taking photos of that precious moment?

With a heavy lump in my chest, I closed up the store and drove home.

38

low

Jamie's reaction proved what I had suspected: she and Freya were no longer friends. This should have delighted me. Other than Max, who floated on the periphery of our world like a spirit, I had Freya all to myself. But that damn baby was still on its way, and there was nothing I could do to stop it.

What had Jamie done to make Freya angry enough to banish her? It didn't take much, that I knew. I almost felt sorry for my employer, but Jamie was pretty, outgoing, charming. She'd move on, find another friend. For me, there was only ever Freya. And I was not going to screw up again. I was going to be everything that Jamie had ever been to her, and more. I'd make Freya need me, rely on me; I would become essential. Freya would never be able to cut me out of her life again.

The object of my devotion was waiting for me, wearing one of Max's flannel shirts and nothing else. The outfit was her idea, but I had to admit it fit perfectly with the milieu. Freya would stand on the deck, the setting sun and a blur of cedar trees behind her. A sexy, pregnant lumberjack. Freya came up with the witty captions, but I might suggest it.

"Hurry," she instructed, without so much as a hello. "We're losing the light."

I followed her out to the deck, where she positioned herself at the railing and struck a pose: back arched, pregnant belly exposed, thigh bent to conceal her privates. Angling myself so the sun's rays were just out of frame, I took a number of shots. With her fair hair and tanned skin glowing in the natural light, she looked like an angel. No, something fiercer and sexier. A fire goddess.

"Why don't we get Max to join you for a few shots?" I asked.

I hadn't seen Max in a while. He always seemed to be out on the water, out for a run, or away dealing with business matters. His presence still made me feel strangely feminine, but I was wearing my photographer's hat. This was about getting a beautiful photo of the parents to be.

"No. No more photos with Max," Freya said. She moved forward and grabbed my camera. She scrolled through the images, deleting those that didn't please her. "When I post photos with him, I get half the likes. And that's when I get nasty comments. People still hate him. He's a liability."

"Maybe you'd like a photo for yourselves," I said. "You could get it framed."

Freya ignored the suggestion. "Once the baby is born, we can post one of those *shirtless dad, naked baby* photos. Gauge the reaction." She raised her eyes to mine. "That is, if we're still together."

"What do you mean?"

She sighed as she handed the camera back to me. "I've been thinking about leaving him."

My stomach churned with panic. "*Leaving* him?"

"Max has got a lot of demons. I know he's trying to deal with them, but . . . I'm not sure he's emotionally or physically present enough to be a father."

I swallowed. "But you'd stay here, right? On the island? With the baby?"

Freya leaned back on the railing. She looked remarkably casual despite the gravity of her words. "I've been thinking about going back to LA. My dad's there. I can hire a nanny and rebuild my career."

"You can do that here," I blurted. "We're taking great photos together. You're getting more sponsorships. People love you again."

"My followers want the *image*," she said. "The hair, the nails, the body. Facetune can only do so much. I won't have time to take care of myself with the baby. And there are basically no domestic workers on the island. I can't even get a housekeeper on a regular basis."

"Order a nanny from one of those foreign agencies," I said. "There are women in war-torn countries who are desperate to come here. They can take care of the baby and cook and clean. Then you can work out. And go to the salon. And get your nails done. And we can do our photo shoots. We can do photos with you and the baby. Everyone will love you. And *it*."

Freya sighed, her eyes on me. "It would just be easier in LA."

"Please. . . ." My voice was hoarse with desperation. "You can't leave. I . . . I don't know what I'd do without you."

But I did know. She had punted me from her life once before, and I had nearly done myself in. If she left for good . . . it could be fatal. I had always tried to hide the depths of my devotion, downplay the intensity of my feelings, but they were on full display now. I was trembling. I felt physically sick.

Freya smiled at me then, and her eyes moistened. It was real emotion, real gratitude; she couldn't fake that. If she'd been that good an actress, she'd have done more than a few commercials and a corny Christmas movie. This was authentic.

"Oh, Low . . . ," she said, stepping toward me, "you're the best friend I've ever had." And then she kissed me.

Freya had stood on tiptoes and pecked my cheek on numerous occasions. But this kiss was different. It was on the lips. And while she didn't quite slip me the tongue, she lingered there, her lips pressed to mine, longer than a friend would. It awakened something inside of me, a feeling that started at my knees, traveled up my inner thighs, and into my groin. It was desire; it was lust. I had never felt so alive.

I had shared my feelings with Freya, and she had reciprocated them. With a warm, moist, lingering kiss. That kiss . . . that kiss would stay with me, haunt me, and, eventually, taunt me.

It would change everything.

39

jamie

As the one-month anniversary of our "break" approached, I pondered the content of my text to Freya. Should I lead with the business angle? Tell her that I was eager to stock more of her pottery for the summer season? It would make me sound less pathetic and emotionally needy. And Freya would be flattered that her pieces were so popular. But it might seem cold and aloof after the heated conversation we'd had. I didn't want her to think all I cared about was our professional relationship, because that was a lie. Eventually, I decided to be honest. Because I could live without Freya's pottery but not without her friendship.

Precisely one month after she'd proclaimed us "on a break," I reached out.

Hey. Been thinking about you and wondering how you're doing. Coffee soon?

My iPhone indicated that she had read the message, but she did not respond.

She was in the middle of something, I told myself. Maybe she was in the studio, working on new pieces for my summer stock. Or she was embroiled in one of her Instagram photo shoots. Or about to have a bath. Or a nap. Or a massage . . . She would answer me soon, I was sure. Freya had to be missing me, too.

But she had still not responded by the end of the day. I locked up the shop, went home, and poured myself a glass of wine. Brian was bustling around the kitchen, making a stir-fry. He was chatty and chipper, talking about the "breakthrough" he and his editor had made on the climax of his novel. I pretended to listen, nodding along, my mind entrenched on my precarious friendship.

"Why do you keep looking at your phone?" my husband asked.

My eyes snapped up, met his intense gaze. I had been checking it unconsciously. "I'm waiting for a message from a glassblower," I said, setting aside my phone. "I'm doing my summer ordering. You're not the only one with a career, you know."

My defensiveness made me sound guilty, I realized. But I was stressed, worried, on edge. And my husband's inquisition was making it worse.

Brian kept his voice level. "Is that really who you're waiting to hear from? A glassblower?"

"Who do you think I'm waiting to hear from, Brian?"

"I don't know. . . ." He stirred the vegetables in the wok.

"Oh my god!" I barked. "Are you still worrying about Max?"

"Max who you had sex with?" he sniped. "Maybe a *bit*."

"I haven't seen him in months. I haven't talked to him—or to Freya—because of you."

He set down the wooden spoon. "Are you seriously blaming *me* for what happened that night? You're the one who was desperate to have sex with someone else."

"I wasn't desperate," I growled. "But you seemed pretty quick to jump into Freya's bed."

"Only because she told me it was what *you* wanted."

"I'm sure it was a real hardship for you."

"It was, actually. I don't take sleeping with another person lightly. Unlike you."

"I don't take it lightly, but it happened! And now it's over! You're the one who can't get over it!"

"I'm over it! You're the one trying to hang on to a sick, toxic friendship."

"It's not sick and toxic! Freya is my best friend. She's my only friend on this stupid fucking island that you made us move to!"

"I didn't *make* you move here," he said, but I had already grabbed my glass and the bottle of wine, was already stalking down the hall to our bedroom.

"Dinner's almost ready!" he hollered after me.

"I'm not hungry!" I slammed the bedroom door.

As I settled onto the bed, glass of wine in hand, Freya's words rang in my head. *If you and Brian are too uptight to handle what we did . . .* It was becoming clear that we weren't handling it, we weren't handling it well at all. This was not the first time these jealousies and insecurities had resurfaced. The distance between us had been growing, the tension and resentment simmering for months. Brian still blamed me for instigating the couples' swap, and I blamed him for ruining my friendship with Freya.

I'd been worried about losing that friendship, but now I realized: my marriage was at risk, too.

40

My mood was not improved the next morning when I opened the store. The hangover didn't help. I knew better than to drink over a half bottle of red wine on an empty stomach. But my condition that morning was irrelevant. There would be few, if any customers. Low would come in at noon to allow me a lunch break and take care of the cleaning duties. I filled the kettle and plugged it in, knowing I had nothing to do but stand behind the till and stew about the mess that was my life. At least I could avoid Brian.

He had slept on the sofa in his office last night. In our eight years of marriage, we'd only spent a handful of nights in separate beds. When we were young and passionate and learning to live together, we'd had some huge fights. Those issues seemed so frivolous now, our outrage back then so misguided and naive. This felt different. There was a *gravitas* to our anger now. We had broken our vows, slept with other people, betrayed each other's trust. This was real.

I suddenly felt a wave of homesickness—not for the life Brian and I had shared in Seattle, but for my life before I even met him.

I wanted to leave the island and go back to Vancouver, to my parents, my high school friends, to a simpler time. It wouldn't be easy, but I could start over there, get back into marketing or even go back to school and learn something new. Rents were high in Vancouver, the price of real estate astronomical, but my parents would let me stay with them until I was on my feet. I could close the door on this messy chapter, this fucked-up experiment, and reinvent myself.

The kettle whistled then, jarring me from my thoughts. As I poured boiling water over a tea bag, I shook away the fantasy. I wasn't ready to leave the island. And I certainly wasn't ready to leave the man I had loved my entire adult life. What Brian and I had was worth fighting for. But I was angry at him. He put all the blame for what happened that night on Freya, Max, and me, and he needed to accept his share of responsibility. If Brian had known the couples' swap would cause such damage, why had he gone along with it? Why hadn't he rejected Freya's seduction? Why hadn't he come to the guest room and taken me home before we'd done things that we couldn't take back? Brian had no right to act so innocent, so holier-than-thou. He had slept with my best friend. The thought made me even queasier.

The door tinkled then, and I hurried out of the back room to greet a welcome customer. But it was only Low, arriving for her eleven thirty shift.

"'Morning," I muttered.

"Rough night?"

Shit. Did I look that bad? Were my anger and hangover so obvious? I was about to deny it but then thought . . . why? Low wasn't going to judge me. Low didn't care about me at all.

"Kind of," I said.

My assistant didn't respond, just picked up the dustcloth and went straight to work. I sipped my tea, watching as she headed to Freya's remaining pieces. She always took care of them first, always carefully, even lovingly. As she wiped the inside of a beautiful, jade-green bowl, I spoke.

"Is Freya making more pottery?"

Low kept her eyes on her work. "We're too busy with her Instagram. Social media is her first love. She only got back into pottery because she wasn't allowed to post anything after Max's trial."

She was being more forthcoming than usual, so I continued. "Do you still make pottery?"

Low kept dusting. "Freya said I can use the studio, but it's not the same without her. She doesn't have that much energy now. She's only got a month and a half till the baby comes."

"Two and a half months," I corrected her.

My employee looked up and met my eyes. As usual, they were unreadable. "Right."

I drank the last of my tea. "I'm going to run some errands and grab lunch," I said, shrugging on my raincoat. "Text me if it gets busy."

"I will. But it won't."

The flat gray sky and cold drizzle fit my outlook perfectly. I huddled into my North Face jacket, the hood restricting my view of the deserted streets and naked sidewalks. I had no errands to run, but I needed to get away from Hawking Mercantile. At times, my supposed *dream job* felt like a prison, complete with physical and financial shackles. I was irritable, depressed, and hungover, and I needed to get out of my cell. And I needed fries.

When Freya and I ate lunch at the Blue Heron, we always ordered salads or Buddha bowls, but I knew there was a burger on the menu. I'd looked at it, coveted it on occasion, but hadn't wanted to order it in front of my slim, healthy friend. Today, I had no one to impress. I was going to drown my sorrows in grease.

Shaking the raindrops from my hood, I entered the quiet restaurant. It was 11:40—on the early side for lunch, and the horrendous weather had kept would-be customers at home. The waitress, a fiftyish woman with a rosy face, recognized me.

"Table for two, hon?"

"Just me today," I said, self-pity clogging my throat. *Just me.*

"Sit wherever you like," she said, taking a tray of dishes toward the back. "I'll be right with you."

Freya and I had always sat near the window, always enjoyed taking in the view with our salads and lively conversation. But today called for a dismal back corner to accompany my burger and silence. I was moving toward a vacant table when I saw him. Max Beausoleil was standing near the bar, his hands in his pockets, waiting for a take-out order. I wanted to turn around, to duck into the restroom, but he looked up then and saw me.

"Hey," he said, and goddammit, my stomach fluttered. I'd put what we did out of my mind, but my body still remembered.

"Hi." I felt self-conscious of my bedraggled state, my wan pallor, my sour breath, until I looked into his handsome face. Max's right eye was bruised, a dark crescent under his lower lashes, turning shades of yellow, purple, and green as it healed. "What happened?" I blurted.

His response was instant, practiced. "I was canoeing. Got an oar in the eye."

"Ouch."

"Yeah."

I swallowed. "How's Freya?" Did he know that his wife wasn't speaking to me? Had she told him that Brian and I couldn't han-

dle what we had done that night? That guilt, jealousy, and insecurity were tearing us apart?

"She's good," he said. "She was craving an acai bowl."

"I'm glad she's eating healthy. For the baby." I forced a smile.
"You must be getting excited."

"Yep." But he didn't sound excited; he sounded eager to leave.
He looked toward the kitchen, willing his order to come.

"I'm going to grab a table," I said. "I'm on my lunch break. I
need to order some food."

"Good to see you, Jamie."

"You too," I said as I backed away. "Take care of that eye."

Alone at the quiet table, I tried to compose myself. Max still
made me feel nervous and guilty and attracted and confused. But
today, he roused something else in me. Concern. Even pity. What
had happened to his eye? Was it really an accident with an oar?
I thought about those puncture marks on his chest, healed to a
four-pronged scar. How had that happened? Was someone hurting him? Was he hurting himself?

My mind couldn't fathom a situation of abuse or self-harm.
Not with this gorgeous couple who looked so perfect from the
outside. But Max's injuries were odd, their explanations unsatis-
factory. He was still at the bar; I could sense his presence. I considered going back to him, to discern if he was really okay. But
I couldn't bring up the scar on his chest without addressing the
taboo subject of our night together. My face got hot just thinking
about it. And then my phone buzzed.

I picked it up thinking it was Low. We must have gotten an
unforeseen rush of business. But it was Freya. My heart pitter-
pattered as I read her words.

Sorry for the delay. Misplaced my phone.

I've missed you. Would love to see you.

Come for lunch next week?

Relief flooded through me, and the corners of my mouth twitched into a smile. Freya had missed me, just as I'd hoped. She wanted to see me. I was back in.

I'd love that!!!

Three exclamation points was too much. I deleted two and hit SEND. Freya's text had instantly dissipated my funk, and I couldn't hide my delight.

The waitress dropped a menu on the table, then, but I didn't need to look at it.

"I'll have the Buddha bowl, please."

"Sure, hon."

I looked toward the bar. Maxime Beausoleil was gone.

41

low

Freya wanted to do a live video in her pottery studio. "I want to show off my artistic, wholesome side," she said. "I've had some nasty comments saying I'm too shallow and superficial to be a mother."

It was a form of virtue signaling, but it was an effective one. Freya was always beautiful, but when she was at the wheel, her delicate hands creating art, she was magical. No one could watch her work without becoming mesmerized, almost hypnotized. And no one would say an unkind word when they saw her talent. I knew that Freya craved the acceptance and validation of strangers. Despite her many gifts, her life of privilege, she needed it.

My digital camera did not record video, so I'd have to use Freya's iPhone. It was newer and better than my phone. But I brought my tripod for stability. And I'd cleaned out my bank account and ordered a portable studio lighting kit online to ensure the most flattering environment for the video. It came with two lights on stands that I could set up in the dim space. We were filming in the afternoon when the light was low. If I did my job right, I could get a sensual, *Ghost* kind of vibe.

As I drove to her house, I felt a giddy sense of anticipation. We would spend the day in the studio again, where our friendship had been born. That space would always hold a special place in my heart. Jamie had asked if I missed making pottery. I'd shrugged off the question, but I did. Photography was my creative outlet now, but it wasn't tactile like pottery. I missed getting my hands dirty, missed the earthen smell of the clay. Unlike traditional film, digital photography meant no waiting, no surprise at the end. When I dipped a vase or a bowl in glaze, fired it in the kiln, I never quite knew what would come out. My mind flitted to my beloved pinch pots, their crushed bodies in the garbage bag, but I shook off the memory. I should never have made Freya so angry. I knew better now.

I parked at the bottom of the drive and lugged my equipment toward the pottery shed. Freya had asked me to meet her there at three, but when I tried the door, I found it locked. Peeping through the windows, I saw that the space was dark, the wheels covered in canvas, the clay sealed away in plastic bags. At first, I thought I had gotten the date wrong, but I would never mess up a session with Freya. She must have fallen asleep. Or maybe she was feeling sick.

Propping the lights and tripod against the building, I marched toward the house. As I passed the matching SUVs, I spotted the small blue Mazda. It was Jamie's car, previously concealed from my view by the larger vehicles. My stomach constricted, and I tasted something metallic on my tongue. It was jealousy. Jamie and Freya were friends again. What did that mean for me?

As I reached out and rang the bell, I tried to calm my racing heart. Freya had told me I was the best friend she had ever had.

And she had kissed me on the mouth. I didn't need to feel threatened by Jamie. What I had with Freya was much deeper, more intense than a simple friendship. And Freya needed me now. Her Instagram was her top priority, and I was essential to its success. Jamie was extraneous.

The door opened and there Freya stood, tanned and gorgeous in a white button-down maternity shirt. "Hey, Low." She appeared confused by my presence.

"Hi." My voice was somewhat strangled. "I thought we were filming you in the studio today. You told me to come at three."

"Shit," Freya cursed. "I totally forgot. I'm sorry, hon. Jamie's here."

"I'll go get set up," I suggested. "You can meet me there when you're done with her."

"She came for lunch," Freya explained. "We had a lot to catch up on." Then she leaned toward me and whispered. "Now I can't get rid of her."

But I wasn't buying it this time. I knew that Freya would go back inside, roll her eyes, and say the same about me.

That was Low. She always shows up here wanting to photograph me. I can't get rid of her.

She was playing us off against each other. Why hadn't I seen it before?

"Right," I said, backing away, trying to hide my pain.

But Freya didn't seem to notice. "Thanks for understanding, doll. I'll text you to reschedule."

With that, she closed the door in my face.

42

I drove home fast, recklessly, my camera equipment rattling in the bed of my truck. Freya had no respect for me or my time. True, I had nothing else to do, but I'd spent my hard-earned money (plus sixty bucks I'd stolen from Leonard) on lighting equipment to make her look beautiful. And she didn't even care. She'd dismissed me like a servant, chosen time with Jamie over time with me. I hated her.

"Anger is just misplaced fear," my mom and dad were fond of saying. When I was little and would throw a tantrum, they'd ask: "What are you afraid of, darling?"

I'm afraid I'm going to bite you if you keep talking to me in that condescending tone.

But now, it made sense. I was scared of losing Freya, terrified of returning to the lonely, solitary existence that predated her. If she chose to banish me, to replace me with Jamie again, I would have no one. The thought filled me with heaviness and darkness.

Pulling into our rutted driveway, I noticed an unfamiliar car parked next to the chicken coop. It wasn't unusual for my parents or Gwen to have visitors; friends who joined them for potluck meals, or drinks. These friends could sometimes turn into lovers when invited to one of the infamous "sauna parties." But since Eckhart had been born, my family's social life had shriveled in the face of his demands.

With my lights and tripod under my arm, I struggled into the house. As soon as I opened the door, my mom called to me. "Swallow? Is that you?"

"Yep," I replied, kicking off my shoes and propping my equipment in the entryway.

"You have a visitor."

There was only one person it could be.

"Hi, Low," Thompson said, as I entered the living room. He was seated on a chintz armchair facing my mom, who was breastfeeding Eckhart, but he jumped to his feet. What was he going to do? Hug me? Kiss my cheek? Shake my hand? I took a step back.

"What are you doing here?" I muttered.

"You haven't returned any of my texts or DMs, so I thought I'd stop by. Do you want go for pizza or something?"

"It's three thirty. I'm not hungry."

"We could go for a drive. Or watch TV. Or play a video game." He looked toward my mom. "We can go to my place, so we don't disturb the baby."

"I'm good," I said.

My mom suddenly pulled her breast from Eckhart's mouth with a loud suctioning sound. "Can I talk to you in the kitchen for a sec?"

Uh-oh.

Alone in the kitchen, Eckhart reached out for me. I'd been ignoring him since Freya had taken me back, but apparently, he still remembered our time together. I took him and jiggled him on my hip, as my mom launched into her whispered lecture.

"Why are you being so rude to that boy?"

"I'm not being rude, I'm being honest. I'm not hungry. And I don't want to watch TV or play video games."

"You complain that you don't have friends, and then you reject a perfectly nice, age-appropriate companion."

I hadn't audibly complained about my lack of friends since the ninth grade, but I was unable to point that out since my mom wouldn't stop talking.

"Why do you want to spend all your time with a pregnant woman twice your age? I thought she was teaching you pottery, but now . . . what? You take pictures of her?"

"I'm her photographer," I grumbled, as Eckhart pulled at my hair. "For her Instagram."

"Has she hired you?"

"We have a *partnership*."

"You used to photograph Eckhart and nature and animals. Now, you only shoot Freya. It's like she's the only thing that interests you. It's not healthy."

"Freya is famous on Instagram. We're building her brand together."

My mom shook her head, her expression chagrined. "None of that is real, Swallow. It's superficial nonsense. You know that."

I was instantly defensive. "What would you know about reality? You hide out in your free-love hippie universe and pretend that there's no such thing as social media, or celebrity. But it exists, Mom. And it matters. You'd get it if you weren't so . . . *irrelevant*."

I watched my mother's face turn red with anger, hurt, and disappointment. She looked like she couldn't decide whether to slap me or burst into tears. But she did neither of those things. She spoke in a trembling voice.

"Go eat pizza with that boy, or so help me . . ."

She took my brother from my arms and stormed out of the room.

"Fine!" I called after her. "God!" I thumped back into the living room, where Thompson, who had clearly heard everything, sat looking pale and frightened.

"Let's go," I barked.

He jumped to his feet and followed me out of the house.

43

We drove to the pizza joint in separate cars. I wasn't planning to stay long. But eating pizza with Thompson was preferable to being at home with my outraged mother, who by now would have told my dad, Gwen, maybe even Vik about my insolence and moral turpitude. My parents were probably strategizing an intervention at this very moment. I would hide out with Thompson until they all cooled off. Hopefully, they'd smoke a joint to de-stress themselves and then find the whole thing laughable.

I arrived first and slid into a booth without ordering. Thompson would want to buy me a piece of pizza; it made him feel chivalrous. Plus, I had no money since having ordered the lighting kit for Freya.

My stout colleague soon joined me. "This is where we sat last time," he said, slipping into the seat across from me. "I guess this is *our* booth."

I managed not to roll my eyes.

"I know you said you weren't hungry, but can I tempt you with a slice?"

"Sure," I said.

"Meat-lovers and a Coke?" He tapped his head like this was some great feat of memory.

"Yep."

While I waited, I checked Freya's Instagram. She had a new post: a selfie of her and Jamie cuddled up on her white sofa. My stomach turned sour as I took in the image of the two women. Freya held the camera, looking natural and pretty and pleased with herself. Jamie was smiling, but I could see that she was self-conscious. The lighting was terrible, the perspective off. Freya and I were supposed to be creating a beautiful, professional-quality page, not posting crappy selfies. But the worst part was Freya's comment.

So happy to have this one in my life. Her support means everything.

#bestfriends #backtogether #grateful

My face burned with betrayal. Freya had never posted a photo with me. She'd never thanked me or mentioned me beyond a photo credit. She said we were *partners*, but she was using me. My mom was right. My friendship with Freya wasn't real or healthy. None of it was.

Thompson returned with a red plastic tray laden with food. I put my phone away and pulled myself together. I wasn't about to share my hurt with this short outcast from my high school. He handed me my pizza and drink, but I'd lost what little appetite I had had.

My so-called date tried to make small talk, but I wouldn't engage. I picked bits of sausage from my pizza, my thoughts entrenched on the selfie of Freya and Jamie, Freya's words of love and devotion for her best friend: Jamie, not me.

Then Thompson said something that grabbed my attention. "I couldn't help but overhear your mom's concerns. About Freya Light."

"My mom only met her once," I muttered. "She doesn't know anything about her." I was still defending Freya. Why?

"Still . . .," Thompson continued. "I can sort of see why she'd be concerned. Freya and her husband have quite a scandalous past."

I didn't like his salacious tone. "And they've suffered for it," I snapped. "Max pled guilty to assault. And they paid that dead hockey player's family millions."

Thompson was suitably chastened. "Of—of course," he stammered. "It must have been a lot to go through. Plus, Max's paternity suit."

A tidbit of sausage dropped from my fingers. "What?"

"You didn't know about that?"

I hated to admit that Thompson knew more about Max and Freya than I did, but he had caught me off guard. "When was this?"

"Early in his hockey career. He and Freya were newlyweds. A woman sued Max for child support. She said her baby was his after a one-night stand at a hotel in Calgary."

"Max has a child?"

"No." Thompson looked triumphant. "He said it wasn't his, because he's sterile. His lawyer submitted test results."

"But he can't be sterile. Freya is pregnant."

"I guess he lied." Thompson took a bite of pizza and then continued through the mouthful. "Or else Freya's baby is a miracle."

But it wasn't a miracle.

And it clearly wasn't Max's.

"How did you find this out?

"It's all online," Thompson said, slurping some Coke. "It's buried under all the stuff about the Ryan Klassen incident. But if you go back far enough, it's there."

"Thank you, Thompson," I said sincerely. "I needed this."

He beamed at me. "I'll buy you pizza any time, Low."

But Thompson had given me more than pizza. He'd given me power.

44

I couldn't take Thompson's word for it. Even though he was the most earnest person I'd ever encountered, I needed proof. The library was open until six, so I left the pizza place and drove directly there. The librarian shot me a look of annoyance as I hurried toward the computer section. She'd probably hoped to close early, but too bad. I was on a mission.

The Ryan Klassen incident would dominate the results if I didn't tailor my search, so I typed:

Maxime Beausoleil, paternity suit, Calgary

Up popped an article from the *Calgary Herald*. Leaning in, I devoured the content. A young woman named Paula Elphin claimed she'd had sex with Max while his team, the LA Kings, was in town to play the Flames. There was a photo of her leaving court: attractive in a busty, bottle-blond kind of way. But she was no Freya. Would Max have cheated on his wife with a random puck bunny? Would Freya have cared if he had? This Paula woman had found herself pregnant shortly after their encounter and had contacted Max for child support. When he refused, she sued.

It wasn't a big news story; Max was barely famous then. But Calgary was a hockey-loving town, and local interest was piqued. To add to the drama, Max had refused to provide a blood sample, which could have cleared up the paternity in utero. Instead, his lawyer had submitted a doctor's letter attesting that Max had contracted a severe case of mumps at seventeen, which had rendered him infertile.

Opening a new window, I read up on *mumps orchitis*, the complication Max had suffered. Complete infertility was quite rare, but subfertility (seriously reduced fertility) was a common complication. I knew he'd grown up in a remote community, may not have had access to the health care a larger center could have provided. The disease had progressed to his testicles and cost him the ability to have children.

The judge must have been skeptical because he'd ordered a paternity test once the baby was born. A follow-up article—short and sweet—published the results. Paula Elphin's baby was not Maxime Beausoleil's child. Max hadn't lied. He was sterile.

Logging off the computer, I tipped back in the chair. I was smiling . . . beaming, actually. This information changed everything. It gave me power . . . awesome fucking power. Because now I knew, without a doubt, that Freya's baby was Brian Vincent's child. It had been conceived the night of the couples' swap. And Jamie and her husband had no idea.

This knowledge would allow me to reassert my significance in Freya's life. I didn't want her to *fear* me (okay, maybe I wanted her to fear me a little bit), but I wanted her to *appreciate* me. Because it was me, not Jamie, who had her back. I was her #bestfriend. She should be #grateful for *me*.

I drove home quivering with excitement. My parents would be waiting for me with concern and consternation, but I didn't care. All I could focus on now was telling Freya that I knew her secret. I would have to do it delicately—she couldn't panic or become angry at me. She couldn't cut me out of her life before I explained that I would keep her safe. I would take her baby's paternity to my grave. The dynamic of our entire relationship was about to shift. I would go from the role of sidekick/servant to that of guardian and protector. Because, if Jamie found out the truth, she would blow up Freya's world.

But I wouldn't let that happen. As long as Freya treated me right.

45

My parents reserved their lecture for the next morning. They had obviously spent significant time discussing the nature of my relationship with Freya and had developed a theory. They accosted me in the kitchen, still littered with breakfast dishes, the smell of coffee taunting me from behind the scrim of concerned adults.

"We all think you should be spending more time with kids your own age," my dad began, his eyes darting from my mom to Gwen for moral support.

"Like Thompson," my mom piped in. "He's so sweet. And he clearly likes you."

"I'm eighteen," I grumbled. "You can't organize my playdates."

The adults shared a look that I couldn't read. Then my mom said, "Yes, you're eighteen. You're legally an adult."

My dad picked it up. "That's why we were wondering if your friendship with Freya is—"

My mom cut him off, blurting. "Is your relationship with Freya *sexual?*"

"Jesus," I snapped, "You guys are sick." But my face turned three shades of red, revealing my guilty conscience. I couldn't forget that I'd lurked outside, watching Freya make love to Brian, and Max make love to Jamie. Freya's kiss still lingered on my lips, still kept me up at night, along with vivid fantasies of a romantic future with her. But my relationship with Freya wasn't sexual; it was more complex than that.

"You know we're accepting of your orientation," said Gwen.

"We wouldn't necessarily expect you to have a traditional, heteronormative relationship," my dad added.

But my mom fell apart. "You're not emotionally mature enough to be involved with a grown woman! A married woman!"

"She's eight months pregnant, for Christ's sake!" Gwen shrieked.

"She's using you!" my dad bellowed. "She doesn't even pay you for your photography!"

Somehow, I remained calm. "I don't expect you guys to understand."

"We're trying to, Swallow!" My mom was on the verge of tears. "Tell us what the hell is going on with you and that woman."

But they'd never get it. So, I strolled away from their chorus of protests.

My bedroom was off-limits to me. Eckhart, who started his day at 5:00 A.M. was down for his morning nap, so I went outside and walked toward the beach-access road. As I sauntered, breathing in the pungent tinge of goat and pig feces in the cedar-scented air, I thought about leaving home. About moving in with Freya and Max. I hadn't forgotten that Freya had been incensed when she'd found me squatting in her pottery studio, when I'd witnessed her attack on Max, but everything was different now. Once she knew that I knew what I knew . . . she would want to keep me happy. And close.

When I reached the beach, I sat on a driftwood log and texted her.

When should we do the pottery video?

She replied instantly.

Now. Before my stomach is too big to get near the wheel.

An afternoon shoot would have given me the opportunity to use my new studio lights, but I didn't want to linger at home. It was only a matter of time before my parents regrouped, launched another attack on my "abnormal" friendship. Their words would have no impact, of course, but they would irritate me. The harmless but annoying buzzing of the male mosquito. I texted back.

I'll be right over

The keys were in my truck, so there was no need to go back into the house. My tripod was inside, but I could do a handheld video. I drove directly to Freya's. Parking in the driveway, I considered heading straight to the pottery studio but decided to go to the main house first. I rang the bell. After a few moments, Max answered the door. He wore faded jeans and a T-shirt, had a mug of coffee in his hand. He looked sleepy and rumpled and gorgeous.

"Hey," I said, noticing that his right eye was bruised. I tapped my own eye. "What happened?"

"Tree branch in the face."

Right. "Is Freya here?"

"She's in the studio."

The smell of his coffee was tantalizing. My family had blocked the coffee maker with their judgment and concern, leaving me woefully uncaffeinated. "Could I get a coffee?" I asked. Max had always made me nervous, even girlish, but now that I knew his secret, I felt more confident.

"Sure."

I followed him inside.

As the former athlete made me a latte from their high-end machine, I watched him. He knew that Freya's baby wasn't his, *couldn't* be his, but he was keeping her secret. Could he love another man's child like it was his own? Was he that desperate to become a father? He'd always seemed indifferent to the baby's pending arrival, but maybe I had misread him. Maybe Freya had convinced him that their baby was a miracle. Or maybe, Max just went along with whatever Freya wanted.

He handed me the steaming mug of coffee and watched me take my first sip. And then he said, "Do you think Freya's ready?"

"For what?"

"The birth. The baby. All of it."

"She doesn't have much choice," I said with a chuckle.

But Max didn't smile.

"She never talks about it. It's like she's in denial about what's going to happen. Childbirth can be traumatic. And a baby needs constant care and attention."

"Do you want me to talk to her?" I offered, my chest warmed by my own altruism.

"Could you? I want to make sure she's mentally and physically prepared. Freya isn't . . . naturally maternal."

"Once the baby comes, the hormones will kick in and she'll be a great mom." I wasn't entirely convinced, but I was enjoying my role as sage.

"I hope so."

"And the baby will have its daddy," I said, watching his reaction. "You'll be there for both of them."

He breathed out through his nostrils. "I'm not sure I'm cut out for this, either."

"Why not?"

I wondered if Max would confess to me, admit that Freya's baby wasn't his. We were not close, but the secret must have been eating at him. Opening up to me would give him some relief. And strengthen my position in their family unit. But Max just muttered, "I'm not really dad material. Not after what I did to Ryan Klassen. Not after all I put Freya through."

"Leave it with me," I said, setting my half-empty mug on the counter. "I'll make sure Freya's prepared."

I headed for the door.

46

The studio was sweltering despite the February chill. Freya had cranked the heat to allow her to wear a unique pottery uniform. Instead of her usual smock and baggy jeans, she wore a fitted white tank top that strained over her belly, and a colorful sarong wrapped low around her hips. Her hair was pulled up into a messy but artfully arranged bun. The clay was wedged, packed into a ball, and waiting on the wheel. Her metal container of water and a sponge were on hand. She was ready for me.

"Hey, babe," she said, all sweetness and light. "I'm sorry about yesterday. Jamie and I had a lot of catching up to do."

#bestfriends #backtogether #grateful

"About what?" I groused. "It's not like she's done anything interesting in the past month."

"She wanted to talk about the baby," Freya said, with a slight eye roll. "You know she's barren, so this is the closest she's going to get to having one of her own."

Closer than she thinks. Jamie thought she was this baby's pseudo aunt. She had no idea she was its stepmother.

"Jamie wants us to do a step-by-step birthing plan. But she's going to be in the delivery room with me, so I figure she can take charge of things."

The last thing I wanted was to witness Freya's delivery. I'd caught unfortunate glimpses of my siblings' home births and they'd scarred me for life. But Jamie's role as amateur midwife annoyed me. I didn't like the thought of her coaching and supporting Freya through this disgusting, but purportedly special, event.

"Let's get started," I retorted.

Freya gave me a quizzical look, but obliged. She positioned herself at the wheel, flicked it on, and within moments she was transformed. I would later learn that Freya, in Norse mythology, was the goddess of fertility, the most beautiful of all the deities. I watched the sensual, artistic pregnant woman at work. Her name fit her perfectly.

I walked around her, taking a series of short videos from varying angles and of varying lengths. Her hands worked slowly, delicately, lifting the clay, shaping it, creating a tall, paper-thin vase. Midmorning sun shone through the studio windows, bathing her in an ethereal light. Once posted, this video would illicit nothing but praise for Freya's talent and beauty. No one would mention Max's lethal hit, the ugly lawsuit, Freya's social media obsession. When she was throwing, Freya was untouchable.

The fluted vase complete, she stopped the wheel and looked up at me. "How'd I do?"

For the first time, I noticed the weariness on her face. Her eyes were puffy, her skin wan under her flawless makeup. I saw her vulnerability in that moment, her insecurity, and it only made her more beautiful to me.

"You were magic," I said.

She smiled at me, grateful and relieved. "Thank you." She took the wire garrote and sliced her creation off the wheel. As she placed it expertly on a wooden bat, she said, "You've been amazing, Low. But we need to take a break."

My stomach plummeted with dread. "Did my mom call you?"

She looked up, bemused. "No . . . But that's going to be my last post for a while."

I was relieved my parents hadn't contacted her, but . . . "Why?"

"I'm fat and disgusting. I don't want people to see me like this."

"You're still beautiful," I assured her. "Just in a different way."

She ignored the compliment, wiping her hands on a towel. "Why would your mom call me?"

I lowered myself onto a stool facing her. "My parents kind of freaked out on me today. It was about you." I saw her brow crinkle. "They think we're like . . . lovers or something." My delivery was tinged with incredulous humor, but my cheeks were burning, my pulse racing. Just saying the word *lovers* prompted a mixture of embarrassment and delight.

Freya laughed. "Oh, shit. Really?"

It was a joke to her. She couldn't imagine being with me that way. But that kiss . . .

"I know," I covered. "I told them it wasn't like that. That we're just good friends. But they think our friendship is *abnormal*. And unhealthy."

She set down the cloth. "I can see their point."

What?

"I'm so much older than you. I'm about to squeeze out a kid any second. Your parents are probably wondering why the hell you're hanging out me."

Because you're my best and only friend. Because we have a soul connection. Because you kissed me.

Freya said, "If we don't see each other for a while, they'll cool off."

"I don't care what they think," I replied. "And I'm an adult. I do what I want."

She sighed. "I'm exhausted, Low. I need some time alone before all hell breaks loose. And this would give you a chance to spend some time with kids your own age."

She was dismissing me again. Sending me away with a smile. I watched as she detached the splash pan and headed for the bucket of clay refuse. She dumped the mud into the pail, then rinsed the tray in the sink. Her expression was weary but content, like we'd just had a normal conversation, like she hadn't just stabbed me in the heart. She turned the water off and faced me.

"And then, after the baby's born, we can legitimize things."

I'm embarrassed to say that her words filled me with hope. I wasn't sure what she meant, but as a girl raised by multiple parents, I knew there were possibilities. I could be Freya's girlfriend. Or Freya and Max's girlfriend. I'd only recently felt stirrings of sexual desire, but I wanted to be a part of this. Whatever this was.

"I've been thinking a lot about it, and . . . I'd like you to be our nanny."

Fuck.

She smiled at me as she pumped lotion into her hands, worked it between her fingers. "We're so comfortable with you. And you know so much about babies. We'd pay you, of course. And then your parents couldn't be upset."

What I felt in that moment was a disappointment so crushing I could scarcely breathe. For the first time, I knew the truth. Freya didn't see me as a friend or a soul mate. She viewed me as an employee. A kid she could hire to take care of her brat while she worked out and got her nails done and hiked/drank wine/had lunch with her real friend, Jamie. Her #bestfriend. I was not an emotional person, not prone to tears and outbursts, but I felt my chin wobble.

She was watching me, waiting for a response. I would tell her that I knew the truth about her baby's father. I would demand that she let me move in with her, insist that she treat me like a friend, an equal. Freya would be angry at first—I knew this about her. She would scream and yell, throw pottery at me or even slap me. But then she would take me back. She'd have no choice.

But she wouldn't love me; not the way I wanted to be loved.

"You're hurt," Freya said.

She knew me after all. She could read my pain.

Freya moved toward me. "I still want you to be my photographer, Low. We'll still do our photo shoots when you're not taking care of the baby. You can take pictures of the kid, too. You'll be my nanny *and* my artistic partner."

I croaked a single word in response. "Okay."

"Thank God." Freya smiled at me, a bright, genuine smile. "Max and I were starting to freak out a bit." She placed her clean hands on her bump and sighed. "Will you post the video for me? I need to go lie down."

I wouldn't see her again for three weeks.

47

jamie

It could have been the promise of spring in the air, the cro-cuses peeping their sleepy heads aboveground, tightly furled buds appearing on the naked trees. It might have been the slight uptick in business as tourists came to the island for long week-ends, braving the still unpredictable weather and sporadic ferry schedule. But I knew that my positive outlook and lightened mood were due to my reunion with Freya. Everything else was just gravy.

She had invited me to lunch and put my world to rights. As it turned out, she had been pining for reconciliation as much—if not more so—than I had.

"I really missed you this past month," she said. "I actually con-sidered moving back to LA."

"Oh my god," I gasped. "I thought about going back to Van-couver."

Freya grasped my hand and squeezed it. "I'm so sorry for what happened that night. I was wrong to disrespect your values. Let's forget about everything and never fall out again."

"Deal," I said.

"Thank God." She leaned back in her chair and rested her hands on her belly. "The baby and I need you."

My throat clogged, and my eyes got moist. "I need you, too." The show of emotion was embarrassing but real. Before I could fall apart entirely, the doorbell rang, allowing me to compose myself. Freya returned shortly.

"It was just Low," she explained with a roll of her eyes. "She's a very *enthusiastic* photographer."

I'd been jealous of Low and Freya, but not anymore. Low was just a kid with a crush; I could see that now. Freya and I were grown women.

"Poor girl," I said, feeling for my awkward assistant. "I hope she can find some friends her own age."

"I know," Freya agreed, tucking into her salad. "I've been pushing her in that direction. It's for her own good."

"It is," I said. But I knew it would be hard for Low to make new friends when her world seemed to revolve around photographing Freya.

Our level of intimacy had not been damaged by our recent estrangement. In fact, we were even closer after we reunited. No subjects were taboo anymore, nothing needed to be hidden or avoided. Our husbands may have felt differently (I know mine did), but I no longer cared if we were "couple friends." Our female friendship was all that mattered.

We texted constantly. Freya was open and funny. She felt like an elephant. She had terrible gas. She was horny but couldn't stand to be touched. When the store was closed, we met for leisurely strolls or lunch at the Blue Heron. It was easier to meet on neutral territory. But one Saturday, Freya summoned me to her house on my lunch break.

"Can you come over? I'm so bored, but I'm too fat to get dressed."

When Low skulked into the store at eleven, I took my leave. I didn't tell her where I was going, but she knew. I could see it in her narrowed eyes, her tense posture. And like Low, I had no one else but Freya.

I'd picked up Buddha bowls for us, and Freya opened a bottle of rosé. "The baby's basically cooked," she said, as she poured herself a small glass. "A bit of wine won't hurt it." A May due date meant she was early into her third trimester. I'd read so many books on gestation that I would have abstained completely if I were expecting. But I wasn't about to object. As close as I felt to her, I was still afraid of setting her off.

I tucked into my bowl of grains and greens. "Have you had a chance to talk to your doctor about a birthing plan?"

"Not yet."

"There's still time," I said, keeping my tone light to hide my concern.

"There's been a lot going on," she said, sipping her wine. "With Max."

Now that everything was out in the open, I didn't have to feel awkward and sweaty at the mention of his name, but for some reason, I still did. "Do you want to talk about it?" I asked, in as casual a tone as I could muster.

"He's been fighting."

"With whom?"

"Anyone who wants to take him on," Freya said. "When he's away with the boys, they go out to bars. He's always been a target. The tough guy. The guy who killed Ryan Klassen. But now, he instigates things. And then he doesn't fight back. He lets himself be beaten. He wants to be physically punished for what he did."

The black eye I'd seen that day in the restaurant made sense now. And, perhaps, the puckered scar on his chest. . . . "Has he talked to someone? A therapist?"

"He's not that kind of guy," Freya said as she chewed. "Even if he were, this backwater is sorely lacking in mental-health services."

I knew that to be true. But Max traveled frequently; he could find help on the mainland. This sounded serious. I was about to offer this suggestion when Freya spoke.

"How can he be a good father when he hates himself so much?"

I looked at my friend and saw tears in her eyes, dimples of emotion in her chin. It was rare to see this display of feeling from Freya. She delivered intense, heartfelt words with a breezy casualness. She shared tales of her childhood pain as if she'd read about them in a book. But she was hurting now. She was worried.

"The baby will change him," I said quickly. "It will become the most important thing in the entire world, and he'll realize he has to get help. He'll have to forgive himself in order to be a good dad."

"Do you really think so?"

"I know so," I said with an adamance I could not back up. But I believed that this baby was going to be transformative. Freya and Max would become the people their child needed: warm, doting, adoring. It was biology: nature's way of ensuring the propagation of the species. And everything felt good and right and possible at that time.

Freya smiled at me. "You always know what to say to make me feel better."

I returned her fond gaze, feeling pleased and warmed. Everything was going to be all right. I would make sure of it.

48

The e-mail came in about a week later, via Hawking Mercantile's website. I had set up a contact address for customers and potential suppliers. The sender's name was unfamiliar, the address a generic Gmail account. I thought it must be spam; I almost deleted it. The only words were:

Please read this.

And then a link.

I was alone in the kitchen, my laptop set up on the small pine table. We had had an early dinner, and now I was paying invoices while Brian watched TV in the living room. If I'd asked his opinion, he would have told me not to click. He'd warned me many times about phishing and viruses. But I didn't call out for advice as my mouse hovered over the words and I debated whether the message was safe and legitimate. Something told me to take the risk. And so, I clicked.

An article from the *Calgary Herald* filled my screen. I had an aunt in Calgary, had visited her on a few summer vacations when I was growing up. It was an archived story from several years ago, about NHL hockey player Max Beausoleil. He'd been involved in a paternity suit; a woman had sued him for child support. My brow crinkled with confusion and concern. Did Max have another child out there? Did Freya know about it? Why had they never mentioned it?

As I continued to read, I learned that Max had disputed the mother's paternity claim. An attractive blonde, Paula Elphin, maintained that they'd slept together when Max played for the Kings. He was newly married to Freya then. Of course he'd deny it. Even if he had Freya's blessing to sleep around, the optics were bad. But it was his defense that made my pulse race and the back of my neck break out in a sweat.

Maxime Beausoleil claimed to be sterile.

His lawyer had submitted a doctor's note into evidence. Complications from mumps, it said, a rare but plausible cause of infertility. The baby couldn't possibly be Max's—or so he declared. But the judge hadn't bought it, had insisted on a paternity test. At the time of writing, the results were pending.

I immediately searched for a follow-up article. I had to know if my best friend's husband had a child out there. Perhaps its existence explained Max's long and frequent absences? But why had the kid never come to visit? It would be in elementary school by now. I knew that Freya had hated children, but her pregnancy had changed things, had changed *her*. This child, if it were Max's, would be welcome now.

But if it wasn't his . . .

A specific Google search provided the answers I sought. The test results proved that Max was not the father of Paula Elphin's baby. So did that mean Max was sterile, as he'd claimed? The judge had ordered only a DNA test, not a fertility test. Max's ability to father children was irrelevant to the court. But it was not irrelevant to me. Because if Maxime Beausoleil was not the father of Freya's baby, who was?

And who had sent me this article?

Suddenly, Brian was behind me. "Almost done?" he asked cheerily.

I turned to face him, my chagrin and confusion evident. "I—I just got this e-mail."

"From whom?"

"I don't know."

Brian took a seat, and I slid the laptop to him. He read the first article, his brow furrowed with confusion. Without a word, he clicked to the second piece, his face growing darker as he read the results of Max's paternity test. I saw him put the pieces together in his brain, watched him scramble with the possibilities.

"What does this mean?" I asked, my voice hoarse.

Brian stood. "It means we need to talk to Max and Freya."

49

brian

My hands held the wheel in a vise grip, and my foot felt heavy on the gas. I was conscious not to speed, not to be reckless as we drove toward the cliffside home. If my driving reflected a lack of urgency, a sense of calm, it might translate to my wife and me. But Jamie was practically vibrating in the seat beside me, nerves and apprehension coming off her in waves. And I felt sick to my stomach. Because this encounter, this confrontation, was going to be brutal. It was going to change our lives, one way or another.

Neither of us spoke, neither of us articulated what that article could mean for us. And for the baby. After my initial suspicions about its paternity, I had put the child—and its parents—out of my mind. Freya had provided the dated ultrasound image, and it had looked authentic. But it could easily have been doctored with some Wite-Out and a scanner. I had wanted so badly to believe its veracity, been desperate to disconnect from that toxic couple and put the night of the swap behind us. But if Max could not father children . . .

Despite our struggles, I still wanted to be a dad. Jamie may have grieved longer and more openly, but I still ached for a child. I'd always envisioned myself with a little girl on my shoulders, tossing a baseball with my son. But not this way. Please, God, not this way.

Freya had charmed me at first, I'd been a pawn to her beauty and sex appeal, but now I saw through it. She was manipulative, even scheming. She got off on playing with people. I'd watched my wife career from jubilance to despair and back to restrained delight as Freya embraced her, dumped her, then lured her back in. I should have been angry at Max for sleeping with my wife, but he was just Freya's puppet. That night was all her doing.

Had Freya wanted to get pregnant? Had she orchestrated the couples' swap so she could conceive? She wasn't the maternal type, didn't seem to have a clue about kids. But this pregnancy had reignited her Instagram career. And got her so much attention—from Jamie, Max, even Low who, as far as I could see, was Freya's volunteer PA. But would Freya go this far? Would she get pregnant with my baby just to fuck with us all? She'd have to be a psychopath.

And now, this woman I despised was carrying my child. I knew it in my gut, had known it all along if I'd been honest with myself. I glanced at my wife, and she looked back, meeting my eyes. She knew it, too.

What were we going to do about it?

50

jamie

We eased down the long gravel drive toward Freya and Max's home. My stomach was in knots, the smallest bump in the path making me nauseous. I wanted to tell Brian to turn around, tell him we needed to go home to discuss and strategize. But we were here now, and there would be no turning back. We needed answers. If we had somehow gotten this wrong, if the baby was Max's, they would never forgive us. But if we had gotten it right . . .

I was anxious, terrified, but I felt something else . . . a glimmer of hope. This baby might be my husband's child. Was there a way that Freya and I could both be mothers? I know it sounds weird and "out there" but we lived on an island with a progressive, highly alternative culture. Low's family was the perfect example. They shared their children and their partners with ease and aplomb. Everyone was loving and happy and devoted. Except Low . . . but I wasn't sure her misery could be blamed on her family's makeup.

And Freya wasn't jealous or possessive. She'd let me sleep with her husband without a second thought. Perhaps she would let me mother her child, too? Joint custody would take the pressure off her. She'd have time to exercise, to pamper herself, to travel. She and Max could work on their marriage and his self-hatred issues without the demands of a baby. Over time, they might find that they preferred the child live with us full-time. They could visit. They could take it to Disneyland. But Brian and I would be its real parents. I would be its mother.

But if Freya had wanted us to be a part of the baby's life, why had she lied to us? Why had she hidden her child's paternity?

Brian stopped the car behind the white Range Rover and turned to face me. "Who could have sent you that e-mail?"

"I don't know," I said. "Maybe someone with a grudge against Max and Freya?"

"But why did they send it to *you*? It has to be someone who knows I slept with Freya. It has to be someone who's concerned about the baby."

I swallowed. There was only one person I could think of who didn't want them to have that child.

"Could it be Max?" I said.

"Could it be Freya?" Brian suggested.

We both sat there, mulling the possibilities. Max had never seemed excited about the baby. Freya could have gotten cold feet. They were the only ones who knew the infant's true paternity.

"What about Low?" Brian suggested.

"No," I said instantly. "She's an odd kid, but she wouldn't do something like this. And besides, she doesn't know what we did that night. Freya wouldn't tell a teenager that we had a couples' swap. That would be sick."

Brian nodded slowly, then he unbuckled his seat belt.

"There's only one way to find out."

51

When Freya opened the door, she looked pleasantly surprised to see me. But I watched her pretty face as she clocked my agitation, my husband's tense presence at my side. The delight on her features quickly evaporated, replaced by darkness and dread. This was clearly not a social call.

"Hey," she said flatly.

"Hi," I replied, my voice strangled.

Brian said, "We need to talk to you and Max."

She hesitated, and for a moment, I feared she'd slam the door in our faces. But she stepped back and ushered us inside.

"Jamie and Brian are here," she called, her lack of enthusiasm evident in her tone. She sounded resigned, like she'd expected us to show up on her doorstep demanding answers. And maybe she had?

Max walked into the room then, wearing faded jeans and a clinging T-shirt that showed off his physique. But I felt no pitter-patter of attraction, no blush of remembrance. We were here on business. A child's future hung on this encounter.

"What's up?" he said, matching his wife's cool but accepting presentation.

Brian spoke directly to Max. "We just got an anonymous e-mail with a link to your paternity case. The one where you stated—in court—that you're sterile."

Max's handsome face turned into a scowl. "Who sent you that?"

"Someone who thought we should know that the baby"—Brian gestured toward Freya's bump—"isn't yours."

I turned to Freya then. "Is it Brian's child?" My words wobbled with emotion. And cautious optimism.

But Freya ignored me and turned to Brian. "Max lied in court. That slut was trying to get money out of him. It seemed the easiest solution."

"The paternity test proved it wasn't Max's baby," Brian countered.

"Yeah, because he didn't sleep with her," Freya snapped back. "Not because he's sterile."

My husband turned to Max. "So you never had complications from mumps? You lied about all of it?"

"I had mumps," Max stated. "And I had complications. But I'm not sterile. I just have lower-than-average fertility."

"We have sex every day," Freya said. "Sometimes twice." She looked at Brian with a disdain. "We still have a higher chance of conception than one lame night with you."

I was simultaneously relieved and insulted that Freya considered my husband a lousy lay. But that was irrelevant right now. "There's an easy way to solve this," I said. "You can take a paternity test."

"Fuck you," Freya barked. "I'm not risking my baby getting stuck with a needle to put your mind at ease."

"There are noninvasive ways to test paternity in utero," I said.

"They can take your blood and extract the baby's DNA from it. It's perfectly safe."

Freya looked at me, her lip curled into a sneer. "You're loving this, aren't you?"

She'd sensed my hope, but I was far from loving this. "Yeah, it's wonderful," I snapped. "My best friend is pregnant with my husband's child, and she's been lying about it for months."

"I told you it's not his fucking baby! You're so desperate to be a mother that you're trying to steal my child. You're sick. You're pathetic."

Anger welled up inside of me and made my voice shake. "Then prove it," I said. "Because if the baby *is* Brian's, it will be a hell of a lot better off having *me* for a mother than you!"

Freya's eyes widened with shock, and her face paled with chagrin. My words were cruel, they would irrevocably destroy our friendship. But it felt good to stand up to her, to hurt her even. She thought I was weak and cowardly. She thought I worshipped her so much that I'd cave in, back down. But I would fight for the truth about this baby.

She took a step back as if I'd slapped her.

"Oh shit," she said. "I think my water just broke."

I saw the wet patch on her designer maternity jeans, watched it spread down her legs. "It's too early," I said, my voice hoarse.

"Fuck," Max muttered.

"Is it too early?" Brian asked. "If the baby's mine, you're only a couple weeks from your due date."

"It's not fucking yours!" Freya screeched, her face red, eyes wild. She was hunched over, clutching her belly. She looked angry. And terrified.

"We need to go to the hospital," Max said, putting his arm around his wife's shoulders.

"I'm so sorry," I said, tears pricking my eyes. Had my verbal attack caused premature labor? Was the baby in jeopardy because I couldn't control my rage? "Can I do anything? Does she have her bag packed?"

"Stay the fuck away from me, Jamie!" Freya yelled as Max grabbed a small suitcase from the front closet and escorted her to the door. "You're not getting anywhere near me, or my baby!"

52

max

We took my car; Brian had parked directly behind Freya's white Range Rover. The hospital was only a fifteen-minute drive from our home, but Freya's contractions seemed to be pretty intense. At least, that's what I could deduce from the vitriol she spewed at me through gritted teeth.

"You sent that fucking e-mail, didn't you? You told Jamie that it's not your baby."

"No, I didn't."

"You're the only one who knows I slept with Brian! It has to be you, you fucking traitor!"

"It wasn't. You must have told someone."

"Who would I tell? I have no one here!" Then she let out a fierce, guttural scream as a contraction hit her.

"Breathe," I said.

"Fuck you!" she responded.

When the pain had passed, she continued her rant. "You never wanted this baby! You're trying to give it away!"

"I'm not," I said, which was the truth. But she was right; I'd never wanted it. Freya and I weren't meant to be parents. Years ago, I would have welcomed a child, but not now, not after all the ugly shit we'd been through. I'd known that my chances of fathering a child were "practically zero" when I married Freya. If I'd wanted a family, I would have chosen a different wife. It sounds harsh, but Freya was not mother material. Freya was sexy, beautiful, witty . . . but she was not selfless; she was not loving. She was not cut out to be someone's mom.

Neither was Paula Elphin. I barely knew her, but a person who would lie in court about having sex with an athlete just to get child support . . . well, she was hardly a positive role model. Thank God I hadn't slept with her. She'd been all over me in the bar that night, but I was a newlywed, madly in love. Freya wasn't possessive, but I wasn't interested. When Paula accused me, my lawyer thought my sterility would be the quickest and easiest way to make it all go away. We hadn't expected the judge to order a DNA test.

"I have contracts!" Freya growled. "I have sponsors! If we have a paternity scandal, I'll be ruined again."

"Jesus Christ. That's what you're worried about?"

She hit me then, her hand connecting with my jaw. It smarted; Freya was small, but her rage made her strong. The pain made my eyes water and my face throb. And then I felt that familiar release. It was like scratching at a rash you weren't supposed to touch. It was damaging, could cause infection. But it was such sweet relief, like it always was, if only for a moment. Freya had come up with a cover story for her battery, had told Jamie I'd been fighting in bars. But the only person who abused me was my wife. And I let her because I deserved it, even craved it in a fucked-up way. I wanted more, wanted her to claw and scratch and punish me. But not now.

My wife was about to give birth to another man's baby.

53

jamie

What could we do but follow them to the hospital? We could hardly go home and twiddle our thumbs while Freya was in pre-term labor. If, in fact, it was preterm. If the baby was fine, big and healthy, that meant the child could be Brian's. But if it was tiny, in need of medical intervention, we would know the timing was off, that the baby couldn't have been conceived that night in July when Brian slept with Freya. And we would know that we were responsible for the infant's premature delivery.

The thought was too horrible to contemplate. I would never forgive myself if the baby was born unhealthy because of our confrontation. Even if it wasn't Brian's child, even if its mother loathed me now, I still cared about that baby, loved it even. But if he or she *was* born robust and strong . . . Did that mean the child was my husband's? How could we prove it? And if we did, what happened then? Freya would not be interested in peacefully co-parenting; she'd made that abundantly clear. We were the enemy.

The whole mess seemed unfathomable. How had one night

of fun and debauchery upended our lives? Threatened our marriages and destroyed our friendships? People did stuff like this all the time with no repercussions. It was common practice on the island, practically de rigueur in the seventies! But we had experimented one goddamn time and it had blown up in our faces. And now, a tiny life hung in the balance, its future precarious.

Brian's voice broke through my reverie. "There they are."

We had reached the hospital and could see Max's black SUV parked near the front doors. He was helping his wife out of the vehicle, his big hands gentle and caring on his delicate passenger. Freya clutched her belly, her face contorted with pain, and something else. Fear. Freya was terrified. She had not prepared herself for what was to come. She needed me.

"Park here," I instructed, as Brian pulled into an adjacent lot.

We would not be allowed to leave our car in the emergency spaces close to the door. We weren't patients or family. Before the vehicle had even stopped, I was out of it and jogging toward her. Despite everything that had happened, the lies and subterfuge, I would help my friend through this. I would hold her hand and coach her through the delivery. I would be there when my husband's child slid out into the world, having been carried for so many months by my best friend.

"Freya," I called as I approached. "It's going to be okay. I'm here for you. We can get through this together."

She looked up then, and I saw the hatred on her lovely face. "No. You don't get to be a part of this."

I stopped in my tracks. "I just want to help you through labor. You're not prepared."

"You're not a mother," she snarled. "You know *nothing*."

My heart twisted in my chest. "I-I've read all the books," I stammered. "I know all the steps. I can coach you."

She laughed at me then, a cruel, mocking bark. "If you come near me, I'll call the police."

Max had her small suitcase in one hand, his other arm wrapped around his wife, supportive and protective. "Go away, Jamie. She doesn't want you here."

As they moved toward the hospital, Freya continued her verbal assault. "You're delusional, Jamie! You're dangerous! Stay away from me and my baby."

People were staring now—nurses, patients, visitors. I didn't look, but I could feel the weight of their eyes on me. They thought Freya was afraid of me. They thought I was a monster harassing a poor pregnant mother.

Brian joined me then and slipped his hand into mine. "It's okay," he said softly. "It's going to be okay."

We stood and watched as Freya and Max disappeared inside.

54

low

My mom and Vik were in the kitchen talking in soft voices. I could barely hear them over the bubbling vat of white beans on the stove, but I pressed my body flat to the wall and strained to listen.

"I was visiting Bill Pickering," Vik was saying, "he's in the hospital with a broken femur. I was leaving, when it all kicked off."

"Freya and Jamie were yelling at each other?" my mom asked. Her voice was hushed, though she didn't know I'd returned to the house. Since the intervention about my "inappropriate relationship," I'd taken to spending most of my days at the beach or in the forest, taking photos, or sometimes going for pizza with Thompson. Anything to get me away from all the parental judgment and concern.

"Is Freya the blond one?" Vik asked. My mom must have nodded, because he said, "She was really angry at the brunette. Jamie wanted to come into the delivery room, but Freya said she'd call the police. She said Jamie was dangerous."

"Oh my god," my mom said, at the precise moment I gasped.

They wouldn't hear me over the boiling beans and their own conversation, but I clapped my hand over my mouth anyway.

"Freya was definitely in labor," said Vik. "A contraction hit her, and she screamed bloody murder."

I didn't need to hear anymore. I scooped up my truck keys and ran for the door.

I drove the dark and winding route to the hospital with my mouth curled into a permanent grin. The anonymous e-mail I'd sent to Jamie had worked. She had confronted Freya about the baby's paternity, and now, Freya hated her. Considered her a mortal enemy. Gratitude and relief filled my chest, made it feel warm and light.

Vik had said Freya was protective of her baby, had accused Jamie of being a danger to it. That was slightly concerning, but it had to be the hormones. Eventually, Freya would see that motherhood was a giant drag, and she'd be better off handing the whining, drooling, pooping creature over to its father. Jamie would be a better mother to it. She had no life except for the store, which, let's face it, was hardly taxing. Without the baby, Freya could soar to greater heights, even greater fame.

Her fans would want to see the baby, of course. It couldn't disappear from her life completely—as much as we might want it to. But weekend visitation would allow us to take enough photos of the child to make Freya look like a loving mother, while preserving her brand as a sexy, independent woman. She'd get cool sponsors like makeup companies, fashion designers, and vodka distilleries, not just boring baby food and diaper brands. She'd get invited to resorts and on cruises, and I'd go with her. We would travel the world together, our relationship deepening through our shared experiences.

I had been right to wait a couple of weeks to send the e-mail. It would have implicated me if I'd been dismissed with tears in my eyes and, moments later, Jamie and Brian had turned up demanding answers. I hadn't expected the confrontation to put Freya into labor, but the baby would be fine. It was only a couple of weeks early, if it had been conceived the night of the swap. Which it had been. Because Max was sterile. And Freya was lying.

The tiniest niggle of concern tickled the base of my brain as I pulled into the hospital parking lot. If the baby had somehow been conceived later, as Freya and Max claimed, it might not survive. I wanted to get rid of the thing, but not that way. I wasn't a monster. I may have fantasized about Freya miscarrying, but this would be too gruesome. But I pushed my concerns aside as I turned off the ignition and hurried across the darkened parking lot toward the building. Freya needed me, now. Whatever happened.

Jamie and Brian were loitering outside the main doors, looking fretful. As soon as she spotted me, Jamie rushed up to me. "Low. Freya's in labor."

"I know."

"Did she call you?"

"Yes," I lied. Freya was no longer speaking to Jamie, so she'd never find out that it wasn't true.

"Thank God. It's been hours. She needs someone in the room with her, someone who knows about labor. Can you be there for her?"

"Of course." I didn't relish seeing the object of my devotion screaming, puking, and pooping (yeah, I knew about labor), but I enjoyed usurping Jamie's position.

Brian had joined us now. "Low, we need some information."

"Like what?"

"The baby's weight and length would help. Or if the doctor says anything about it being premature."

"We just need to know that the baby's okay," Jamie said.

"I'm sure it's fine," I replied, noticing the concern, even fear, on her face. "It's only a little early."

I was moving toward the automatic doors when I heard Jamie say, "Wait!" My shoulders tensed. "It *was* you."

I almost didn't stop, considered pretending I hadn't heard her. But I turned toward her. "What was me?"

"Did you send me the link about Max's paternity case?"

"No."

"Freya told you about that night, didn't she? You know Brian is the baby's father, not Max."

Her eyes were full of tears of gratitude. She thought I had done this for her. She thought I was on their side. God, she was naive. But I couldn't admit that I'd sent the e-mail. If Freya found out, she'd banish me.

"I'll let you know how the baby is," I said. And I hurried inside.

55

Somewhat thankfully, the nurses would not let me into the Freya's room. "It's been a difficult labor," the heavyset warden of the maternity unit explained. "She's been trying for hours. They're performing an unscheduled C-section."

"Why?" I asked. My mom had given birth in the living room without incident. "Has something gone wrong?"

"Tiny mother, big baby," she said dismissively, returning to her paperwork.

Big baby. That probably meant it was not premature. That probably meant it was Brian's child.

I lingered in the hallway, waiting for some news. A couple of hours passed before a handful of people emerged from the operating room, men and women in scrubs chatting casually among themselves. A man with dark eyes and a shiny bald head looked approachable. I hurried up to him. "Can you tell me how she is?"

"Mother and baby are fine," he said, in an unfamiliar accent.

"Thank God. Was it born early? The baby? Is everything okay?"

His smooth brow furrowed. "Are you family?"

"Yes." I lied. "I'm Freya's niece. Can I see her?"

He didn't question the fact that this gangly, unattractive girl was related to the gorgeous couple in the delivery room. "You can visit her when she's moved to the maternity ward. But I'll tell her you're here."

"My name is Low," I said quickly, afraid she wouldn't figure out that the hovering niece was me.

The man popped into the room and out again. "Have a seat in the waiting area." It was a command.

So I sat on an orange Naugahyde sofa and waited. Even as the minutes ticked into hours, I had no doubts that Freya would want to see me. I was her best friend, even more than that. And she had no one else. No family. No Jamie. Just me. And Max, who was standing by her though he knew her baby couldn't be his. The pair seemed locked in some kind of sick, codependent partnership full of lies and abuse and emotional distance, and yet . . . they had each other's backs.

As if summoned by my thoughts, Max appeared in the entry-way. He looked pale and worn; the toll of witnessing his wife give birth to another man's child was etched on his face.

"Hey," he said softly.

I stood. "Is Freya okay? Can I see her?"

"She's fine. She had a baby girl."

She had a baby girl. Not *we*.

"Come with me."

I followed his hulking form down the buffed hallway feeling petite and girlish next to him. Max still elicited a little thrill in me. Once the baby was out of the picture, he would fade into the background, or disappear completely. But for now, I didn't mind having him around.

The number on the door was eighteen. Max pushed it open and held it for me to enter. Freya was propped up in a narrow hospital bed, her face fully made-up, her white-blond hair brushed to a sheen. She wore a pale pink robe . . . the robe I'd seen on her the night she'd attempted to stab Max with a fork. Other than some puffiness around the eyes, you would not have known she'd just been in labor, had just had a child cut out of her stomach.

She greeted me with a weary smile, and my heart filled up.

"I'm so glad you came."

Freya wanted me here at this seminal moment. I was the most important person in her life.

I noticed the tiny bundle sleeping in a clear plastic bassinet next to Freya's bed. The baby was tightly swaddled in a white blanket, a few blond curls peeping out of the pink cap on her head. I moved closer, taking in the full pink cheeks, the long lashes, the rosebud lips. She was beautiful, not shriveled and purple like Eckhart had been. I'd wished the child away so many times, but she was perfection. Just like Freya. I felt something like awe as I stared at her . . . awe and fear. Because Freya might fall in love with this pretty baby.

"Her name is Maggie. After Max's mom."

I looked over at Max and met his dark eyes. We both understood the significance of this moniker. It was a bold move; a fighting stance. It meant that Freya was determined to pretend her baby was Max's. That she would never admit that Brian was the real father. And she was not going to hand her child over to Jamie's loving maternal arms. Freya was going to fight for her child.

Damn it.

"Pass her here," Freya instructed me. I reached into the bassinet and scooped up the little bundle. Maggie didn't stir as I settled her in her mother's arms. Freya gazed down at her daughter, her face alight with maternal adoration. She looked radiant, beatific, almost saintly. Love emanated from the pair like a visible halo. Then Freya looked up at me.

"Do you have your camera?"

"Uh . . . no."

"Why not?"

"I heard you were in labor. I raced over here."

"Take a photo with your phone then."

"It's in the truck."

"Well, go get it," she snapped, handing the baby to Max, who returned her to the bassinet. "Before Maggie wakes up and starts screaming her head off."

Dismissed, I scurried down the polished hallway—past doctors, nurses, and patients, absorbed in their own dramas. Freya's curt tone had hurt me, but in a way, I was relieved. Her bonding moment with Maggie had been nothing but an act, a stunt for the cameras. She wanted to keep Maggie for appearances only, was going to fight Brian and Jamie on principle alone. But she didn't know that they had a secret weapon in their struggle for custody.

Me.

When I burst through the sliding doors, I expected to see my boss and her husband waiting patiently in the cold, crisp night, but Jamie and Brian were gone. Maybe a security guard had shooed them away. Or Max may have called the cops. Or perhaps the hours without word had worn them down. But they should have stayed. They should have been more devoted to their baby. As I stalked across the darkened lot, I felt a prickle of concern.

I slid into my truck and reached for my phone in the glove box. With trembling fingers, I texted Jamie.

The baby is healthy. Seven pounds two ounces. Not a preemie.

And then, for good measure. . . .

She looks like her dad

spring 2020

56

jamie

On the fifth day after my husband's daughter was born, we saw a lawyer. Her name was Nancy Willfollow—her office a renovated heritage home on the edge of town. She had been a customer at my store on occasion, breezing into the shop in her shapeless black Eileen Fisher togs. Despite the slow pace of island life, she exuded an air of frazzled efficiency. She had three sons away at boarding school and a retired landscape architect husband who devoted himself to the care of their home and garden. Perhaps the townspeople of Hawking had more pressing legal issues than I thought?

My cheeks burned as Brian told the fiftyish woman about the night he bedded Freya upstairs while I was in the basement guest room with Max. It was entirely possible that Nancy and her landscaping husband were swingers. They might have moved to the island specifically for its open-minded, sexually adventurous culture. The attorney's features remained blank, unreadable, but I was mortified, nonetheless. It could have been worse, I told myself. It's not like we were using whips or chains or animal costumes. But still . . . the conception of Brian's child sounded taw-dry and sleazy.

My husband slid a print-out of the news story about Max's paternity case across the polished walnut desk. "Maxime Beauso-leil said, in court, that he's sterile."

We waited as the lawyer's eyes roamed over the article. She read slowly, thoroughly, taking in every word, as Brian and I fidg-eted in our seats, glancing at each other and back at her.

Finally, Brian said, "The baby has to be mine. The dates line up. And Max is infertile."

"But we need to prove it," I added. "Can we make them do a paternity test?"

Nancy finally looked up from the page. "You could take this to court. If there's enough evidence, the judge might compel them to test the baby. But there's still no guarantee you'd get custody rights or even visitation."

Brian said, "Even if we prove she's *my* daughter?"

I winced inwardly at my husband's words. He didn't mean to exclude me, but this was his fight.

"That would be a separate trial. The judge would want to determine the best interests of the child."

"Freya and Max aren't meant to be parents," I interjected. "They never wanted kids. They're . . . superficial and self-absorbed." As soon as I said it, I realized how benign it sounded. Superficial and self-absorbed people reproduced all the time.

"Is the child in danger with them? Do they abuse substances? Is there violence in the home?"

We couldn't mention the magic mushrooms without impli-cating ourselves. But Brian took another tack.

"Max has a violent history. He broke a man's neck during a hockey game. The guy later overdosed on opioids."

"I heard about the case," Nancy said, sounding unimpressed. It was on the ice and in the past. It had little bearing on Max's ability to be a dad.

"Freya told me he picks fights in bars," I added quickly. "He feels like he deserves to be punished, so he instigates things and then he doesn't fight back. I saw his black eye."

Nancy nodded slowly. "It sounds like you might have a case."

My heart leaped. Brian reached over and squeezed my fingers.

Nancy said, "I don't go to court anymore since I moved here, but I can refer you to a colleague on the mainland." She reached for a pen and paper, but then paused. "Pursuing this will be expensive. Trial lawyers charge upward of four hundred bucks an hour. You'll need to travel to hearings, stay in a hotel. It will be a significant financial outlay."

My eyes flitted to my husband, and despair reflected back at me. We couldn't afford a lengthy court battle in another city. Brian had handed in his manuscript and received another installment of his advance, but it was just enough to live on until business picked up at the store. We didn't have the resources to fight for this child.

Nancy clocked our concern. "Alternatively, you could do what they call a curiosity test."

"What's that?" Brian asked.

"If you can get access to the baby, you can do a cheek swab. You send it off to a lab with your DNA. The results won't be admissible in court, but they might give you leverage with the mother."

"Freya's not a reasonable person," Brian said. "She already knows this baby is mine, but she refuses to acknowledge it."

"Maybe presenting her with scientific evidence will change her mind," Nancy offered.

"It's worth a try," I said hopefully.

"It's not." Brian's contradiction was curt. "And we don't have access to the baby, anyway."

Nancy let a breath out of her nose. "Court is going to cost you—a lot of money and a lot of hours. By the time you get a result, the child could be a couple of years old. It could be difficult to form a bond with her."

Panic fluttered in my chest and tears pooled in my eyes. We were so close to having a child, a little girl who was biologically Brian's baby. And the opportunity was being ripped away from us. Pressing my lips together to quell my emotions, I stood. "Thanks," I managed to mumble, "We'll discuss it." And then I bolted for the door.

Brian joined me outside minutes later, where I stood blowing my nose and swiping at my tears.

"You okay?" he asked, rubbing my back.

"We can't lose this baby because we don't have enough money to fight for her," I said. "Nothing is more important than Maggie."

My husband ran his hands through his cropped hair. "I could ask my brother for a loan. . . ." Brian's brother was a tech multi-millionaire in Silicon Valley. He was also an arrogant douche.

"How would you explain it?" I asked. "I got my wife's best friend pregnant while I was high on 'shrooms, and now we want access to the baby."

Brian did not laugh. "I'll make something up."

"How will you write your next book? How will I run the store? Even if we prove the baby is"—I stopped myself from saying *ours*—"yours, we might need a second trial to get custody or even visitation." I stuffed the snotty tissue into my pocket. "We need to work this out with Freya and Max. We can do the curiosity test. Once we prove, beyond a doubt, that you're the father—"

My husband cut me off. "They *know* I'm the father, Jamie. Max is sterile. He can't have children. We're not dealing with reasonable people here."

I swallowed hard. A plan was formulating in my mind, a sneaky plan that could blow up in my face. I could share it with Brian and risk him talking me out of it. Or I could add it to the secrets and subterfuge that had nearly destroyed us. Brian made the decision for me.

"How would we get the baby's DNA? If we try to get near her, they'll use it against us." He sighed then, his eyes staring out at the quaint main street, deserted, as usual. "She's a horrible human being." He was talking about Freya; I didn't need clarification. "I wish we'd never met her." Then he stalked off toward his truck.

Part of me agreed with him. Part of me wished Freya hadn't walked into my shop that day, that I hadn't suggested coffee, that I hadn't fallen under her spell. I wished we'd never gone to their waterfront home that night, that we hadn't drank the mushroom tea, that we had never swapped partners. But part of me was grateful that we had. Because now we had a chance—no matter how tenuous, no matter how slim—to become parents.

And I still believed in Freya then. I still thought that we could make her see sense, that we would be able to work this out with mutual respect and understanding. Freya may have been selfish and shallow, but deep down, she had a good heart. And she would do what was best for her child. That's what I thought then.

I was so naive.

57

low

Freya and the baby came home from the hospital after six days. The baby was healthy—happy and thriving—but the same could not be said for her mother. Freya had been kept in for a few extra days due to a minor infection. When she returned home, she was exhausted and glum. She was struggling to breastfeed and resented the enthusiastic lecture about its benefits that the nurses had given her prior to release.

"Fucking nosy do-gooders," she snarled, as I bounced the hungry baby and Max prepared a bottle of formula.

"My mom breastfed all her kids for way too long," I quipped. "She used to meet Leonard at recess for a quick top-up."

"I bet her tits are down to her knees," Freya muttered.

Max or I did most of the feedings. Even though she wouldn't breastfeed, the nurses had wanted Freya to bottle-feed her child, said it was important for bonding. But she wasn't interested. Besides, she was usually asleep. She had been through physical turmoil, was recovering from surgery. But when her napping continued into the second week, it seemed a sign of avoidance and apathy. Freya had once mentioned her own mother's postpartum depression, and I wondered if she was following in her maternal footsteps.

"Can you move in?" Max asked me, the weariness of caregiving showing on his face, "As soon as possible."

He needed me. Desperately. I won't pretend I didn't like it. "I'm already here all day," I said, enjoying my power.

"I need you here at night. I'm exhausted."

"My parents won't like it."

"I'll pay you," he said quickly. "How does thirty bucks an hour sound?"

It sounded like more than double the money I made at Jamie's shop. And while being Maggie's nanny was far more onerous than selling knickknacks to tourists, I could handle it short-term. And it would let me live here, with Freya and Max. To entrench myself into their lives and their home. And when Maggie was gone . . . ? Well, by then Freya and I would have reached a new level of intimacy. She would realize she couldn't live without me, and she wouldn't let me leave.

"I'll do it," I said.

Lucky for me, my parents were embroiled in a new drama that had shifted their focus from my role in the Light-Beausoleil household. Vik had met a woman at a silent meditation retreat and invited her to move into his trailer.

"He's disrespecting the basic tenets of our relationship," my mom said. She was sitting in the living room with my dad and a cross-legged Gwen. "Honesty and openness."

"How well can he even know her?" Gwen sniped. "They were silent for most of their relationship."

I heard my dad's voice. "It's new-relationship energy. He's experiencing a desire for monogamy, but he'll soon see that it's not worth sacrificing what we have."

My mom sounded petulant. "He always said he liked living alone, said he wanted his own space. What's so special about this Angela?"

I had just come downstairs with a backpack full of my belongings. I walked into the living room. "It's good to know you're human after all."

My mom glared at me. "What are you talking about, Swallow?"

"You're all jealous," I said. "You feel possessive of Vik and threatened by this Angela person. It's normal. It's human nature."

"No, it isn't!" my dad cried. "Pure love isn't about ownership and control!"

"Monogamy is a societal construct!" Gwen shouted. "It treats women like chattel!"

But my eyes were on my mom, and she was surprisingly quiet. Then she pointed at the backpack looped around my forearm. "Where are you going?"

"I'm moving in with Freya and Max. They need help with the baby."

"You can't *stand* babies."

She was right. And while I pitied baby Maggie, that hadn't changed my feelings toward infants in general. But Freya's daughter would soon be gone, living with her father and Jamie. At least most of the time. And I would be entrenched in Freya's life: her live-in photographer, her social media manager, and her best friend. Maybe even more. . . .

"They're paying me," I explained. "A lot."

The adults shared a look. While they proclaimed to be socialists, they understood the value of a buck.

"Don't be a stranger," my dad said. My mom hugged me and let me walk out the door.

* * *

If I was to be employed as a full-time nanny, I would have to quit my job at Hawking Mercantile. Resigning also gave me the opportunity to check in with Jamie, to ensure that her plans to gain custody of Maggie were progressing. I'd always kept an emotional distance from my boss, but now I needed to connect with her. I needed her to trust me, to see me as her ally. I had been feeding her information via text: informing her of the baby's name (and its link to Max's mother); apprising her that Freya refused to breastfeed; letting her know that Max was struggling, even with my help. But I hadn't seen Jamie in person since that night at the hospital.

I parked directly in front of the store and entered the deserted shop. Jamie was behind the counter, scrolling disinterestedly through her phone. My boss—soon to be former boss—did not look well. Her skin was dull and dry, and there were circles under her eyes. She wasn't sleeping, wasn't taking care of herself. She needed to pull it together. She had a battle ahead of her.

"I'm sorry to see you go," she said, when I told her Max had hired me to help Freya. "How's the baby doing?"

I sighed. "Okay, I guess. Except . . ."

I saw the concern, even fear in her eyes. She hadn't even met the child and she was already fiercely protective. "Except what?"

"Freya wants nothing to do with her. She doesn't feed her, doesn't cuddle her. The only time she ever touches her is when we do a photo session."

"Jesus Christ," Jamie muttered. "What is wrong with her?"

"Not everyone's cut out to be a mother," I said.

"She doesn't have that luxury," Jamie cried. "She has a child who's depending on her." Her face crumpled up and tears filled her eyes. "This could be damaging the baby's development."

I hammered the nail in. "Yeah. She doesn't seem as alert as my brothers were at the same age."

Jamie looked at me intently. I could see her internal deliberations, wondering if she could trust me. "I need you to do me a favor."

"Sure," I said, keenly. "What is it?"

"I ordered a DNA test," she said. "If you'll swab Maggie's cheek, we can prove that she's Brian's child."

"And then what?" I asked, but I knew what. They would take the baby away.

"We'll try to work out some kind of custody arrangement with Freya and Max. We're not trying to take Maggie away from them, but we're her parents, too. We deserve to be a part of her life."

A *big* part, I hoped. "What if they won't be reasonable?"

"Then we'll go to court," Jamie said. "We'll demand visitation rights. We might even sue them for custody."

Now she was talking. "I'll do it," I said, taking the plastic envelope she proffered. And then I smiled.

"I just want the truth to come out. I just want what's best for Maggie."

58

I had ample opportunity to swab the baby's cheek. In fact, once I was settled into the guest room, I spent hour upon hour alone with Maggie. My presence seemed to lift Freya out of her funk somewhat (a sign of her strong feelings toward me, surely), and she rejoined the world of the living. She still slept a lot, but she also went for mani-pedis and massages, and embarked on a series of laser treatments meant to firm sagging skin at the town's only medi-spa. Her demeanor was decidedly improved. Though she still showed little interest in her daughter, she was no longer hostile toward her. She would tousle Maggie's soft blond hair as she passed by, even hold her little hand and marvel at her beauty.

"So pretty," she'd mumble, like her child was an inanimate object, a ruby necklace or a Birkin bag. Then she'd say, "You two have a nice day!" and leave.

Max was slightly more present, but he had returned to his previous habits: kayaking, running, riding his motorcycle . . . Sometimes he was gone for three or four hours, but he always returned and took the baby from me. He would talk to her and cuddle her, playing with this little stranger as if she were his own. But there was a wistful sadness on his face, even as he smiled and gurgled at the pretty child.

I had collected Maggie's DNA quickly and efficiently while Freya was being lasered and Max was on his motorbike. But the tube sat in my bag for over a week. I was eager to deliver it to Jamie, eager for her to prove that Maggie was Brian's baby and take her away. She was a good baby—cheerful and unfussy— but she was still a baby. She still needed constant attention, still pooped, and puked, and screamed when she needed something. But I hadn't had an opportunity to get away from the house.

Since her parents could not be relied upon, I would have to bring Maggie with me. There was a newborn bucket car seat in the garage. I would strap the baby into my truck, load a bag with diapers and bottles and burp cloths and rattles, and then I would text Jamie and arrange a meeting. There was a small picnic area on the north side of the island's only lake. The mosquitoes were bad out there this time of year, so it would be abandoned. It had better be. Because if anyone saw us, if anyone told Freya . . . The thought made my forehead sweat and my bowels loosen.

Freya had warned me about Jamie. "There's something you need to know. . . ."

I knew everything, of course, but I looked at her with wide, innocent eyes, tilting my head like a curious puppy.

"Jamie's got this crazy idea that Maggie should live with her and Brian."

"Oh my god. Why?"

"Because she's delusional. And dangerous. You know she can't get pregnant, so now she's obsessed with my baby. You need to keep Maggie away from her. If she shows up here, call the police. And then call Max and me."

If Freya found out I'd taken the baby anywhere near Jamie, I'd be fired. And kicked out of her home. And banished from her life. And if she found out I provided a sample of her daughter's DNA . . . Well, I wasn't sure what Freya was capable of. I just knew I had to be very careful.

And then, one morning, Freya announced that she was going away.

"Away where?" I demanded. Maggie wasn't even a month old. Freya had only recently started leaving the house. Now she was taking a fucking vacation?

"One of my old friends is having a bachelorette weekend in Sonoma."

"But all your old friends turned on you."

"She's using me to bump up her Insta, but I don't care. I really need a break from all of this."

All of what? I wanted to ask. I did everything around the house and everything for the baby. Freya spent her days getting massages and laser treatments. Now she needed wine tasting and fine dining? But I bit my tongue and fed Maggie a bottle while Freya packed.

Max announced that he would take his wife to the airport on the mainland. "I'll get the last ferry back tonight," he said. "I'll be home by seven."

"Fine," I snapped, unable to keep the hurt out of my voice. I felt abandoned by them both. I felt like the hired help—which technically I was, but not for much longer.

Max didn't seem to notice. "Does Maggie have everything she needs? Diapers? Formula?"

"She'll be fine," I grumbled.

Freya hugged me goodbye at the door, long and tight. "Thanks for taking care of the baby." She released me and held both my hands in hers. "Honestly, Low, if you weren't here supporting me and helping me through all this, I'd probably kill myself."

Max picked up his wife's suitcase. "Don't say that."

She kept her eyes on me. "It's true. I'd throw myself off a cliff into the ocean. I couldn't take it. All the hormones and the baby's crying and neediness. You've saved my life, hon. Literally."

If Max wasn't hovering, watching us, she would have kissed me again. I could feel the energy between us, the pull of attraction. And my resentment melted away in the face of her tribute. How could I be angry when she was articulating every word I needed to hear? I was essential to her survival. She would die without me.

"Have a good trip," I said. She gave me a last, quick hug and they left.

Their absence gave me an opportunity to deliver Maggie's DNA sample to Jamie. I fetched the car seat from the garage and dropped the tube into the diaper bag. Maggie had yet to be taken on an outing, but I was familiar with the backward-facing safety device. I popped her into the seat, adjusted the straps, and installed her in the back seat of my truck. Then I drove to Hawking Mercantile.

The plastic bucket seat bumped against my shin as I walked into the shop. Jamie was with a customer, but her eyes widened when she saw me. Her gaze flitted to the baby, and I saw her swallow. She hurriedly rang up the woman's purchase—one of Freya's bud vases—and expediently wrapped it in natural-colored tissue paper. Jamie's hands were shaking as she handed the brown paper bag to the customer and watched her leave. As soon as the elderly woman had gone, Jamie rushed over to us.

"You came," she said, stating the obvious. But she wasn't looking at me. Her eyes were on the little girl snoozing peacefully on the floor. Jamie knelt down and spoke softly to her.

"Hello, honey." She gently stroked her downy head. "It's so nice to meet you."

Maggie didn't stir, even as Jamie touched her cheeks, her hands, her feet. I could see the emotion in Jamie's eyes, hear it in her voice as she murmured sweet words to the sleeping child. It was getting to be a bit sappy, so I broke in.

"I brought the swab." I reached into the diaper bag and extracting the sample.

Jamie stood. "Thank you. You'll never know what this means to me."

"Don't tell Freya I did this," I said. "Ever."

"I won't. If you promise not to tell Brian."

"Brian?"

"He wants to do everything by the book. He wants to get a lawyer, and go to court, and have a judge demand a paternity test. But I can't wait that long."

"But how will you get his DNA if he's not in on this?"

Jamie gave a sheepish smile. "Deep sleeper. Mouth breather."

She was that determined. That desperate.

"Once Freya sees these results, once she knows *for sure* that Maggie is Brian's child . . . I think she'll be reasonable. All we want is access. We're not trying to steal her away from her mother."

"I hope you're right," I said, hoisting the car seat. "I'd better get Maggie home before she gets hungry."

Jamie walked us to the door. "Thank you for coming. I know you took a big risk."

"Not that big. Freya and Max are out of town."

Her pretty face darkened. "Where are they?"

"Freya's gone to Sonoma for a bachelorette party."

"Are you all right alone with Maggie? Can I help?"

"I'm fine. Max will be back tonight."

I allowed Jamie one last stroke of her husband's baby's soft cheek, and then I left.

Mission accomplished. Now all we had to do was wait.

59

My cell phone rang at 4:45 P.M., as I was picking up burp cloths and rattles and black-and-white infant toys in preparation for Max's return. But his name appeared on my phone screen, sending an ominous wave through me. My intuition told me this was not good news.

"I missed the last ferry," he said. "Traffic was a nightmare."

It could have been worse: a car/boat/plane crash . . . but I was irritated. I'd been anticipating spending the evening alone with Max. Not in a romantic way—I'd long since realized a sexual preference for Freya—but I could have subtly mentioned the benefits of sharing custody with Jamie and Brian, if not handing Maggie over to them altogether. And I needed a respite from the baby. Other than the trip to Jamie's store, it had been another long, dull day of feeding, burping, and changing diapers.

"I'll crash at a hotel tonight," he continued. "And since I'm here . . ."

Shit.

". . . I thought I'd spend the day tomorrow. Catch up with some friends. But I'll be on the evening ferry. For sure."

"Great," I snapped. "Sounds fun. Have a nice time." I hung up the phone and threw a bamboo baby rattle across the room in frustration. It hit the plaster with a clatter and shake, the bulb splitting, spreading tiny beans all over the hardwood floor. Maggie let out a startled squeak from her crib on the other side of the wall. Shit.

Don't wake up. Don't wake up. Don't wake up.

Thankfully, after a few hiccupping coughs, Maggie returned to her slumber, oblivious of my tantrum.

I realized that hunger might be contributing to my sour mood. My last meal had been snatched around eleven as I'd prepared for my trip to Hawking Mercantile. I went into the kitchen, ignoring the dirty dishes littering the counters and filling the sink. A look in the fridge revealed two prepared baby bottles, a jar of pickles, a carton of oat milk, a bag of chia seeds, and a box of greens. The cost of a restaurant delivery this far out of town would be astronomical. My stomach growled angrily, and I felt a surge of desperation. I could make a spinach, pickle, and chia-seed salad, or I could call my mother.

"They left you alone with a two-week-old baby?"

"She's three weeks."

"How can they leave their daughter when she's so tiny? It's not natural."

This was coming from a woman who breastfed a first grader, so I took it with a grain of salt. "Can you bring me some food? I don't want to drag Maggie to the grocery store."

"They left you with nothing to eat? When are they coming back?"

"Can you bring me something or not?" I grumbled.

"I'll send your dad over."

Within the hour, he was there, carrying a ceramic bowl covered in beeswax-coated fabric and warm naan bread wrapped in a tea towel. I could smell curry and cumin and turmeric.

"Brought your favorite."

It was dal, of course, but I wasn't about to complain. "Thanks, Dad." I took the warm container from his hands and hurried into the kitchen for a bowl and spoon. My father trailed after me, taking in the piles of dirty dishes, the mounds of filthy burp cloths, the empty formula containers littering the counter.

"What's that smell?"

My aromatic dinner masked all other odors, but I knew the source. "I haven't had a chance to take the garbage out."

He plugged his nose. "Are there diapers in it?"

I nodded and shrugged.

"Where is it?" he muttered.

"Under the sink."

When he returned from depositing the bag in the outside garbage cans, he said, "Mind if I look around a bit?"

"Sure." I understood his curiosity. This home, despite its chaotic state, was still awe-inspiring.

I ate a third of the lentils and two pieces of naan and put the rest in the fridge. Max had promised to return tomorrow, but I couldn't rely on him. And I didn't want to bother my parents for another food delivery, didn't want to hear them disparage Freya and Max as selfish, irresponsible parents and employers. If I had pickles for breakfast and half the leftover dal for lunch, Max could pick up dinner for us. If he didn't return, I'd finish the dal and naan.

My dad returned to the kitchen. He was holding fragments of the rattle I'd thrown across the room. He didn't ask any questions, just moved to the cupboard under the sink and threw the pieces into the now empty bin.

"It's a stunning house," he said.

"I know."

"Call us if you need any more food."

"I will."

"Or if you just need a break. Or some company."

A lump of self-pity formed in my throat. "Thanks."

He gave my arm an affectionate squeeze and then left.

60

Freya returned looking relaxed, happy, and a little hungover. "God, I needed that," she said, sinking into the white sofa.

"Glad you had fun," I said, only the slightest edge to my voice. I was holding Maggie, jiggling her gently on my shoulder. "We were fine here. Alone."

"Good," she said, oblivious of or ignoring my tone. "I need to do a photo shoot with Maggie."

I had been anticipating this suggestion. Freya had made the critical error of chronicling her wine tasting, her sunbathing, and her culinary adventures on Instagram and YouTube. Some of her followers appreciated her glamorous photos, but others were ruthless.

Leaves her newborn baby to get drunk in wine country. #motheroftheyear

I'm sure the nanny is having a great time right now too.

People this selfish should be sterilized.

These attacks gave me a sense of satisfaction. I wanted Freya to feel guilty for leaving Maggie and me. I wanted her to regret her trip to Sonoma so much that she never left us again. The trolls were saying what I couldn't.

"I thought I might try breastfeeding her," Freya said.

"Really?" I asked. "Do you even have any milk left?"

"It's just for the photo," Freya said. "Even if she won't latch, you can make it look like she's nursing."

The shoot was damage control. Maggie was just a prop.

"Sure," I complied. Because I was invested in Freya's celebrity.

She dragged herself off the sofa. "I need to shower and do my makeup. Make sure Maggie's hungry so she takes the breast."

Two hours later, Freya reappeared looking fresh and natural. Her hair was softly tousled, and you could barely tell that she had used a curling iron. Her face appeared wholesome and makeup-free; I knew it took a lot of skill (and a lot of makeup) to create that look. She wore a white eyelet peasant top: the epitome of demure sexiness.

"Let's do this," she said, lifting Maggie from the bouncy seat that kept her placid. It was the first time she had touched her daughter since her return.

"Support her head," I said automatically.

Freya gave the child a cuddle and a kiss and then said, "I don't like her outfit. Does she have anything white?"

White was a highly impractical color for a onesie, but I recalled seeing a summery dress in the nursery. "I think so."

"Actually, maybe she should be naked. Skin on skin is good for kids, right?"

"Right."

Freya lay the baby down and unbuttoned her onesie. I stood by with my camera, watching the businesslike precision with which Freya undressed her tiny daughter. Then she yanked down her top, exposing her perfect, non-lactating breast. She picked up the baby and pressed her face toward it.

Maggie had always been bottle-fed. She had not even taken to the pacifier that I'd offered her numerous times. So the human nipple Freya was now waving in her face was not of interest. I took a few shots, but the baby turned her head away, squirming in her mother's arms.

"Come on, Maggie," Freya cajoled, "take it."

But Maggie let out a squawk of defiance, her little body stiffening with irritation. As I pressed the shutter button, Freya tightened her grip, pressing the back of the baby's head toward her breast. "Do it, you little brat."

And then, she *shook* her.

It was a small movement, not enough to seriously hurt Maggie, but it was rough. And it was scary. Maggie let out a piercing scream of shock and distress, and something surged in me. A mother-bear protectiveness. I suppose it's natural that I would have developed a bond with the baby after our many hours together, but the visceral reaction took me by surprise. I dropped my camera onto the armchair.

"Give her to me."

"No," Freya snapped, clutching the little body now racked with sobs. "Just take the fucking picture."

"Let me calm her down first."

"I'll put a blanket over her. No one will know she's upset."

"No."

"Do it," she commanded, her eyes flaming at me. "Or I'll find another photographer. And another nanny."

It was an ultimatum. Comforting Maggie could get me banished from her life. And Freya's life. Though the child's anguish tore at my heart, I reached for my camera. Then the doorbell rang.

We both froze. Only Maggie kept wriggling and screeching. My eyes met Freya's ice-blue gaze, and I saw the same dread I felt. There was no way of knowing who was at the door, but somehow, we knew it was trouble.

61

The woman on the doorstep appeared only a few years older than I was, but she wore a cheap pantsuit and a severe bun, clearly an effort to be taken seriously. She held a briefcase in her hand, an old-timey rectangular one. She was even smaller than Freya, who was now standing in the open door, facing her.

"Freya Light?" she asked over Maggie's continued screams. I bounced her gently and made shushing noises in her ear, but she was too traumatized to settle. We were standing several feet behind Freya, lurking in the foyer. She had dispatched Maggie and me to the nursery, but I had disobeyed her. I had to know who was at the door and what was going on.

"Yes," Freya answered, her tone hostile.

"My name is Britney Chin. I'm with the Hawking branch of Child Protective Services."

My stomach lurched. CPS had never checked on my younger brothers. This was not just a routine visit. Britney elaborated.

"We've had a call from someone who is concerned about your child's welfare."

"Who was it?" Freya snapped, which was probably the wrong response.

"That information is strictly confidential," the young woman replied, and I could tell that this was exciting for her, possibly even her first case. Her enthusiasm did not bode well. "May I come in?"

Freya said nothing but stepped back to allow the petite CPS worker inside. It was too late to duck into another room; that would have looked guilty. But Maggie was still sobbing, was wearing only a diaper in the spring chill, was covered in tears and snot and drool. The woman took us in.

"And you are?"

"She's the nanny," Freya answered. "My husband and I are with the baby most of the time, but we have some professional obligations. We wanted to make sure all of Maggie's needs are met."

"Why isn't she dressed?"

Again, Freya responded. "We were changing her when the doorbell rang."

"She's very upset," Britney observed.

I took this one. "Colic," I said.

This seemed to satisfy Ms. Chin, and she moved into the kitchen. Luckily, Max had done the dishes and stocked the fridge upon his return. She'd find nothing incriminating there. Freya trailed after her, snarling at me as she passed. "Get Maggie dressed and calm her down."

I took the baby back to the living room, where her onesie was discarded on a chair. Dressing her would set her off again, so I swaddled her tightly in a blanket, and bounced her on my shoulder. Over her dwindling snivels, I could hear Freya and Britney moving to the main-floor nursery. After several minutes there, they climbed the stairs to the upstairs bedrooms. I had snooped through Freya and Max's master bedroom on more than one occasion. It was simply too tempting when I was left to my own devices. There was a lot of lingerie, a few run-of-the-mill sex toys, but nothing that would condemn them as parents.

And then, they were headed to my basement quarters. My heart pounded against Maggie's little body as I heard Freya and Britney descending the stairs. It was a disaster in there. I never made my bed or picked up my dirty clothes. But it wasn't embarrassment that had me trembling, it was fear. Because I had things to hide. Serious things.

There was a small bag of weed, but it was concealed in a rolled-up pair of wool socks, buried deep in a drawer. I wasn't a big stoner but sometimes a toke helped me through a long, dull day of babysitting. There was a lighter and rolling papers, too, but they were also well hidden. If discovered, they would be damaging. They might even get me fired. But if they found the photographs, my entire world would come crashing down around me.

Most of them were on my phone, and I was pretty sure Britney Chin did not have the authority to make me enter my passcode so she could search the device. But I had asked Thompson to print a copy of each photo, so I could hold them, touch them, stroke them. He had complied, handing them over to me with a disturbed look on his face. Under my mattress were five four-by-six photographs of Freya and Max making love on the living room floor. No . . . they weren't making love. It was too intense, angry, and violent to be called that. They were photos of them *fucking* while Freya periodically hit, bit, and scratched him.

I'm not a voyeuristic perv; the photo shoot was not pre-meditated. I had been roused from a deep slumber by thumps and bangs and Freya's angry shrieks. I'd considered ignoring the cacophony. They wouldn't thank me for my interference if it was just another squabble like last time. But something—concern or curiosity—had drawn me out of bed and up the stairs. By then, the cries had ceased, morphed into gasps and moans, the thumps into a rhythmic knocking. What I saw from my vantage point on the second-top step was rough and wrong . . . and so hot.

I'd had my phone in my hand—I must have grabbed it on autopilot in case I needed the flashlight app. Crouching lower on the stairs, I took a video of the action, and several still shots. It was for my viewing pleasure . . . for flexing my recently discovered sexuality muscle. And it was collateral. If things went wrong with Freya again, if she tried to boot me from her universe, I would have ammunition.

But if Britney Chin found the photos under the mattress, all hell would break loose. Was rough-sex porn starring a baby's parents grounds for the child's removal? What if the rough sex porn had been secretly documented by the nanny? Did that make it better or worse? I didn't know. But I knew that Freya would fire me. I knew she'd find my phone on the dresser and she would smash it, drown it, destroy the evidence. She'd come for my camera, too. It was still on the chair, and I scooped it up by the strap. But I couldn't protect it and hold Maggie at the same time. I waited, my heart in my throat, for Freya's angry voice. And then I heard their feet coming up the stairs.

The women entered the room and, while their expressions were grim, it was clear they had not found the photos or the marijuana. Britney strode purposefully into the living area, the last unexplored space. Maggie was dozing now, exhausted from her previous outburst, and I breathed a sigh of relief. The CPS worker scoured the room, but I knew we were in the clear.

"What is this?" Britney asked. She was holding a handful of tiny pellets.

"I—I don't know," Freya stammered.

"A rattle broke," I said quickly, hoping they wouldn't ask me to explain how. "I was going to vacuum."

"This should have been cleaned up immediately," Ms. Chin remarked. "They're a choking hazard."

"The baby can't even crawl," Freya said, with a roll of her eyes. "How would she get one into her mouth?"

Britney seemed mildly flustered. "You haven't done any baby proofing."

"We will," I said quickly. "In the next couple of weeks."

The tiny woman consulted her clipboard. "I'll check back in fourteen business days to see that you have." Then she looked up at us. "I'll have to file a report when I get back to the office, but I don't see anything here of grave concern." She almost sounded disappointed.

Freya escorted her to the door, closing it behind her with a resounding slam. When she returned to the living room, her eyes were dark with anger.

"Who the fuck called CPS?"

"I don't know." It was the truth, but I felt caught out. "Maybe some online troll?"

"Child Protection wouldn't send someone out because I went on a fucking vacation," she growled. "It was Jamie. It has to be."

It made sense. She was the only one with motive.

"Did you tell her I was a bad mother?" Freya asked.

"Of course not!" I cried, my voice trembling with fear. "I would never say anything bad about you, Freya. You're a great mom. Maggie loves you. You're just settling into it, getting used to it."

But she was no longer listening to me. She collected her car keys off the side table and stalked out of the house.

62

jamie

Hawking Mercantile had returned to summer opening hours. It was only spring, but I felt hopeful that business would pick up with the warmer weather. And I wanted to work six days a week, wanted to stay at the store until five thirty on weekdays, seven on Fridays and Saturdays. Staying busy distracted me from waiting for the DNA results, worrying about Maggie's well-being, and the dull ache of guilt I felt for lying to my husband. Again.

Brian still insisted on going through the proper channels in our fight for access to Maggie. He still maintained that we would find the money to pay the lawyer, to travel to the city as often as necessary, to go to court when and if we needed to. We'd had a telephone consultation with a lawyer in the city named Julian Walsh. Speaking at the speed of an auctioneer (Mr. Walsh charged in fifteen-minute increments), Brian explained that Freya was keeping his child from him. The attorney had affirmed for us that the first step was proof of paternity. We were to provide an affidavit—basically a numbered statement of facts pertaining to the case that we would take to Nancy Willfollow for witnessing.

We would then submit it to Julian Walsh, who would file it with the court.

"You might not even need to attend," he told us, and my husband and I had shared a hopeful smile. If our evidence was sufficient, the court would compel Freya to provide Maggie's DNA for testing.

But that could take months. And then, once we'd proven that Maggie was Brian's daughter, there would be another court hearing to determine visitation. By the time we had access to our child (yes, I thought of her as *ours* now), she could be two years old.

I was going to circumvent the whole process. One night last week, as my husband snored after half a bottle of red wine, I had swabbed his cheek. Low had provided Maggie's sample, and I had mailed them off immediately. The kit said four to six weeks—an eternity—but when the results came back, I would take them to Freya. And we would work everything out.

I couldn't forget how Freya had admired Low's family's dynamics, their honesty and openness. It might have been scandalous in more conservative communities, but two couples coparenting would not be a big deal in Hawking. Once Freya was presented with irrefutable proof of Maggie's paternity, she would let us into the child's life. Maggie could have two homes, two moms who dropped her at school, two dads who alternated soccer and dance practice.

I won't pretend that I didn't envision a premier role in our daughter's life. Brian and I had always wanted to be parents, we were born to raise children. Freya and Max simply weren't cut out for it. They wouldn't remember Maggie's pediatrician and dentist appointments, wouldn't limit her screen time, or ensure she got enough vitamin D. When she got older, they'd forget to pack her school lunch, ignore her homework assignments, skip parent-teacher interviews. Maggie needed us, too.

It was quiet that afternoon, a Tuesday. I was preparing an ad for the Hawking Exchange—the island's version of Craigslist—to replace Low. Without help, I would struggle with the tourist-season rush. It would be months before the store got busy, but I knew from experience that it would not be easy to find another shop assistant. There were not a lot of teens like Low Morrison, content with a slower-paced job that was really 80 percent dusting. My thoughts drifted to the odd, taciturn teen who had spent nine months in my employ. I missed her, in a way. Maybe I didn't *miss* her. Maybe I was just grateful that she had swabbed Maggie's cheek for me, had slipped away to deliver the sample, had fed me information about Freya's lackluster parenting. Low was on my side in this battle. I didn't know why, but I thanked her for it.

And she was caring for Maggie. While the tall, angular girl wasn't warm or nurturing, she was competent. She had three younger siblings, so she knew the baby drill. She knew when to feed Maggie, when to change her and put her down for a nap. Freya was clueless. And selfish. The child would be in jeopardy if not for Low's capable presence.

The bell above the door jingled then, and I closed my laptop anticipating a customer. But it wasn't a patron. It was a seething ball of fury with pale-blond hair and a pristine white outfit. It was Freya, and something had enraged her.

"You fucking cunt."

I was rendered speechless by the venom and vulgarity. Had Low told her that I'd submitted Maggie's DNA sample? But Low couldn't have outed me without revealing her own complicity. Could Freya have discovered it some other way?

"Your plan backfired," she sneered at me. "They found *nothing of concern.*"

A moment of relief was chased away by confusion. "I don't know what you're talking about, Freya."

"You called Child Protection Services on me."

"No, I didn't."

"You're delusional, Jamie. You know, that right? The fact that you're barren has fucked with your head."

Anger heated my belly. "I didn't call them," I snapped. "I guess someone else knows you're a terrible mother."

She came at me then, and I thought she was going to attack me, but she stopped just short of where I stood. "You and Brian will never get near my daughter," she spat. "You will never be her mother."

"Maggie is Brian's child! He has a right to be in her life!"

Freya stepped back and I thought I sensed the slightest softening, a receptivity in her posture.

"We were friends once," I tried, my voice gentler. "I—I loved you like a sister. We can work this out. For Maggie's sake."

She cocked her head slightly to the side. "Why would I want someone like *you* in my daughter's life? You're so basic. And boring. You've wallowed in self-pity for so long that you've lost any semblance of a personality. You're pitiful."

"At least I'm not a narcissist," I shot back. "At least I'm not so shallow that I crave the constant validation of a bunch of online strangers."

She smiled then, a mirthless grin, and narrowed her eyes at me. I hadn't thought my rebuttal through, and I felt a sudden flicker of panic. And fear.

Freya's tone, unlike her words, was calm and casual. "Even if you prove that Maggie is Brian's, even if the courts take your side,

I'll run. I'll take Maggie and I'll disappear. I'll take her and I'll drive off a cliff. You will never, *ever* be a part of her life."

It was an admission. She knew the truth. But Freya would fight us till the end. She was unhinged, suffering from postpartum depression, even psychosis. I had to get the baby away from her. She wasn't safe.

The bell jingled as Freya stormed out of my store.

63

low

Max returned to the house about an hour after the woman from CPS had left. He'd been windsurfing. Or kayaking . . . some water sport that had wet his dark hair with salt spray. He wore a tank top and board shorts. He looked like he'd just walked off some Hunks of Summer calendar, but I barely noticed.

"Hey," he mumbled, his eyes scanning the rooms for his wife and her daughter, and finding only me, seated at the dining table. "Where is everyone?"

"A woman came," I said, swallowing the dread that was clogging my throat, "from Child Protection. Freya thinks Jamie called her. I think she went to the store to confront her."

Max's face darkened. "Where's the baby?"

"Asleep in her crib."

He ran his hands through his damp hair, making his biceps bulge. "Should I go after her?"

"Yes!" I cried. "What if Freya does something to Jamie? Beats her up or something? She was so angry. . . ."

"She'd never attack Jamie."

How could he be so confident when he knew, better than anyone, Freya's violent side?

"She might smash up the store," I said. "She could get arrested! CPS could take Maggie!"

A few weeks ago, this option might have suited me fine, but I'd grown to care for the little creature. I didn't want to look after her 24-7, but I didn't want her in the system. Hawking probably didn't even have a system. They'd send Maggie to the city, where she'd get swallowed up by the foster care behemoth. She belonged with her father and Jamie.

"Shit . . . ," Max muttered and moved toward the side table and his car keys.

But the sound of an SUV pulling up out front stopped him in his tracks. A car door slammed, and small feet crunched across the gravel toward the door. My heart thudded in my chest. Freya was back.

A gust of angry energy preceded her into the home. The confrontation had not diffused her rage. Had Jamie admitted to calling CPS? Or denied it? Which would add more fuel to Freya's fire?

She spoke to Max first. "Child Protection Services was here."

"Low told me."

"Jamie swears she didn't call them," she said, tossing her keys on the table. "I believe her. She's too bland to lie convincingly."

"Then who called?" Max asked.

"I don't know. But it doesn't matter because we're leaving. It was a mistake to move here in the first place, and now everything is totally fucked-up."

"Where are we going?" Max said to her departing back as she moved to the kitchen.

We both trailed after her.

"We'll go back to LA," she said, flicking on the coffee machine. "You know I've been thinking about it for months. This thing with CPS was the last fucking straw."

"It's not that simple," he said, as she rummaged in the fridge. "We'd have to sell the house. In this market, that could take months. Even years. And we won't get much bang for our buck in LA."

Freya emerged with a carton of oat milk. "I don't care if we live in a dumpster in LA. I'm not raising my daughter in this hillbilly backwater."

I had stood by, listening in mute horror, but I stepped forward then. "You can't leave."

It was clear from the look on Freya's face that she had forgotten I was there. "This doesn't concern you, Low. Go home."

"I live here."

"Not anymore." She poured the nondairy beverage into a mug and slammed it into the microwave. "We won't be needing your services."

"You can't just . . . let me go."

"We'll pay you two weeks' severance," Max mumbled.

But this wasn't about money. "I'll go with you," I suggested. "I hate it here, too. I can look after Maggie in LA."

"You wouldn't fit in there. You're too . . ." Freya's eyes roved over me and I steeled myself for an unkind assessment. But she said, "You're an island girl. This is where you belong."

The microwave dinged, and she turned away from me. If she had thrown scalding oat milk in my face it would have hurt less.

"Maggie needs me," I countered. "We've bonded." I swallowed my fear and added, "She barely knows you."

Freya set down her coffee mug and turned to face me. "*You* called CPS."

"What?" My face blanched, which I feared would read as guilt. "No."

An incredulous laugh erupted from her. "Are you jealous of my baby daughter, Low? Are you trying to get rid of her so you can have me all to yourself?"

Now my face was burning, and I knew my cheeks were fuchsia. Freya was onto me. She had read my thoughts and emotions. But I had not made that call.

Max addressed his wife. "Stop."

But she didn't stop. She kept coming at me. "You're obsessed with me, aren't you, Low? And Max, too. You've got some deluded fantasy that we're soul mates. That we're in *love*."

"I don't."

"Do you watch us fucking? Do you take pictures of us and then masturbate to them?"

"Jesus Christ, Freya," Max said.

But she knew. She knew about the photographs hidden in my bedroom. Had she seen them? Or could she simply sense my lust, my fascination?

Freya almost smiled as she watched me grapple with her accusations. And then she narrowed her eyes at me. "Pack your shit and go home to your sex cult."

Obediently, I hurried from the room.

64

It didn't take me long to gather my belongings. I'd been living there less than a month and had been too busy with the baby to really make myself at home. I shoved my clothes, my bag of weed, and a few trinkets into the backpack. And then I reached under the mattress for the photographs. I'd intended to use them in an instance exactly like this.

Take me to LA with you or I'll post these online!

But I couldn't do it. I couldn't give her the satisfaction of knowing she was right about me: I was a voyeur and a pervert. I grabbed the photos and stuffed them into my bag.

Lugging my backpack up the stairs, I moved to the living room to collect my camera from the low teak coffee table. Had the breastfeeding photo shoot really been this morning? It felt like an eternity ago. I could hear Freya and Max arguing.

"You're upset. You're not thinking this through."

"You didn't think it through when you moved us to this island full of freaks and losers!"

I drove home in a fog. I was losing her. Them. Forever. It couldn't be real. Maybe I was in shock because the next thing I knew, I was parked in my driveway. My dad and my brothers were chopping kindling. My mom was pushing Eckhart on a rickety swing. I slowly got out of the truck with my backpack.

"Low!" Wayne ran over to me and wrapped his arms around my waist. "You came home."

His words were a punch in the gut. I didn't want this to be my home.

My mom approached, "Are you okay?"

I didn't want to tell her; she wouldn't understand. But the words fell from my lips. "Someone called Child Protection Services about Maggie. Freya thinks it was me."

"I'm sorry," my mom said, reaching out to stroke my arm. "But it's for the best."

"How is it for the best?" I snapped.

"What matters is that the baby is safe and well cared for."

"She is safe. I was caring for her."

My dad had joined us by then, the hatchet still in his hand. "I didn't like what I saw when I brought you the dal. You were in over your head."

"*You* called CPS?" I shrieked. "I was fine! I was happy! How could you do this to me?"

My mom sounded stern. "We did this *for* you, Swallow. A teenaged girl is not equipped to look after an infant on her own for days on end. It's too much."

"We were looking out for the child," my dad added. "She's what really matters in this situation."

"*I'm* what matters. Me!" I shrieked. "You've never cared about me! You've never put me first!"

"Stop being so melodramatic," my dad said, but I was already storming toward my truck.

"Come back here and talk about this," my mom called after me. But I slammed the vehicle door and backed out of the driveway, narrowly missing the goat.

65

My first instinct was to drive back to the Light-Beausoleil household and profess my innocence. But in a way, it was still my fault that CPS had been called to check on Maggie. I had complained about being hungry and alone; I had asked my parents for help. If I'd just eaten those fucking chia seeds, everything would be fine right now.

I drove around for almost an hour, despondency seeping into the marrow of my bones. There seemed no way forward for me, and no way back. Freya was leaving. She blamed me for all her problems. I couldn't follow her to LA, but I couldn't imagine staying here without her. And I was not going back to my family, who had betrayed me.

My aimless route took me to the interior of the island, and I found myself approaching Hyak Canyon. A drastic, devastating plan began to take shape in my mind. I pulled into the canyon's empty parking lot and up to the guardrail. My truck idling, I envisioned crashing through the barrier and hurtling over the edge. It was a deep gully and more than one careless or drunk driver had plunged to their death. If I did it now, before Freya left for LA, she'd hear about my tragic demise and regret her treatment of me. She'd weep at my memorial service, might even make a speech. After the cremation, she'd take some of my ashes to LA with her and throw them off the Santa Monica Pier. Better yet, she'd wear them in a locket around her neck. Forever.

They say suicide is a coward's way out, but I beg to differ. Maybe it depends on the method. Plummeting to the bottom of the canyon, while tragically poetic, was also terrifying. What if I didn't die instantly? What if I lay at the bottom of the canyon, badly injured, for days? Thirsty and bleeding and alone? Who would find me? And how? I'd told no one where I was going. My parents would think I'd gone back to Freya's. Freya thought I'd gone home. No one would search for me. No one cared.

I needed courage to go through with this . . . liquid courage.

Thompson Ingleby lived nearby. I had never been to his house, but he'd described the location, its proximity to the canyon. And he'd mentioned the distinctive train car that sat in their front yard, heavily graffitied by his older brother and his friends. Pulling back onto the road, I drove north for less than five minutes before their homestead came into view. Among the broken-down cars, trucks, and tractors was the train car, GRAD 2017 and FUCK OFF prominently tagged on its side. Nice touch.

As I drove down the rutted drive, I was greeted by two large barking dogs, intent on eating my tires. Hopefully Thompson would emerge and shepherd me inside. Being torn apart by snarling mongrels was not the way I wanted to go out. I stopped my truck but kept it running while I waited for rescue.

A short, sinewy man in a dirty white undershirt walked onto the porch and glowered at me. He had a pistol in the waistband of his filthy jeans, and his hand rested on it, anticipating trouble. When he saw the tall, pale kid in his driveway, he whistled through two fingers and the dogs obediently galloped to his side. He disappeared back into the house with the animals, and moments later, Thompson came out. I turned off the ignition and opened the car door.

"Hi." Thompson couldn't hide his delight. "This is a nice surprise."

"I came for a drink," I said. "Can you get some of that grain alcohol?"

"Umm . . . sure." He glanced over his shoulder. I could tell he didn't want me to go inside his house. Neither did I. "I'll get it and we can go down to the barn."

Ten minutes later, we were perched on sawhorses in a dilapidated building cluttered with farming equipment, car parts, and empty beer cans. Thompson handed me a jar half filled with a cloudy liquid. The smell made my eyes water.

"Cheers," he said, clinking his jar to mine. We drank then and both shuddered at the taste. The alcohol burned in my throat, chest, and stomach, but I felt myself relaxing, the anxiety seeping out of me. I hadn't eaten since breakfast, the day's dramatic events tying my guts in knots. The strong alcohol on an empty stomach hit me hard. After a few more gulps, my loss and sadness became more profound, more painful. I resigned myself to my tragic fate.

We drank in silence, Thompson matching me sip for sip. I had a reason to be getting wasted at six in the evening, but Thompson was being chivalrous again. I guess he didn't want me to drink alone. Soon, I felt ready to execute my plan. And if I drank much more, I wouldn't be able to pilot my truck back to the canyon. Setting my jar down on the concrete floor, I turned to say goodbyes.

"I think I know why you came here," Thompson said, his face pink, very pink. "We've been friends for a few months now. The chemistry has always been there, but it's been building." He was slurring slightly from the booze. "I don't think either one us can ignore it anymore."

Oh no.

He was leaning in, his straggly soul-patch whiskers straining toward me. He was going to kiss me! I would have considered it four years and six inches ago, but not now. No. No way. I shoved him in the chest.

"Back off."

He looked genuinely shocked. "But I thought . . ."

"No," I said firmly. "There is nothing between us. I'm in love with someone else."

At first, he appeared confused, like I'd spoken the words in Cantonese. But then his expression darkened. "Is it Max? Or is it Freya?"

I may as well tell him. It would all come out when I was dead. "It's Freya."

He shook his head sadly. "You worship her and adore her and do everything for her. But she doesn't care about you at all. That's not love, Low. That's obsession."

"You don't get it. You don't know what we have."

"You're her nanny. She pays you."

"Fuck you," I muttered. "What would a short little dweeb like you know about love anyway?" The comment may have been unnecessary, but it hammered the message home.

Thompson jumped off the sawhorse. "I'm not sure our friendship is such a good idea anymore."

"Probably not."

He pressed his lips together like he was keeping some cruel, hurtful words inside. And maybe he was. Finally, he mumbled, "Let yourself out." And he hurried out of the barn.

Drunk and alone in the filthy chaotic workshop, I felt a lump of anguish crushing my chest. I'd had one person who cared about me, one person who saw something beautiful in me, and now he hated me. But, like everyone else, Thompson would be better off without me. And that made what I was about to do easier . . . emotionally at least. I was still afraid of dying a slow and painful death. Or surviving with permanent, debilitating injuries. But there was no other way.

And then, like a sign from above—or maybe below—I saw it. Tossed carelessly on the workbench, barely visible in the clutter of tools and beer cans and carburetor parts, was a handgun.

It was not unusual for the island's rural homesteads to have a weapon. There were numerous critters that could get into crops, build dens under houses, eat through sacks of grain. And if Thompson's family really was smuggling cigarettes/cooking meth/growing illegal weed as was rumored, they'd have even more need for protection. My pacifist family didn't have one, but I wasn't daunted by it. I had watched enough TV to know how a pistol worked. I picked up the gun and found it loaded with two bullets.

I only needed one.

66

max

Freya had been making a show of packing since Low stormed out of the house. She was throwing things into the cardboard boxes we'd kept in the garage after we moved in. She was drinking, too: vodka on the rocks. I'd lost count of how many times she'd refilled her glass, but I could tell by her unsteady movements, that she was getting drunk. I'd given Maggie her bottle and her bath and settled her down for the evening. When I returned to the kitchen with the baby monitor in my back pocket, I found my wife on the phone.

"It's just until we get set up," she said, overarticulating each word to hide her inebriation. "A month . . . two at the most." There was a pause as she listened, sipping her drink. "The baby won't be a problem. I'll hire a nanny." After a moment she snapped, "Yeah, it's three adults and a baby. It's not like you don't have the fucking room."

It had to be Freya's dad in LA on the line. The conversation wasn't going well.

"Your new wife can kiss my ass," Freya growled. "You know she's only after your money, you stupid old fart." She hung up and threw the phone across the room.

I knew not to engage with Freya when she was in this state. She would be irrational, easily enraged, and cruel. My best strategy would be to slip out of the room, to hide myself away until she passed out. Before Maggie, I used to let Freya take her anger out on me. It became a sick sort of release, a toxic, sexual game. But since the baby had been born, I wasn't into it. Only once, since we'd brought our daughter home, had I let Freya attack me, had we ended up having sex on the living room floor. That time, with a child slumbering in the next room, it had felt wrong.

I turned to go, but I was too late. "That was my dad."

I turned back. "I figured."

"He doesn't want us to stay with him. Not with the baby."

"We'll figure something out."

She sipped her drink. "This is your fault, you know. All of it."

"Okay."

"Okay?" She laughed and moved toward me. "You destroy my fucking life, and all you can say is *okay*?"

"Sorry."

"Apology *not* accepted." She smacked me then, upside the head. "I hate you!"

I stepped back, my head stinging. "You're going to wake the baby."

"Fuck the baby!" *Smack.* "I hate the baby!" *Smack.* "I hate my life!"

Her blows were harder than usual, her drunken rage improving her strength.

"Stop," I said.

"You love this, you sick fuck."

"I don't," I said, holding an arm up to fend off her blows. "Not anymore."

"You don't get to end this game," she growled, reaching into a box filled with tools I had kept in the kitchen pantry for unexpected repairs. She withdrew a claw hammer. "*I* end it."

If I had known what she was going to do, I'd have defended myself. I was twice her size, after all. But the hammer took me by surprise. Freya could be cruel and violent; she'd utilized a weapon before. But it had always been something fairly benign, like a plate or a wine bottle. Once, she had stabbed me in the chest with a fork. A hammer was different. A hammer was potentially lethal. And I didn't think she was capable of murdering me. Not until I saw her eyes, dark and empty. Not until I saw her swing the hammer at my head with all the force in her body.

At first, I felt nothing, just a loud, shrill ringing in my ears. The pain came a few seconds later, sharp and pulsing. I'd suffered numerous head injuries, but this was different. This was critical. My vision blurred, and then everything started to go black. It was blood, pouring into my eyes from the wound above my temple. And it was darkness closing in on me, taking me under, snuffing out my life. The last thing I saw was Freya's beautiful face, contorted by rage, hate, and alcohol.

It was the last time I would ever see it.

67

low

My truck rattled along the winding road that traversed the northern tip of the island. It was a quieter route, with virtually no traffic. I was too drunk to be driving, and despite my suicidal intentions, I didn't want to take anyone out with me. And I no longer wanted to end it all in a car crash. I had a new plan and it was perfect.

With Thompson's dad's gun, I would shoot myself in front of Freya. Unless she begged me not to. Unless she promised to love me like I needed to be loved. But she wouldn't. She hated me. No, she didn't hate me. She was indifferent to me. That was worse.

Maggie would be asleep, so I didn't have to worry about traumatizing her. If Max was home, he'd be collateral damage. But he had already effectively killed a man. Watching me die would be no worse than that. Perhaps a little messier. I planned to splatter myself all over Freya's bright white sofa. It would serve her right.

I made it to their waterfront home in one piece and parked in the driveway. Ignoring the front door, I stumbled around to the back deck. The sliding glass door would be unlocked, allowing me access. The gun was in my left hand, the hammer cocked, ready to fire. I would draw this out just long enough to see Freya quake and cry, not long enough to change my mind.

But when I yanked open the glass door, I was met with a horrific sight. Max was lying on the floor, his head in a small pool of blood. Freya stood over him, clutching a bloody hammer, trembling with rage, fear, or shock.

"Oh my god," I gasped. "What happened?"

Freya looked up, and her blue eyes looked cold and blank. "Low . . ." was all she said.

"I'll call an ambulance." I tucked the pistol into my waistband and pulled my phone from my pocket.

"It's too late," she said, in the same strange monotone. "He's gone."

"Y-you killed him," I stuttered, looking at the hammer. There was blood on the head, some skin and bits of dark hair.

Freya looked at it like she was seeing it for the first time. And then her eyes met mine. They were still blank and lifeless, but I saw her knuckles turn white as she gripped the hammer tighter, I saw her elbow draw back. Freya had to get rid of me. I knew what she had done.

Despite my suicidal mind-set, I didn't want to be beaten to death with a claw hammer by the object of my thwarted desire. Grabbing the handgun out of my jeans, I pointed it at her.

"Don't come any closer."

The hammer dropped to her side, and her face softened. "I would never hurt you, Low. You know that. . . . I love you."

"Y-you don't."

"Of course I do." Her voice was gentle, almost musical. "We have something special, you and me. We always have. And now, it can just be the two of us. Like you've always wanted."

"Not like this."

"Max would have killed me. I had to defend myself." She set the bloody hammer on the counter. "You knew he was violent and troubled."

The gun wavered in my hand. I lowered it an inch.

"I told him I couldn't leave you. I told him to go without me. But he got so angry."

My head was spinning, the grain alcohol swirling my thoughts. I had wanted to be with Freya, but I couldn't ignore Max's dead body on the floor. But if it had been self-defense . . .

"I didn't want it to be like this, hon, but maybe it's for the best. Now, we can go to LA. We can build an amazing life together, as partners, and best friends. Maybe more . . ." She still wore the white top she'd donned for our morning photo shoot, but there was a light spray of blood across the chest. And yet, she still looked beautiful despite her husband's body at her feet. "That is . . . if you still want me."

I did. Of course I did. But Max . . .

"Help me carry him to the kiln." Freya had clearly thought this through. "We'll say he took the boat out and never came back. No one will miss him. There'll be no evidence."

Could I do this? For a life with Freya, could I incinerate Max's body?

"We'll get a house on the beach," she said, moving toward me. "Just the two of us. It will be everything you ever wanted." She was almost on me, her lips slightly parted. She was going to kiss me again. I would be firmly under her spell.

And then, from under Max's body, I heard a squawk. It was Maggie's voice coming through the monitor, reminding us that she was there. That she was a part of this. That it would never be just Freya and me.

Freya's eyes bore into mine, and she smiled, a very small, very cold smile. She grabbed the hammer and moved toward the nursery.

"Stop!" I yelled. At least I think I did; the word may have been screamed in my head only because it had no effect on Freya. She kept stalking toward Maggie, the bloody hammer in her hand.

And so I shot her. I had no choice.

68

If I'd had two dead bodies to deal with, this story would have a very different ending. But Max was still alive . . . unconscious but alive. It would take more than a hammer to the temple to take out a man who'd already endured so much abuse. His breath was shallow and raspy, but it was regular. He would wake up soon. I had to act fast.

Freya lay in a crumpled heap at the entry to the hall. The bullet had entered her back and lodged in her heart, killing her instantly. There was almost no blood; she had bled out internally. Even in death, Freya was perfect and pristine.

First, I had to attend to Maggie. The gunshot had startled her, and she was sobbing uncontrollably. Her wails came in stereo: from the monitor under Max's body, and directly from the nursery. With the gun in my waistband, I hurried to her, picked her up, and rocked her gently. My presence calmed her, and soon enough, she nuzzled into my neck and fell asleep. I placed her tenderly back in her crib. Then I went to dispose of her mother's body.

With an eye on Max, I pocketed the shell casing and wiped up the tiny pool of Freya's blood with a paper towel. I was entirely sober now, adrenaline coursing through my system, allowing me to do what had to be done. I scooped Freya into my arms and carried her to the studio. She was such a tiny woman, but she felt remarkably heavy. I stumbled inside and went straight to the kiln room with my lifeless cargo, setting her down on the concrete floor. Freya had taught me to fire the gas kiln. It was not as simple as an electric kiln, but she insisted the results were better, especially when doing salt or soda firing. With the shelves removed, the receptacle was the perfect size for my petite victim. Max would have required dismembering; I shuddered at the thought.

I took the diamond rings from Freya's fingers, the phone from her pocket, and placed her gently inside. Then I sealed the kiln and cranked the heat to the max, cone 10. Eventually it would reach 2,300 degrees Fahrenheit, significantly hotter than a cremation oven. Within a few hours, all that would be left of the gorgeous woman who had hurt so many people, who'd destroyed so many lives, would be a dusting of ash.

A wave of nausea hit me then, and I hurried outside to vomit behind a juniper bush. Tears streamed down my cheeks, but there was no time to fall apart. Wiping my mouth on my sleeve, I went back to the studio to turn off the lights and close the door. Freya had always insisted that all firings be monitored; gas kilns could be dangerous. But I couldn't hang around, for obvious reasons. And the top of the line appliance had a thermocouple safety shut-off valve that would kick in eventually. I crept up to the house and peered through a kitchen window. Max was awake now, sitting on the floor with his head in his hands. He had been out for over fifteen minutes; this could be a serious brain injury. But if anyone knew how to deal with a concussion, it was Max.

He'd call paramedics if he needed them. He'd summon me to
look after Maggie, if he couldn't cope. And he would wonder
where his wife went.

But he would never know the truth. No one would.

So why didn't I call the police? Why didn't I tell them I'd shot
Freya to protect Maggie? Because they wouldn't have believed
me. When the cops interviewed my parents, they would have
told them about my "inappropriate" friendship, their sexual concerns. Thompson would have told them I was obsessed with
Freya, distraught because she wouldn't love me back. I had gone
to her house drunk and with a loaded gun.

And who would believe that a woman would murder her
own baby with a hammer?

Nobody.

69

jamie

As I did every morning, I poured a cup of coffee, sat at the kitchen table, and looked at Freya's Instagram. It was an exercise in torture: seeing my former best friend on her trip to wine country, looking gorgeous on her oceanside deck, snuggling with her adorable daughter. It made me feel sick, sad, and jealous. But it was the only way I could catch a glimpse of Maggie, to ensure that she was safe and thriving. Our pricey lawyer had instructed us to stay away from the trio while our petition for a paternity test traveled through the courts. Low had not fed me any information for a few days, and I was still waiting for the results from the secret DNA test. Social media was my only connection to our child.

Freya's post, that morning, was a photo of her with the baby. But this image was different than the rest. Maggie, wearing only a diaper, appeared to be screaming. Freya, dressed in a sexy white outfit, was struggling to breastfeed her. Her expression was overwhelmed, angry, and disappointed, all at once. The caption was long and cryptic.

**You see my photos and you see a beautiful woman
with a beautiful baby and a beautiful home. But you
don't see the loneliness and despair. You don't see the
hurt and sorrow. No one wants to hear about the dark
side of motherhood. No one wants to talk about the
difficulties of bonding with your child, of breastfeeding,
of playing the role of mommy when you don't feel it.
I can't tell anyone about the black thoughts where I
want to hurt my own child, when I want to make her
disappear. And when I say my baby would be better off
without me, no one wants to listen. No one wants to
hear it. But it's the truth. And I will do what is best for
my daughter. Goodbye.**

#postpartumdepression #sacrifice #sorry

I took the phone to Brian's office, where he was working on his latest novel.

He read it, his brow furrowed, then looked up at me. "What does it mean?"

"It's a suicide note," I said, my voice barely a whisper. "I'm sure of it."

"No," he said. "Who would leave a suicide note on Instagram?"

"Lots of people," I said. "Freya."

He knew I was right. I could see it in his eyes.

"I have to call Max," I said. "I have to go over there."

"You can't. Any contact could be seen as harassment. It could be used against us in court."

"But if Freya is dead . . ."

"But if she's not . . ."

Neither of us spoke for a few moments, the weight of what

Freya may have done settling on us. Finally, I said, "Low might know something."

Brian nodded. "It's worth a try."

But Low had been banished, she said, when I phoned her. "I don't know what's going on with her. She wasn't coping. She was freaking out. But when I tried to help her, she sent me away."

"Do you think she would . . . *kill* herself?"

"She talked about it. A lot. I didn't think she really meant it. . . ." I heard Low sigh. "I'll try to talk to Max. I'll keep you posted."

And so, we waited.

"We'll know the truth, soon enough," Brian said. "Small towns like to talk."

But that day passed, with no answers and no whispers. And then another. Low didn't respond to my texts. I didn't reach out to Max. I convinced myself that Freya was fine. Her Instagram post was just a cry for attention. She was being overly dramatic, as was her habit, manipulating people into worrying about her. I screenshotted the post to use as evidence of her instability in our custody fight.

It was on the morning of the third day, when Brian and I were having toast and coffee in our pajamas, that a vehicle crunched down our drive. Visitors to our home were rare in general, and even more rare at 6:45 A.M. We both moved to the front of the house and peered out the window. Crawling toward us was Max's black Range Rover.

My heart was in my throat as I watched the big athlete get out of the vehicle and walk around to the back door. He moved slowly, like he was in pain. Or in mourning. Or both. Reaching into the back, he withdrew a bucket car seat. And in it was our beautiful baby.

"He brought Maggie," I whispered, tears filling my eyes.

"Don't get your hopes up," Brian said, practical and cautious. "We don't know why he's here."

I hung back as Brian opened the door and ushered Max and the baby inside. Max had a bulging diaper bag on his shoulder, and my chest fluttered with hope. There would be no need to pack so much gear for a short visit.

He eschewed pleasantries. "Freya's gone," he said.

Brian's eyes flitted to mine. Then he said, "Gone where?"

"She just disappeared." He swallowed. "The police think she jumped off a cliff into the ocean."

"Oh God," I cried. While I had suspected suicide, hearing it articulated was devastating. Tears pricked my eyes for the loss of the woman I'd once loved, the woman I'd thought was my best friend, the mother of the beautiful little girl before me.

"They've dragged the coastline near our property, but they haven't found her."

Brian said, "Could she have left? Gone back to LA or somewhere else?"

"Her wallet and credit cards are still at the house. Her parents and old contacts haven't heard from her. Only her phone is missing. I don't know if you saw her Instagram post . . ."

"We did," I said. "We've been concerned."

"I would have called you, but the police have been interrogating me." He shifted the car seat into his other hand. "I've been cleared."

Brian and I both nodded. "Good."

Max took a labored breath. "I want Maggie to live with you."

"Really?" I gasped, not sure I could believe my own ears.

"She doesn't belong to me. I know that. And I can't take care of her on my own. She deserves two parents who will love and adore her."

"We will," I said, the tears spilling over. "I promise."

"Thank you," Brian said, clearing the emotion from his throat. "We'll be the best parents we can be."

"I'm moving back up north," Max continued. "I need to be close to my family. I need some quiet. I've put the house on the market, but you can come and get her furniture. We've got everything she needs."

I nodded slightly, but I was too overcome to speak.

"I called my lawyer in the city about custody. Freya named me as the baby's father, so my attorney said a formal adoption will be the easiest. The paperwork shouldn't take too long."

He set down the car seat and knelt to peer in at Maggie. "Have a good life, little one." He stroked her soft cheek with his big fingers.

Maggie gurgled and smiled at him. My heart twisted in my chest.

"She'll be happy here," Max said to us. "This is right." Without looking back, he left.

That's how Maggie became ours. It was an adjustment, at first, but we joyfully made it. I cared for her in the mornings while Brian wrote. When I opened the store at ten, he took over the childcare duties. At noon, after she had her lunch, Brian brought Maggie to the store, where she napped in the back room. I'd found a new assistant—a lovely senior named Joyce, who was more than capable of managing customers while I tended to my daughter's needs. At the end of my shift, I took Maggie home for dinner, a bath, and bed. I was exhausted but happy. The baby was happy, too. She never made strange with us; she never seemed to miss Freya and Max. It was like she, too, knew this was where she belonged.

Two weeks after we became parents, a manila envelope

arrived at Hawking Mercantile. I barely glanced at the unfamiliar return address; I knew it was from Max's lawyers. These would be the documents required to make our parenthood official. Excitedly, I slid my thumb under the sealed flap and pulled out the pages. But they weren't custody papers. They were the results of Maggie's paternity test.

We didn't need them now. Maggie was *our* child and biology was irrelevant. And Brian wouldn't thank me for going behind his back, for ignoring his advice. I would destroy the report, put it through a shredder or toss it in the fire. But first . . . I had to look.

It stated, unequivocally, that Maggie was *not* Brian's child.

I sat down heavily on the stool behind the till. Maggie was Max's daughter. Freya had been fighting to keep her child from us because we had no claim to her. But Freya had lied about the date of conception. Faked the ultrasound images. Perhaps she'd been unsure of her daughter's paternity, too. But now, I knew the truth. As I slipped the papers back into the envelope, I wondered if Freya had had other lovers I didn't know about. But no . . . we had been friends when Maggie was conceived. I would have known if she had been sleeping with other men.

Joyce must have noticed my shock, because she asked, "Are you okay?"

I forced a smile. "I'm fine."

And I was fine. This didn't matter. This didn't change anything. The adoption papers would arrive soon, and Maggie would be legally ours. One day, she would want to know about her birth parents, might want to test her DNA. One day, we would bring Max back into his daughter's life, but not now.

Now, she was ours.

70

low

I don't like to say that the Hawking police were *stupid*, but they were stupid. They were so fixated on Max, on his fight with Freya, and on searching the main house, that they barely inspected the studio. They walked through it, climbed up into the attic, and opened the kiln. When they found it empty but for a tiny pile of ash, they closed the lid and walked away. They may have known that a cremation oven leaves approximately one cubic inch of ash per pound of body (I knew this because Freya had been commissioned to make an urn a few months back). But they didn't know that incinerating a person at significantly higher temperature reduces that residue. And if they had sifted through the fine dust that once was Freya, they would have found it: a small misshapen disk the size of a large thumb print. It was an alloy of copper and lead, melted and then hardened. It was the bullet that had been buried in her heart.

It was the only souvenir I kept of the woman I'd loved so fiercely. Her phone and her rings were at the bottom of the Pacific, along with the gun and the shell casing. I'd taken Vik's aluminum fishing boat out for the afternoon and jettisoned the evidence off the side. (No one thought my trip was unusual. Before Freya, I used to spend hours alone on the water under the auspices of fishing.) I burned the sex photos of Freya and Max, and then I laid low for a couple of weeks, photographing my siblings, enthusiastically eating my mother's dal, acting normal. When I knew that no one could ever link me to Freya's disappearance, I returned to the scene of the crime.

The FOR SALE sign was already planted on the verge as I pulled into the driveway. Max was in the garage, packing up his boating gear, but he emerged when he heard my vehicle.

"You're leaving," I said, as I got out of my truck.

"Yep. The police cleared me. Did they talk to you?"

"For about five minutes. They wanted to know about Freya's 'state of mind.'"

Max nodded. It was clear to everyone that she'd been suicidal. "I'm going back to the Yukon," he said.

"And Maggie?"

"She's with Brian and Jamie. They're her parents, now. She'll be better off."

I nodded my agreement.

We were both taciturn types, so there was a long tense silence while thoughts raced through my mind. Max had been unconscious when I shot Freya; he couldn't know that I had killed her to save his daughter. Unless . . . somewhere in his injured brain, he had heard the gun go off. Unless, his sightless eyes had flickered open and witnessed what I had done. Did he know that I had considered, however briefly, incinerating his body, and running off with his wife?

"Take anything you want," Max said. "From the house or the studio. Freya would have wanted you to have it. *I* want you to have it."

Okay, so he didn't know.

I said, "I don't want anything of hers."

"She cared about you, Low. As much as she was capable of caring about anyone. She hadn't had an easy life. It fucked her up."

I'll say. But I didn't. I forced a tight smile. "Good luck, Max." I wandered down to the studio.

That's when I scooped Freya's ashes out of the kiln and found the pellet that had ended her life. There were shelves of her pots, vases, and dishes, at various stages of finish. They were delicate and beautiful, made by her talented hands. But I didn't want reminders of that toxic relationship and its violent end. Even if I had, I couldn't take them where I was going. No, I wasn't here for me. I was here for Maggie.

Selecting a small bud vase, glazed in robin's-egg blue, I deposited a sprinkling of Freya's ashes in the bottom. It was not an urn, exactly; no one would know that the fine powder inside was anything but dust from the studio. But I would take it to Maggie. She should have a little piece of her mother.

I drove to Jamie's store. When I entered, I was greeted by an elderly woman with a big smile. "Hello," my replacement said. "Can I help you find something?"

What a keener. I'd let customers browse for a while before I pounced on them. "Is Jamie here?"

The smile slipped from her face as she recognized me, as she put the pieces together. I knew what she thought, what everyone in town thought. That I was part of the sordid sexual shenanigans that led to Freya's suicide. That the five of us had had daily orgies until Freya found herself pregnant by her best friend's husband.

"She's in the back room with the baby."

I brushed past her. "I know the way."

The door to the storage room was slightly ajar, so I pressed it open. The space had been transformed into a kind of nursery, with a playpen and a rocking chair. Jamie was seated with Maggie in her arms, giving her a bottle. The expression on her face was pure bliss.

"Hey," I whispered.

She looked up and smiled at me. "Low."

"I brought this. For Maggie." I unwrapped the newspaper protecting the vase and set it on a shelf.

"It's beautiful. Freya was so talented." Jamie's eyes were misty. "To think she felt so desolate and overwhelmed that she . . ." She couldn't say it.

"But it all worked out for the best," I said lightly.

She half shrugged, half nodded. She didn't want to articulate the truth.

"I'm leaving," I said. "In a few weeks."

"Where are you going?"

"My friend Thompson and I are moving to Seattle."

"Thompson?" She cocked an eyebrow and her lips twitched with a smile.

"It's not like that," I snapped. Thompson and I were *not* romantically involved. But I had gone to the drugstore to apologize for my behavior in the barn that day.

"Sorry for being a drunken asshole," I'd muttered. Thompson was still hurt, still angry. He'd given me the cold shoulder, and so I had slunk away. So much for trying to be a decent human being.

But a few days later, after he'd heard about Freya's disappearance, he had shown up at my house. "Sorry for your loss."

"Thanks."

"I know how you felt about her. This must be really hard."

"You were right. It wasn't real," I said. "I'm trying to let it go and move on."

He kicked the ground with his ratty sneaker. "Want to get some pizza?"

It's not like I had anything else to do. "Sure."

It was in "our booth" that I told him I was leaving the island, that I needed a fresh start. He had chewed thoughtfully for a moment before he said, "Want a roommate?"

"I'm not into you," I said quickly.

"Yeah, I got that," Thompson said, with the slightest roll of his eyes. "But I could use a change of scene, too. We could split the rent on a two-bedroom place."

I had taken a sip of Coke. "You're *sure* you're not in love with me."

"Super sure."

And so, I had agreed.

But now Jamie was looking at me like I was about to elope. "Thompson wanted to move, and I needed a roommate," I said. "I'll start college in the fall."

"That's amazing." Jamie's face lit up. "I'm so proud of you."

"It was always my plan," I lied.

It hadn't been, as you know. I'd been scared to leave the island, afraid I wouldn't fit in in the big wide world. But Freya had changed me. For better or worse. She had pushed me to the brink of my sanity, forced me to commit an unthinkable act, and I had done it. I had killed the woman I loved to protect a baby from certain death. *And* I had gotten away with it. There was no need to feel fearful or intimidated anymore. By anyone.

I was formidable.

Maggie had finished her bottle and was dozing in her mother's arms. Jamie carefully rose from the chair and placed her baby in the playpen. I watched the sleeping child for a moment. She looked so much like Freya. Would the resemblance haunt Jamie and Brian? Would Maggie inherit the cruel, sociopathic-bitch gene? Or would the love of two solid (if a little dull) parents allow her to grow up stable, confident, normal . . . ?

Jamie ushered me out of the room and back into the shop. There were a couple of customers, but the old lady had them well in hand.

"Thanks for bringing the vase. And for coming to say goodbye."

"Sure."

"She put us through a lot," Jamie said. "But sometimes, I still miss her. I'm sure you do, too."

I pressed my lips together and gave an ambiguous nod. And then I left. I got in my truck and drove back to my family's homestead.

Did I miss Freya? Of course I did. But her death freed me from so many negative feelings. I was no longer racked with jealousy, envy, and insecurity. I didn't have to worry that Freya loved Jamie more than me, that Maggie would usurp my position in her life, that Freya was taking advantage of my adoration. That's not why I shot her; I was protecting Maggie. But I had released us all from her web of cruel manipulation.

And I now shared the most special bond of all with her, an eternal connection. I had taken her life. I had held her corpse in my arms and turned her beautiful body into ash. I was the only one who knew what really happened to Freya, and I had the melted bullet to prove it. Maybe I'd make it into a pendant and wear it over my heart.

She would always be close to me.

acknowledgments

So many people work so hard to turn a manuscript into a book. I'm grateful to everyone who helped *The Swap* on its journey, starting with my wise, funny, passionate editor, Jackie Cantor. Her wisdom, insight, and ability to rein me in when I get too crazy made this book so much better. Thanks to Jennifer Bergstrom and her incredible team at Scout Press: Molly Gregory, Jessica Roth, Sydney Morris, Anabel Jimenez, Aimée Bell, Sara Quaranta, Jennifer Long, Liz Psaltis, Abby Zidle, Diana Velasquez, John Paul Jones, and everyone else behind the scenes. Thanks to my eagle-eyed copyeditor, Erica Ferguson, and to designer Chelsea McGuckin for this absolutely stunning cover.

Thanks to my kind, calm, enthusiastic agent of seventeen years, Joe Veltre, the faultless Tori Eskue, and the entire team at Gersh.

Thanks to Simon and Schuster Canada who have done so much for me here at home: Nita Pronovost, Felicia Quon, Kevin Hanson, Catherine Whiteside, Adria Iwasutiak, Rita Silva,

Rebecca Snodden, Sarah St. Pierre, Mackenzie Croft, and co. You are the best! Thanks to the wonderful Fiona Henderson, Anthea Bariamis, Rachael Versace, and everyone at Simon and Schuster Australia, and the team at Simon and Schuster UK.

I'm so grateful to all the booksellers and librarians, the bloggers, bookstagrammers, and Facebook groups who do so much to spread the word about books. (Last time, I mentioned many by name, but then I worried about those I had missed!) And thank you to all my author friends for the support, camaraderie, and laughter (including my early readers Eileen Cook and Roz Nay).

A special thank you to Charmian Nimo, my pottery teacher, who is so patient, talented, and has a great sense of humor. Thanks for suggesting a great way to get rid of a body. And thanks to the metallurgist Clayton Thesen of National Kwikmetal Service who answered my unsolicited (and bizarre) question about melting a bullet.

As always, thank you to my mom, my family, and my friends. And all my love to John, Ethan, and Tegan.

the

swap

ROBYN HARDING

*T*his reading group guide for THE SWAP includes an introduction, discussion questions, and ideas for enhancing your book club. The suggested questions are intended to help your reading group find new and interesting angles and topics for your discussion. We hope that these ideas will enrich your conversation and increase your enjoyment of the book.

introduction

Low Morrison is not your average teen. You could blame her hippie parents or her looming height or her dreary, isolated hometown on an island in the Pacific Northwest. But whatever the reason, Low just doesn't fit in—and neither does Freya, an ethereal beauty and once-famous social media influencer who now owns the local pottery studio.

After signing up for a class, Low quickly falls under Freya's spell. And Freya, buoyed by Low's adoration, is compelled to share her darkest secrets and deepest desires. Finally, both feel a sense of belonging . . . that is, until Jamie walks through the studio door. Desperate for a baby, she and her husband have moved to the island hoping that the healthy environment will result in a pregnancy. Freya and Jamie become fast friends, as do their husbands, leaving Low alone once again.

Then one night, after a boozy dinner party, Freya suggests swapping partners. It should have been a harmless fling between consenting adults, one night of debauchery that they would put behind them, but instead, it upends their lives. And provides Low the perfect opportunity to unleash her growing resentment.

Robyn Harding brings her acclaimed storytelling, lauded as "fast-paced, thrilling, gut-wrenching" by Taylor Jenkins Reid, *New York Times* bestselling author of *Daisy Jones & The Six*, to this dark and suspenseful thriller for fans of Megan Miranda and Lisa Jewell.

topics and questions for discussion

1. When Low is first introduced to readers in chapter 1, what do we learn about her as a character through how she describes her classmates and her first impression of Freya?

2. In chapter 1, Low sees Freya for the first time in her school, posting an ad for pottery classes. Later on, Freya tells Low she posted it to earn money, but her home and lifestyle don't indicate she's financially unstable. Did Freya have other motives for posting the ad for pottery classes and, if so, what were they?

3. The book consistently juxtaposes obsession and jealousy with freedom and sharing. Discuss the idea of monogamy versus polyamory. Are people inherently one or the other? Do these concepts exist in black and white, or is there a grey area in between?

4. How does Low's own perception of herself differ from how Jamie and Max describe her when they first meet?

5. At various points in the story, Max, Jamie, and Brian all allude to Freya's persuasiveness and charm and how they were all ultimately deceived by her into thinking everything was going to be alright (end of chapters 5, 15, and 18). Could this mean Freya was a sociopath?

6. In chapter 8, Low describes the meaning of her full name—Swallow, a highly adaptable, small bird—and the shame it caused her growing up. Freya is the name of a Norse goddess who is accused of infidelity and who incidentally is pictured with birds of prey. How do these names represent the evolution of these two characters throughout the book?

7. In chapter 39, Brian says to Jamie, "You're the one trying to hang onto a sick, toxic friendship . . ." with Freya. This is the first time a character in the book explicitly names the nature of Freya's relationships with others. Discuss why you think this revelation came from Brian.

8. In chapter 66, Thompson says of Low's relationship to Freya, "You worship her and adore her and do everything for her. But she doesn't care about you at all. That's not love, Low. That's obsession." Does Thompson's relationship with Low mirror her relationship with Freya?

9. In chapter 49, Brian asks, "Had Freya wanted to get pregnant . . . this pregnancy had reignited her Instagram career." Do you think that Freya was trying to get pregnant or that it was unplanned, as she claimed?

10. Do you think that Brian and Jamie would have "swapped" with Freya and Max if they weren't under the influence of drugs?

11. Discuss why Low became so attached to Maggie that she was able to overcome her obsession with Freya, even momentarily, to save the baby's life.

12. In chapter 65, after Low's parents called CPS on Freya, Low explodes at them. "'I'm what matters! Me!' I shrieked, 'You never cared about me! You've never put me first!'" Discuss how Low's upbringing affected her relationship with the other adult women in the book (Jamie and Freya).

13. In chapter 68, Low only turned on Freya when she heard Maggie's cry and realized Freya was going to kill her own baby. Where did the mothering instinct come from? Did she kill Freya because she knew she could never have her to herself or because she was trying to protect Maggie?

14. Discuss the relationship between couples Jamie and Brian and Freya and Max. Are the dynamics in one better than the other, or do both exhibit unhealthy ones? Did Max and Freya influence Brian and Jamie?

15. Low describes Freya and Max's relationship as, "locked in some kind of sick, codependent partnership full of lies and abuse and emotional distance, and yet . . . they had each other's backs." Do you agree with that assessment?

enhance your book club

1. Max and Freya's life is turned upside down when Max inadvertently kills another hockey player during a game. Discuss how you would deal with this kind of life-altering event? How would it affect your relationship to the loved one responsible?

2. Throughout the book, each character exhibits pathological behavior. Do you think mental illness played a role in the story? If and when you've experienced similar behavior in real life, has mental illness played a role? Does it make any of the characters more sympathetic when looking at their choices and actions through the lens of mental illness?

3. Low's attachment to baby Maggie was the catalyst to finally break Freya's psychological hold on her. Do you believe in the power of a mothering instinct that strong? Have you ever experienced that in your own life?

4. Low discusses her ambiguous sexuality throughout the book. When she talks about her relationship with her childhood friend Topaz and, later, Freya, she says multiple times that she isn't attracted to them "in that way." But at the end of chapter 38, Freya kisses Low and she feels her first pull of attraction. Did this sexual awakening impact Low's obsession with Freya? Do you think the book would have ended so violently if Low's feelings for Freya had remained platonic?

5. Are any of the characters unreliable narrators? Did you see examples in the book where they gave conflicting opinions or hypocritical advice to others?